THE DIVA
COOKS A GOOSE

THE DIVA
COOKS A GOOSE

KRISTA DAVIS

WHEELER
CHIVERS

This Large Print edition is published by Wheeler Publishing, Waterville, Maine, USA and by AudioGO Ltd, Bath, England.
Wheeler Publishing, a part of Gale, Cengage Learning.

The text of this Large Print edition is unabridged.
Other aspects of the book may vary from the original edition.
Set in 16 pt. Plantin.

LIBRARY OF CONGRESS CATALOGING-IN-PUBLICATION DATA

Davis, Krista.
  The diva cooks a goose / by Krista Davis.
    p. cm.
  "A Domestic Diva mystery."
  ISBN-13: 978-1-4104-3690-0 (pbk.)
  ISBN-10: 1-4104-3690-X (pbk.)
  1. Winston, Sophie (Fictitious character)—Fiction. 2. Women cooks—Fiction. 3. Murder—Investigation—Fiction. 4. Christmas stories. 5. Large type books. I. Title.
  PS3604.A9717D54 2011
  813'.6—dc22   2011001521

BRITISH LIBRARY CATALOGUING-IN-PUBLICATION DATA AVAILABLE

Published in 2011 in the U.S. by arrangement with The Berkley Publishing Group, a member of Penguin Group (USA) Inc.
Published in 2011 in the U.K. by arrangement with The Berkley Publishing Group, a member of Penguin Group (USA) Inc.

U.K. Hardcover: 978 1 445 83736 9 (Chivers Large Print)
U.K. Softcover: 978 1 445 83737 6 (Camden Large Print)

Printed in the United States of America
1 2 3 4 5 6 7 15 14 13 12 11

For my beloved Tante Ingrid,
who loved Christmas as much as I do

ACKNOWLEDGMENTS

Special thanks to Kathy O'Brien, who confirmed the dangers of the method of death in this book. As always, I owe thanks to Avery Aames and Janet Bolin, for their friendship, and for critiquing with love and humor. I am also always indebted to my first readers, Marianne Ryplansky and Betsy Strickland, who keep me on track, as well as Amy Wheeler and Susan Erba for unflagging moral support. I am also grateful to Laura Alden, Peg Cochran, Kaye George, and Marilyn Levinson, who are always there with astute insights and clever ideas to spark my imagination.

Thanks also to my new agent, Jessica Faust, for her enthusiasm and energy, and to my wonderful editor, Sandy Harding, who is always a joy. The very talented Teresa Fasolino has created another warm and wonderful cover for the original edition of this book and even gave us a glimpse of Faye!

A special note of appreciation to Verena Rose, whose gorgeous Ragdoll kittens, officially named Edgar and Agatha, and nicknamed Jasper and Alice, star in this book. What a pleasure to write about Verena's beautiful babies.

Merry Christmas from the Bauer Family

Paul
Inga
Sophie
George and family
Hannah

Christmas Greetings from the George Bauer Family

George
Laci
Jen

Happy Holidays from the Thorpe Family

Tom
Tyler
Dasher

Merry Yuletide from the Chadwicks

Forrest
Ginger
Emma
Edward

Happy Christmas from the Lane Family

Phil
Marnie
Laci and family
Shawna

Season's Greetings from the Scarboroughs

Bonnie
Beau

*Best Wishes for a Joyous Holiday from
Natasha and Mars*

ONE

From "THE GOOD LIFE":

Dear Sophie,
I nearly canceled Christmas last year when my children found their presents. My husband thinks we should hide them in the trunk of the car, but I think that's a hassle. Where can we hide gifts from our snoopy kids?

— Frazzled Mom
in Santa Claus, Arizona

Dear Frazzled Mom,
Car theft is rampant during the holidays, so don't leave gifts in the car! Hiding them in almost plain sight is best. Consider the laundry basket with piles of blankets on top. Another great choice is unused luggage in a storage closet.

— Sophie

If it hadn't been for my brother, George, standing in the middle of the street waving his arms like a maniac, his block would have looked like a Christmas Eve picture from a movie. Strands of Christmas lights sparkled in trees, wound around porches, and traced roof lines. Light snow had begun to dance in the air, teasing that children might rise to a blanket of white on Christmas morning. But the harsh blue of a police car strobe light zapped an eerie glow over the crowd of people milling on lawns and in the street.

"Pull over there." Detective Wolf Fleishman, who sat next to me in my car, pointed to the right. "Next to the Grinch snow globe."

The Grinch would have been hard to miss. Bigger than the people on the lawn, he bobbled inside a clear plastic orb, grinning evilly and lit from below to show off fake swirling snow. The home owners hadn't stopped there, though. Eight huge reindeer pulled Santa across the roof of the house, and a train set, big enough for a toddler to ride on, chugged on tracks through the front yard.

My sister, Hannah, leaned forward in the backseat. "Thank goodness Mom and Dad are all right. I see them on George's front porch. When he called, I was afraid one of them had an attack or something."

Hannah jumped from my car while it was still moving. Normally I would have yelled at her, but I understood her anxiety. Our parents and brother, George, and his family, including his mother-in-law, had spent the evening at my house in Old Town, Alexandria, enjoying our Christmas Eve tradition of feasting on goose. After they left, Wolf, Hannah, and I were cleaning up the kitchen around ten thirty, when George's cryptic call came. He insisted we bring Wolf to his house immediately, then hung up. Hannah had tried to call George back during the forty-five-minute drive from Alexandria to Chantilly, but he wasn't answering his phone.

Once we arrived, Wolf had barely stepped out of my car when George began to gesture like a crazed person and sprang into a frenzied explanation. George's daughter, Jen, launched herself at my car door declaring, "Christmas is over!"

I opened the door, stepped out, and smoothed her hair. "Don't say that, sweetie." But I had a terrible suspicion that she might be right, given the unhappy faces I saw on her neighbors. Not to mention that it didn't take much to spoil Christmas for a twelve-year-old. Even one like Jen, who never failed to remind us that she would be a very sophisticated and grown-up thirteen on her next birthday, still ten months away.

Moving fast so I wouldn't miss anything, I scooted around the front of the car in time to hear George say, "I think everyone in the neighborhood should open their houses to the cops. The thief won't agree and then we'll know who it is."

"Thief? What happened?" I asked.

"Some crumb stole our Christmas gifts. Right out from under our trees. The thief hit the whole neighborhood. We've been wiped out." He'd barely finished speaking when a raven-haired woman, a neighbor, I presumed, clutched his arm and actually batted her eyelashes at him.

George's big frustration in life was that he'd only grown to be medium height. That, coupled with a sweet baby face, made him feel he didn't have what it took to be a tough guy and intimidate people, but women flocked to him like hummingbirds to a red flower.

"How could that happen?" I asked.

George used his free hand to give the woman a reassuring pat on her shoulder but cast an impatient look at me. "Apparently he did it during the community party earlier today. People were either away visiting rela-

14

tives, or at the party. That's why I think it was an inside job. The thief had to know that everyone would be over at the community center. Someone in our neighborhood is a rat. He even raided closets and found most of the" — George stopped his tirade and looked around at the kids — "S-A-N-T-A gifts and stole them!"

Wolf nodded in the direction of a couple of Fairfax County cops. "I'll see what I can find out."

"I told you Christmas was over," said Jen sadly.

Mustering a hopeful voice and trying not to sound like my mother, I said, "There's more to Christmas than just presents." In spite of my efforts, my voice faded with lack of conviction. Presents are a huge deal when you're twelve.

"That's what Grandma said. I made her a Christmas ornament that's all sparkly and now some creep has it."

Her little mouth turned down at the corners and I couldn't help hugging her. "We'll have a fun Christmas anyway."

"Sophie! Sophie!" The woman's voice was all too familiar. Wearing an elegant faux shearling vest and matching hat, she strode toward us. *Natasha.*

Natasha and I had grown up together in

Berrysville, Virginia, where we had competed at everything, except the beauty pageants she adored. Raven-haired, and svelte in a way I could never be, Natasha had cultivated a loyal and enthusiastic following through her local TV show about all things domestic. And since she had hooked up with my ex-husband, Mars, and bought a house at the end of my block in Old Town, Alexandria, Natasha had become a fixture in my life.

"What are *you* doing here?" It wasn't the nicest reaction, but I did wonder what brought her to my brother's neighborhood.

"One of the residents, Tom Thorpe, asked me to decorate the community center. He's one of Mars's political clients."

We hadn't been married for some time, but since Mars was a political consultant, most of his clients were well known. Tom Thorpe didn't ring any bells for me. "I don't think I've heard of Thorpe."

She lowered her voice. "It's not public knowledge yet but Tom's going to be running for office. He's also one of my biggest fans, so when he asked me to decorate, I couldn't say no. Did you see the square? It's absolutely fabulous."

As it happened, I had seen it when the children rehearsed their holiday pageant the day before. In fact, Hannah and I had pondered why someone, apparently Natasha, had chosen life-size pink peacocks with white wreaths on their necks and giant turquoise magnolia flowers as a theme. I imagined the net lighting on the trees and the candlelight parade of the children into the clubhouse to see Santa had been charming, but I had missed the actual production since I had a goose to roast. While the rest of my family watched Jen in the pageant, I cooked our Christmas Eve feast and had it waiting for them.

"Can you believe this?" Natasha asked, indicating the crowd. "We went out to dinner, and when we got back, the cops were here."

A shrill voice cut through the gentle murmuring. Jen perked up at the sound. "That's our neighbor, Mrs. Chadwick. If anyone can find the missing presents, she can. Everybody is afraid of her."

"Your neighbor?"

Jen nodded, grabbed my hand, and pulled me over for a clearer view of Ginger confronting the Fairfax County cops.

I'd met Ginger Chadwick a few times but didn't know her well. She'd struck me as a nervous type, and seemed particularly skilled at complaining. "There was a brand-new, and very fancy, computer under our tree. Do you know what those things cost?"

"You got me the new Mac I wanted?" Ginger's son, Edward, asked with glee. Almost as tall as his father, seventeen-year-old Edward still had that gangly look — thin as his mother, but with long legs and arms. The glow of the Grinch globe cast light on his strawberry blond hair, which fell into a mussed shock on his forehead, as though he hadn't bothered to comb it all day.

The police officer, whose name tag said Sergeant McGregor, looked tired. Wolf, who loved good food and sported a slightly rounded girth, seemed far more imposing. Fair-haired McGregor might have been the one in a uniform, but next to Wolf, he seemed slender and boyish, even though I guessed him to be about forty. He opened his mouth, but he only managed a weak, "Ma'am . . ." before Ginger started in on him again.

"I'm just telling you that we're not talking about crummy toys and cheap as-advertised-on-TV items. Significant high-ticket items were stolen, which I'm positive places this in a felony category, not something you can simply dismiss." She placed her fists on her hips and glared at him. "So what are you going to do about it?"

Wolf, who had been talking to McGregor, winced. It was almost imperceptible, but I caught it and realized how well I had come to know him. I doubted that anyone else noticed that tiny flash of pain. After a rocky start to our relationship, my work as an event planner, and Wolf's job as a homicide detective, had made it next to impossible to get together. But an unfortunate run-in with another detective forced us to meet secretly at my house, late at night, which turned out to be prime dating time for Wolf and me. We didn't get out to restaurants or museums or shows, but we both liked to putter in the kitchen, and snuggling on the sofa with a late-night movie helped both of us unwind from the stress of our jobs. Some of my friends would have been very unhappy to be in a relationship like ours, but it suited Wolf and me perfectly. The best part was that most people butted out of our relationship because they didn't know about it.

One of Wolf's eyebrows arched a hair, and I knew he was about to pull a fast one. "McGregor," he said to the cop, "why don't you start by searching this kind lady's house?"

Ginger Chadwick's mouth dropped open. She leaned forward and shouted, "Mine? I didn't take anything. I'll have you know that

I am a respected member of this community. You should start with some of the other houses. I happen to know that some of our neighbors have holiday guests and families with criminal pasts."

A tall man with a rugged, square jaw and neatly trimmed silver hair that glowed under the sparkling Christmas lights glowered at Ginger and muttered, "Careful, Cruella. I wouldn't throw any stones if I were you."

"Who's that?" I asked Jen.

"Mr. Thorpe. That's his house with the Grinch and the train."

Even though he towered over her, Ginger didn't back off. "Well, if Santa's boot happens to fit . . ."

Huh? I looked to Jen.

"Mr. Thorpe played Santa at the pageant today."

McGregor stepped between them. "Which house is yours, ma'am?"

Ginger's lips puckered with displeasure. She waved toward her house, next to my brother's, and in the dim glow of festive lights, the long, lean silhouette of her son, Edward, was visible sprinting home.

Two

From "THE GOOD LIFE":

Dear Sophie,
I love Christmas — the baking, the wrapping, the decorating — and then I see the tiny Christmas lights and everything sours. My husband and I have a cheer-killing fight every year about those tangled tools of torment. We put up a lot of lights and can't afford fancy reels for all of them. Any suggestions?

— Tangled Up
in Nanty Glo, Pennsylvania

Dear Tangled Up,
There's an easy and free way to keep those lights untangled. When taking them down, hold the nonplug end in the palm of your hand. Wrap the cord loosely around your hand until it begins to form a ball, then slip it off and keep wrapping

the lights around the ball. End with the plug on the outside so you can easily check to see if they still work the following year. They'll stay in a ball all summer and be ready to use next Christmas!

— Sophie

As though it were a party, the entire crowd shuffled across the street behind Ginger and the policeman.

No snow globes or animated displays occupied Ginger's yard. Two-foot-tall lighted pine trees lined her sidewalk. Fancy topiary trees flanked the short stairs to the front porch, and lights glittered in heavy white pine swags on the railing. On the lawn in front of the railing, a family of life-size caroler dolls, dressed in Dickensian fashion, posed, mouths open, as though they were midsong. I didn't see Scrooge, but Tiny Tim, leaning on his crutch, appeared to join in the silent song. Faux streetlights with flickering flames flanked the carolers. On the door, more lights twinkled in a wreath loaded with sumptuous pinecones, pears, apples, and pomegranates. I'd seen the very same wreath at a florist shop in Old Town, but passed on it when I checked the price. Ginger had spent some major bucks on her Christmas decorations.

Natasha leaned toward me. "Nice, but uninspired, don't you think?"

"Very Christmassy." I wanted to point out that it related to Christmas, unlike her pink peacocks. Magnolia leaves and flowers were a time-honored elegant Christmas decoration in the South, but spraying them with turquoise glitter took them to a whole other level. In the spirit of the season, I bit my tongue and excused myself.

I cut across the driveway to my brother George's house, where a Buick was backing into the street. My mother, Inga, and sister, Hannah, watched the goings-on from the porch.

"Is that Dad's car?" I asked.

"Laci is beside herself that Jen won't have anything to open tomorrow morning. She's so distraught, poor dear, that Dad offered to drive her and Marnie around to see if they can find any open stores. It's a hopeless expedition, I fear. She and George bought Jen a new camera and now — it's gone."

Poor Laci. She and my brother, George, doted on Jen, their only child. Who wouldn't be distraught if Christmas was ruined for their children?

"Along with the turkey for tomorrow," added Hannah.

"The thief stole food, too?" It had to be more than one person to have taken so much.

"They even snatched my Sweet Potato Spectacular. I hope you have a lot of leftovers from the goose dinner earlier tonight." Mom held her arms crossed against her chest, even though she wore a puffy down coat. She stretched her fingers toward me. "Let me see your left hand."

I looked at my palm to see if it was dirty.

"The other way," said Mom.

I flipped it over, and she released a sigh big enough to have blown over the gigantic Grinch across the street.

"No ring. I was hoping one of my girls might receive an engagement ring for Christmas."

Hannah snorted and laughed at me. "She must mean you, Sophie. I'm not seeing anyone."

Just what I needed. Even the theft of Christmas gifts couldn't distract Mom from her quest to marry off her daughters. "I'm really very content with my life exactly as it is." It was the truth. After my divorce from Mars, I'd settled into a comfortable existence with loads of friends and a busy event planning career. Not to mention writing my domestic diva advice column. Newspapers all over the country had picked it up, and to my complete surprise, an increasing number of readers wrote to me about their domestic problems.

"I find that hard to believe," Mom protested. "I thought Wolf might pop the question after we left tonight." She paused, and when I didn't respond, she continued. "I understand the neighbor across the street, Mr. Thorpe, is quite successful. He's widowed and very handsome, but he's too old for you girls."

My sister pretended to smack her forehead against one of the porch pillars.

I couldn't help grinning. Now that Hannah and I were both in our forties, not many people thought of us as girls. Eager to change the subject, I asked, "How could anyone take so much stuff without being seen?" I leaned against the railing and watched my brother's neighbors in the yard next door.

"That's what I want to know. Someone *must* have been home on this block. It's almost inconceivable that everyone was out. Even if none of the neighbors were home, someone must have driven down the street, don't you think?" Mom ticked her points off on her fingers as she spoke. "Plus, whoever did this must have pulled into the driveways and made several trips in and out of each house."

"How did he . . . *they* get in?"

"He came prepared," said Hannah, beckoning me.

I followed her into the warm house, fragrant from the lush Fraser fir Christmas tree. Hannah led me to the kitchen but didn't have to say anything. Frigid air blew in though a perfect six-inch round hole in the window of the door. "Wow. They brought a glass cutter and unlocked the door by reaching through the hole? Does every house have this kind of door?"

"Laci said it was a feature offered by the builder."

"Sounds more and more like an inside job by someone who lives around here. Who else would know that all the houses have doors with glass in the back?"

"Soph?" Wolf's voice came from the direction of the living room.

Hannah and I joined him and George. Along with the other cop, McGregor, they stood near the tree, which was decorated with a delightful mishmash of glitzy ornaments — some blown glass, and some that Jen had made out of beads and sequins. I missed the old glitter glue paper chain garland that we had made with Jen when she was younger, but the popcorn and cranberry garland added a delightful homey feel. I could just imagine Jen and her mom, Laci, sitting by the fire, laughing and enjoying the holiday spirit while they created the garland.

Wolf introduced us to Sergeant Zack McGregor. Although he politely acknowledged each of us, his blue eyes lingered on Hannah, and some of his earlier exhaustion seemed to evaporate.

Hannah returned his interest with a coy smile. Not that I could blame her. McGregor might not be a big burly cop, but he'd been blessed with dimples that appeared when he smiled, and enough laugh lines to make me suspect he had a good sense of humor. Sandy hair fell into a good cut that framed his handsome face. Although he was fair and it was the middle of the winter, his skin bore remnants of a fading tan, suggesting he liked the outdoors.

Hannah had removed her bulky winter coat, revealing a green angora sweater with tiny beaded stars cascading from the shoulder to the V-neck. She wore her flaxen hair up, soft tendrils escaping to tickle her neck. No wonder the sergeant gave her a second look.

Sergeant McGregor spoke with George,

asking what was missing. I couldn't help noticing his continued glances at Hannah, who beamed like she'd been handed a new toy. She accompanied them as they toured the house.

I pulled off my coat, left it on a chair, and answered a knock at the door. Forrest Chadwick, a big bear of a man with a gentle voice, waited on the porch. A sprinkling of snowflakes clung to the wave of dark chocolate–colored hair that swept above his forehead. The rest of his hair was neatly trimmed in an expensive cut that screamed executive. A row of white Christmas trees adorned his blue ski sweater, emphasizing his broad shoulders. I invited him in and he headed straight toward Wolf. "I have to apologize for my wife, Ginger. She's high-strung and doesn't deal with setbacks well. Do you think there's any chance we'll find the culprit?"

Wolf, nearly as large as Forrest, but a little trimmer through the middle, said, "Unless Zack or one of his men happen upon something as they go from house to house to take reports, it's extremely unlikely that you'll have your gifts back by morning. I'm sorry."

Forrest ran a fleshy hand over his face. "Why would anyone do this? Who would leave so many children without the joy of

Christmas morning? I don't understand. It's one thing to take a package or two, but wiping us out — that almost seems like a vendetta."

"Is there anyone in the neighborhood who might harbor that kind of anger?" asked Wolf. "Your wife certainly implied there are neighbors with issues."

"We're ordinary folks around here. Everybody has some kind of problem — a kid who got caught joyriding, a spouse who drinks too much, an estranged family member. Nothing that would trigger anything this coldhearted. Is there anything we can do to help find the thief? A lot of our neighbors have little kids who won't understand why Santa didn't come."

"What if everyone contributed a toy or two that their kids have outgrown?" I suggested. "We could collect them here, and the moms and dads could come by to select something."

Forrest clapped me on the back. "Brilliant. Half the fun is opening a package."

"Mom? Could you gather some large boxes for people to put toys in? Maybe sort them by type? Stuffed animals in one, puzzles in another. I'll go to the houses on this side of the street and tell everyone what we're doing. Forrest, will you work the other side of the street?"

I grabbed my coat, and Wolf grabbed my arm. "Be careful."

I made a don't-be-silly face at him. George and Laci loved their neighborhood. It wasn't like I would encounter an ax-wielding sicko.

"Don't give me that look. I know how snoopy you can be. Maybe I should come with you."

"Nonsense. I'm just going door-to-door." As I was beginning to think I wouldn't be able to dissuade Wolf from joining me, George called him, and I took the opportunity to bolt out the door.

The occupants of the houses on the opposite end of the block were grateful and relieved when I told them our plan. As I walked up the sidewalk to the Chadwick house, I saw a line forming on my brother's porch as people brought toys to contribute to the effort.

Ginger Chadwick answered her door eagerly. "Have they found the gifts?" Reddish hair glided to her shoulders as perfectly as if she'd just had it done, but piercing black eyes and the perennially disgruntled set of her mouth dampened her natural attractiveness.

I hated to dash all hope, but when I explained about collecting old toys, her expression changed to one of bored tolerance. "I donate old items to charity."

Her son, Edward, appeared behind her. Far enough back that she wouldn't notice, but close enough to overhear.

"I'm sure your donations are appreciated. We're just doing this so that neighborhood children will have something to open in the morning."

"If anyone donates an expensive brand-new computer, let me know."

Well, that was hardly the Christmas spirit! "I doubt that anyone will manage to find exactly what their children wanted, but we thought it would be nice . . ."

"Who are you again? You look familiar. Where were *you* this evening?"

I resented the implication that I might have stolen anything but I controlled myself. "I'm George's sister." She stared at me without a hint of recognition. "George Bauer?" I prompted. "From next door?"

Boredom reigned on Ginger's face. "Then none of this is any of your business anyway." She shut the door.

I muttered, "Merry Christmas," in a sarcastic tone and turned to leave.

But I stopped on her porch and watched a dark sedan roll down the street — so slowly that it scared me.

THREE

From "Ask Natasha":

Dear Natasha,

Every Christmas it's the same thing. I work until I'm a quivering heap and the joy of the holiday has been sucked out of me. Each year I promise myself it will be different, but between shopping, baking, and decorating, by Christmas Eve, I'm a grumpy Grinch. There has to be an easier way.

> — Mrs. Scrooge in Humbug,
> Arizona

Dear Mrs. Scrooge,

You need a planner. A calendar from which you do not deviate. The key is to make lists, then plan to implement a few items each day. Start the day after Christmas and begin your lists for next year. You'll be surprised how smoothly everything will go once you organize your time.

— Natasha

Had the culprit returned to steal more? Or was he hoping to gain some sick pleasure by watching the chaos he'd caused? I wanted to think it could be a Christmas-lights gazer, but the hour was a little late for that.

I cut across Ginger's yard again, sticking to the shadows. I figured Ginger would be horrified to imagine anyone stepping on her grass but I was unwilling to go too close to the street and the creepy car that seemed to follow me.

I had nearly made it to George's driveway when Edward Chadwick, Ginger's son, loped up behind me.

Awkwardly, he held out a digital camera. "Maybe Santa could bring this to Jen. When her parents replace it with a new one, they can give it back to me. Just don't tell my mom, okay? She wouldn't understand."

His generosity bowled me over. What kind of seventeen-year-old boy would give up his camera, even temporarily, to make a kid happy? "You must like Jen a lot."

He grinned. "She's a pretty cool kid. Hey, can I come with you and help organize the toy drive?"

"Sure, your dad's pitching in, too. Should

you tell your mother where you are?"

"It's okay. She'll assume I'm in my room ignoring her."

I wasn't at all sure that it was okay, but if it wasn't any of my business to help arrange a happy Christmas morning for the neighborhood children, then it certainly wasn't my business to boss Ginger's son around.

My dad's Buick pulled up in the driveway, and from the smiles on their faces as Laci and her mother, Marnie, stepped out, I gathered their mission had been successful.

I gazed up and down the street in search of the dark car, but it had vanished.

Dad handed bags to Edward to carry into the house and pulled more out of the trunk. Laci handed me shopping bags. "It won't be a conventional Christmas, but at least the kids on our block will have something under the tree tomorrow morning." She giggled and whispered, "We found a drugstore. A lot of little girls on this street are getting lip gloss in their stockings."

During my absence, Laci and George's home had come alive. "Rockin' Around the Christmas Tree" played, smiling neighbors poked through boxes in the foyer selecting gifts for their children, and Hannah held a tray of to-go cups of hot cider and cinnamon-spiced decaf coffee. The aromas mingled into a heady scent that made me wish for Christmas cookies to nosh on. I left the bags with Edward, who was already in the process of handing out the contents. Apparently he knew every child on the block and had suggestions for all of their parents.

In the living room, Wolf poked a fire to life next to the twinkling lights of the tree. The mantel glittered with Laci's collection of snowmen, and if I hadn't known better, judging from the way neighbors mingled with drinks in their hands, I'd have thought George and Laci had planned this party.

Smiles and laughter had replaced the unhappy faces we saw earlier. I couldn't help thinking of the thief as a Grinch and the neighbors as the residents of Whoville whose irrepressible spirit helped them overcome their sadness. The only problem was that I didn't think our Grinch would come sliding back to join in the merriment.

An hour later, the crowd dissipated, and Wolf reminded me, "I have to get up early to drive to my parents' house."

Bleary-eyed, I drove Hannah and Wolf back to Old Town through the snow that continued to fall. When we stepped out of the car, my street was deserted. In the wee hours of Christmas morning, my neighbors slept and traffic had vanished. The air held that special soundless quality that only accompanies snow. Wolf wrapped his arms around me, and freezing bits of ice melted on my flushed face as I turned it up to him.

"Promise me you'll avoid Kenner while I'm away?"

Like there was any comparison between my Wolf and his counterpart, the dour Detective Kenner. Kenner thought Wolf and I had broken up and had asked me out several times over the last few months. So far, I'd managed to dodge him. Being an event planner didn't lend itself to dating. I was out most nights working. "Don't tell me you're jealous?" I teased.

"I'm not beneath a little jealousy where you're concerned. It's been a long time since I cared about someone enough to be jealous. I kind of like it."

He kissed me with no-nonsense fervor, leaving me slightly giddy.

"I hate to interrupt, but it's cold out here for those of us who aren't in a bear hug, and we're supposed to be back at George's tomorrow morning for Laci's Christmas Day celebration."

I reached out a hand with the keys so Hannah could let herself into the house, but Wolf released me. "I've got to get cracking. I'll only get a couple hours sleep as it is."

I wanted to watch him walk away in the snow, but Hannah tugged at me like a bored child. I ran out of adrenaline right about the time I stuck the key into the door lock. Even Mochie, my Ocicat, winding around my legs, and the frantic happy wriggles of Daisy, my mixed-breed hound, didn't restore my energy. Hannah went straight up the stairs to bed. I tossed my coat over a kitchen chair, let Daisy out in the fenced backyard for a minute, and fed Mochie. Thankfully, Daisy promptly came back, more eager to be with me than to play in the snow. She escorted me up the stairs to my bedroom, and in minutes, Mochie joined us.

Hannah and I slept late on Christmas Day. When Jen phoned and said, "Mom's putting your cinnamon buns in the oven, aren't you coming?" I had a feeling the rest of my family hadn't slept much.

I stumbled down the stairs, started a pot of coffee, and let Daisy out. Mochie sat by his food dish, watching me expectantly, and Hannah staggered into the kitchen like the Bride of Frankenstein.

"*Ugh.* I am too old to stay up half the

night." She rubbed her face and yawned. "I feel hungover and there wasn't even any liquor, men, or general debauchery involved. Although that one cop was cute."

I smiled at the memory of Wolf's kiss in the falling snow. "Too bad. I called dibs. He's mine."

Hannah's face wrinkled up. "Not that one. The Zack cop." Her eyes finally opened to a normal width. "Oh! Do you think he'll be there today? Do you have any cucumbers? I'm all puffy."

"No cucumbers, sorry. And I doubt he'll come on Christmas Day. He probably has a police wife and four little police children at home."

"Did Wolf tell you that?"

I poured each of us a mug of steaming gingerbread-scented coffee. "No. But most people don't want to work on Christmas."

Hannah slurped coffee and opened the door for Daisy, who shook snow off her dark coat, wagged her tail, and stared at Hannah hopefully. Hannah bent forward for a doggy kiss. In a sugary voice, she said, "Daisy, you have no idea how glad I am that *I* don't have to walk you in this weather."

"I thought we'd take her with us. If Jen's full of energy, she can walk Daisy in the snow." I felt a little bit guilty for leaving

Mochie home alone, but then, sometimes I thought he enjoyed a quiet day by himself. And he surely wouldn't like the snow.

The phone rang again and the two of us looked at each other. "Mom?" I asked.

"I'd bet it's Laci, you know how uptight she is."

I finally answered and gave Hannah a thumbs-up. Laci launched into a frenzied explanation of the fact that the thief took food, as though I hadn't been at her house last night. I promised to bring food with me, and handed Hannah the phone, in spite of the fact that she waved her hands "no."

An hour later, we'd packed the car with food — frozen, fresh, and leftover — and Daisy, Hannah, and I were on our way back to Chantilly. Hannah applied makeup as I drove, and Daisy, who stood in the back of the SUV, hung her head over the console between the front seats.

"Do you think this is too sappy if Cop Zack happens by?"

I gathered she meant her outfit, a red turtleneck topped by a midnight blue sweater, on which Santa and his reindeer streaked across a sky. "You never know what a guy will like. Jen will adore it, though."

"I don't need to impress Jen. *Daisy!*"

I tried to keep my eyes on the road but

prepared to pull over. "What's wrong?"

"She licked my blush."

"That can't be good for her."

"Her? This stuff costs a fortune."

I ignored my sister and focused on the road, slick with melting snow. The brief howl of a siren bleated behind me and a flashing light reflected in my rearview mirror. "Oh, crud! Just what I need. Getting pulled over on Christmas Day!"

"You weren't going too fast, that's for sure." Hannah ran a hand through her hair. "A turtle could have passed us."

I pulled to the side of the road and rolled down the window to gaze up into the gaunt face of Detective Kenner.

"Sophie! I didn't realize it was you." He frowned at me. "Did you drink a few mimosas this morning?"

"No!" My voice got a little bit too loud. I might not be perfect, but I never drive after drinking.

Hannah leaned over, dipping a mascara wand into its container. "She wasn't speeding, either."

"Were you putting on makeup?" he asked.

"I think it's pretty obvious that I'm not wearing makeup."

"Really?" He squinted at me. "I'm afraid you were weaving, Sophie." He crouched a bit, bringing his face even with the window.

Good-natured Daisy chose that exact moment to growl. Her long jowls drew up to show her teeth, not her best expression.

Kenner drew back — fast. "Impressive guard dog you have there. What is she? Some kind of hound?"

"Hound mix." I wasn't about to tell him she was really a sweetheart.

Kenner bounced a fist off the car door. "Then you two have a Merry Christmas, and try not to weave anymore, Sophie."

Hannah and I wished him a Merry Christmas, and I pulled back onto the roadway before he returned to his car.

"Is that the cop who is jealous of Wolf?"

"Apparently. I find it hard to believe that he's smitten with me."

"Me, too. But he must be. You know he pulled you over on purpose when you hadn't done anything wrong. Not much to look at with those sunken cheeks." Hannah reached back to stroke Daisy. "Good girl for growling! Is that him following us?"

I glanced in the mirror, but couldn't tell because the car followed from a distance. It turned off shortly thereafter and we relaxed.

Although the main highways had been cleaned, as we neared George's neighborhood, I slowed to a crawl since the snow-removal trucks hadn't been through yet. It made for a sparkling winter wonderland effect. The huge Grinch still bobbled inside his bubble, and kids dodged around it, throwing snowballs at each other.

I pulled into George's driveway to leave the street clear in case the county truck came through to clean it. Jen bounced over to the car immediately, snow crystals clinging to her jacket, evidence that she hadn't managed to avoid all the snowballs pelted her way. Her cheeks glowed from the fresh, cold air, and I was thrilled to see her happy. The Grinch who tried to ruin Christmas hadn't succeeded. She opened the back hatch, and Daisy leaped out. They chased each other until Jen caught Daisy and they fell, rolling on the fluffy white ground.

The door to George's house opened. My dad, Paul, still sprightly and good-looking for a retiree, hurried to the car with George. "Thank goodness you're here. I thought Laci, her mother, and your mom might start a war over food. You have no idea how close we came to eating omelets for Christmas."

I wouldn't have minded omelets, actually, and wondered how pleased he would be to find that I'd brought bratwurst and pork chops from my freezer. The leftover goose from the night before wouldn't be enough to feed everyone.

Dad and Jen, her dark hair shining in the sun that made a brief appearance, carried bags and boxes into the house.

I pulled the Christmas presents I'd planned to give my family out of the car, and asked George, "How did it go this morning?"

"Terrific. The kids have some weird toys, and the snow helped. Tom Thorpe, who lives across the street, played Santa yesterday at the community party, and he still had the suit. He put it on early this morning and went to all the houses with little kids and shook sleigh bells. There are a few who are convinced Santa was here. Then Edward organized a neighborhood snowball fight. It's actually turned out to be a fun holiday for the kids."

"Tom sounds like a good egg. Is that the guy Mom likes?" asked Hannah.

"What *is* it with her? She's determined to find someone for him. Honestly, it's embarrassing the way she tries to matchmake for everyone." George shook his head and led the way up his walk.

I deposited packages under the tree and ventured, with some trepidation, into the kitchen. The heavenly scent of cinnamon and yeast bread lingered in the air. I helped myself to a bun with sugary cream cheese icing, and realized that Dad hadn't been kidding about the tension in the kitchen.

Strands of hair frizzled around Laci's forehead and her face flushed redder than the velvet bow on the wreath over the kitchen sink. Unlike Jen's pink cheeks, I had a bad feeling the mothers were the cause of Laci's flushed and disheveled appearance.

My brother had married a beauty. Petite and always pulled together, Laci was a bit of a control freak. More than a bit, really. She made lists for everything. A list of contents was taped to her freezer. A corkboard hung in the kitchen with lists for groceries, chores that needed attention, and a gigantic calendar Laci had made on her computer with color-coded information about their activities. At the moment, she stood in front of the stove, holding a list of some sort in trembling hands.

Her sister, Shawna, almost ten years younger, sat at the kitchen table, calmly applying bloodred nail polish, evidently oblivious to Laci's distress. I knew Shawna from The Laughing Hound, a restaurant near my house where she waitressed. Every bit as beautiful as Laci, Shawna wore her lustrous brown tresses longer and dieted constantly in a never-ending battle with extra pounds.

Mom's eyes twinkled as she admired Shawna's manicure. "Shawna's expecting an engagement ring tomorrow!"

Great. Not that I wasn't happy for her, but my mother would take every possible opportunity to remind me.

"I thought he would give it to me last night." Shawna blew on her nails. "Wouldn't that have been romantic? An engagement ring on Christmas Eve? But he didn't, so I think he's waiting for his mother's big Boxing Day party tomorrow. You won't believe what she has planned. I don't want to give away any surprises but it's going to be sweet! Did you know one out of five men pop the question at Christmas?"

My mom, as petite and uberorganized as Laci, gave Shawna an excited wink. "He's not joining us today?"

"It's difficult for people with divorced parents. He's spending the day with his dad. He's genuinely relieved that his mother finally met someone, so she won't be alone today." Shawna slapped a hand over her mouth and turned her eyes to her mother, Marnie. An awkward silence fell over us. Laci had warned me that this would be Marnie's first Christmas apart from their dad.

Mom came to the rescue by changing the

subject. "I hope you brought cranberries, Sophie. It's just not Christmas without cranberries."

"You're not serving pumpkin pie, are you?" asked Marnie.

Laci gulped and mashed her eyes shut. When she opened them, she snapped, "This Christmas, you just have to eat whatever is served." She ripped her list into tiny shreds. "It's not like I didn't plan a nice dinner."

"I just don't want to see pumpkin pie, is all. For the rest of my life, I'll associate it with the day your father left."

From the way Laci's hands clenched the shredded list, I knew I had to find a way to get the moms out of the kitchen — fast. "Mom," I said casually, as if I hadn't noticed anything wrong, "Hannah was wondering if she's dressed right in case that cop, Zack, comes by today. Did you find out if he's single?"

It was cruel of me to sic her on Hannah, but there was no gift, other than an engagement announcement, I could have given my mother that would bring her more pleasure than the notion that Hannah might be attracted to someone. Amazement flashed over Mom's face, and she bolted from the kitchen, still wearing an apron.

Marnie was a little tougher since I didn't

know her well. A perfectionist like Laci, she stood in front of Laci's pantry, scowling. "What an odd assortment of staples you have. If you recall, I offered to buy you a freezer. If you'd taken me up on it, we wouldn't be in this mess."

I munched on the sweet bun, laden with heady cinnamon and nutmeg, and eyed Marnie, wondering what would prompt her to abandon the kitchen. A little bit taller than Laci, Marnie kept in good shape. She didn't have a runner's leanness, though. I would bet on aerobics, yoga, or one of those women-only exercise clubs. She wore a sweater vest featuring polar bears with three-dimensional mufflers embellished with tiny bells. I wasn't quite sure about the connection to the holiday, but one thing seemed clear to me — she'd worn it for Jen.

"George told me Jen had a great Christmas morning," I said. "I'm so glad. But she seemed very flushed and wet from the snow when I came in. You don't think she's coming down with anything, do you?"

Alarm registered on Laci's face, and for a moment, I thought my plan to clear the kitchen might have backfired. Fortunately, Marnie proved to be the devoted grandmother I'd suspected. "I'll check on her, sweetheart."

I grinned at Laci as her mother rushed from the kitchen.

Laci scowled at me. "Is Jen really sick?"

I shook my head. "No. But the cold air has pinked her cheeks nicely. Just enough to distract a doting grandmother. So what can I do to help?"

Laci looked around her nearly vacant kitchen and then stared at me, speechless. For a moment, I thought she might burst into tears. "I have to learn how to do that." She blinked hard before moving into boss mode.

By the time our mothers reappeared, potatoes cooked in a huge pot, the remaining meat had been picked off the goose, a green bean casserole baked in the oven, and a pot of red cabbage with heavenly roasted chestnuts cooked on the stove. I tossed chopped celery into a pan of onions sizzling in bacon grease for a quick dressing. Laci peeled sweet potatoes, but I could see her anxiety ratchet again when the moms reappeared.

I quickly sent them off with instructions to take a head count, set the table, be sure we had enough chairs, pour wine, and pass hors d'oeuvres that I'd whipped together out of cream cheese and smoked salmon. Shawna continued to wave her fingers in the air, careful not to smudge her fresh manicure in case a diamond ring would slide onto one of her fingers.

When we sat down to eat, Forrest Chadwick and his son, Edward, joined us. His wife, Ginger, who had been a no-show, waltzed in at the last minute like an auburn June Cleaver, complete with pearls and frilly apron, carrying a hot roast turkey.

With great fanfare, she placed it in front of her husband to carve. "It's not an expensive, organic, heirloom turkey, like the one I drove four hours round-trip to buy directly from the farm, but at least it's a turkey."

Amid the oohs and aahs, I couldn't help wondering whose turkey we were about to eat. How had she managed to find a thawed turkey on Christmas Day? No one else seemed perturbed, and the mood around the table turned decidedly festive.

We staggered away from our dinner, filled to capacity, in agreement to wait an hour before dessert. Ginger took her leftover turkey home, and Laci permitted our mothers to clean up the kitchen, while she served eggnog and hot chocolate. In honor of the holiday, I blew off all concerns about calories and sipped at eggnog from one of Laci's Spode old-fashioned glasses adorned with a Christmas tree. I stood next to my brother, George, my back to the large window overlooking the street. The packages had been opened, bows and bright wrapping paper still littered the carpet, and a cozy fire crackled. Jen and Edward sat on the floor playing Clue, and Daisy sprawled next to them.

It couldn't have been a more tranquil family scene. Forrest lounged next to my dad, but Forrest's glass held an amber liquid, which I suspected might be Scotch.

"Oh no! Christmas is over," George grumbled under his breath.

It wasn't like my brother to be so negative. "Don't be silly. This is the best part."

"That's not what I mean."

He elbowed me, and I turned around to see what he was looking at. An elegant sedan had pulled up in front of the house. Bonnie Scarborough, the local organizing diva who owned the store Clutter Busters, strode up the driveway, her arm linked intimately with that of a man who looked vaguely familiar.

"Who's the man?" I asked.

George sighed, long and hard. "Laci's dad."

FOUR

From "THE GOOD LIFE":

Dear Sophie,
My fiancé comes from a family of crafting women. No matter what I do, I can't come close to the fancy way they wrap packages. How can I make mine special without having to create bows out of doilies?
— Wrapping Impaired
in Gift, Tennessee

Dear Wrapping Impaired,
Use store-bought bows, and tuck a little holly sprig or twig of glittery faux berries next to the bow. Or tie on a festive foil-wrapped chocolate for a decoration everyone will look forward to receiving.
— Sophie

No wonder George thought Christmas was

over. Bonnie clutched Laci's father, Phil, in a manner that left little doubt a romance was brewing between them. If only we could bar the door. George's eyes, filled with dread, met mine when the bell rang at the front door.

I followed along when he ventured to the foyer. Phil graciously allowed Bonnie to enter first. She shrugged off her coat, revealing a soft peach sweater with a daringly low keyhole in front, heavily trimmed in pearls and sequins. Her peach trousers matched perfectly. Her thin lips wore the same shade of peach. The slightest touch of copper enriched loose medium brown curls that she adjusted with a practiced hand. She'd gone a bit heavy on the makeup, but maybe I would at her age, too. She reminded me of an aging actress trying to keep the years at bay.

Bonnie looked on as George hugged Phil, and then a shriek arose behind me.

"Gampi!" Jen sped past me like a locomotive to embrace Phil.

I hadn't spent much time with Laci's family, other than the requisite parties and dinners connected with Laci and George's wedding, but I vaguely recalled meeting the man who hugged Jen. Jovial with blue eyes that reminded me of ocean waters, Phil sported a girth that suggested he loved butter and bacon. I couldn't quite figure out what was different about him, though. Maybe the separation from Marnie had left him more relaxed?

"Sophie! Happy holidays." Bonnie hugged me. "What luck running into you. I've been wanting to talk to you about a business proposition I have . . ."

But then, behind me somewhere, Marnie said, "Phil's here?" I didn't hear another word Bonnie uttered because my heart sank at the hope in Marnie's voice.

I couldn't imagine what Phil was thinking when he grasped Bonnie's hand and entered the living room.

Laci, Shawna, and their mother, Marnie, appeared to be paralyzed. In shock, really. In a horrible silence that seemed to last far too long, Laci lost her grip on a platter of cookies, and it crashed to the floor.

My mother, Daisy, and I rushed to the rescue. Daisy grabbed a cookie and dashed away. A leg with an iced boot jutted from her lips and it looked like a gingerbread man to me, so I let her enjoy her little holiday treat while Mom and I collected cookies and plate shards.

Unfortunately, the mishap with the platter

of cookies didn't break the awkward moment.

Marnie finally choked, "How could you do this to us?" and disappeared into the kitchen, with Laci on her heels.

"Mrs. Scarborough?" Shawna stared at Bonnie in disbelief.

With my hands full of broken cookie pieces and ceramic shards, I had no choice but to toddle into the kitchen to the trash bin.

Marnie gripped the island counter with both hands. "I don't understand. Phil was never cruel."

Laci stared at her mother and appeared to have stopped breathing.

My mother bustled in and dumped cookies in the garbage. "Well, at least she's age-appropriate, not some twenty-year-old who thinks he has money."

Marnie scowled at Mom. "He does have money."

"Mother!" Laci whined the word as though she was frustrated. "Not that again."

"It's true, Laci. One of these days you'll see." Marnie poured herself a Scotch and sputtered when she drank it. "I hate this stuff. Is there any more wine?" Addressing Mom, she explained, "Phil has an elderly great-uncle who's loaded. He'll inherit a bundle."

I didn't want to defend the other woman. It seemed traitorish. On the other hand, I felt terrible for Bonnie. Surely she hadn't known what a wasp's nest she was walking into. "I don't think Bonnie is a golddigger."

Marnie spilled the wine she was pouring. "You know her?"

"Bonnie Scarborough. She owns a closet store, Clutter Busters, in Old Town and organizes people's houses." I bit back the fact that I'd always heard Bonnie was pretty popular and well liked.

"Well, doesn't that beat all? Sloppy Phil got himself a professional organizer." Marnie snorted in a most unladylike manner.

Shawna burst into the kitchen, her face Christmas red. "My boyfriend's mother is dating my father? Have you ever heard of anything so warped?"

Marnie sucked in air so fast I thought she was hyperventilating. "She's Beau's mother? Oh no!" And then she started to hiccup. "It's only been a month since we separated. He must have known her before. What a fool I've been. I thought he still had feelings for me. Meanwhile, the old goat was out carousing."

"Mom, Shawna." Laci spoke slowly, like she was cautioning them. "Don't do this.

Don't flip out. Not on Christmas."

Flip out? I wondered if they were prone to displays of temper that I didn't know about. In any case, it seemed an appropriate time to leave Laci alone with her mom and sister. I cocked my head at my mom and raised my eyebrows. Fortunately, she understood my message and the two of us returned to the living room, where Jen ripped into a fancy package. The silver paper gleamed with a gold brocade-like pattern. The large bow had definitely been handmade of translucent shimmering gold, and silver flowers glimmered around it. Any adult would have opened it delicately, loath to destroy the pretty wrapping.

But Jen cast the fancy trappings on the floor and eagerly opened a box. "Oh . . . it's a doll."

I hoped neither Phil nor Bonnie picked up the disappointment in her voice. With the exception of stuffed animals, Jen had lost interest in dolls around the age of nine. I leaned over her shoulder to see it and wondered what they'd been thinking. The doll wore a red dress with a matching red bow perched in stiff blond curls that gave the effect of a puffy-faced madam in the Wild West. Even worse, the doll's eyes crossed.

"Take it out and show everyone, dear," said Mom.

Reluctantly, Jen removed it from the box and held it up.

Bonnie didn't seem to notice the stunned silence. "Now that's not a doll for playing with, Jen. You put her on a safe shelf in your room because she's an antique." As though she thought we all knew about antique dolls, she glanced around at us and proudly declared, "All bisque."

I could tell Jen was about as excited as I would have been to receive the ghastly doll as a gift, but she had the sense and manners to thank Bonnie and plant a big kiss on Phil's cheek.

Bonnie made her way to me. "What a nice child. Now, about that business proposition. In January, everything is about organizing. I was over at your website recently — you've done such a lovely job with it — and I thought, why don't Sophie and I make some organizing videos?" She beamed at me. "If we do them right, you might just get your own TV show. I have a few connections. Wouldn't that be fantastic?"

Momentarily speechless, I tried to absorb her suggestion. Organizing did lend itself to videos — and it would be great promotion for both of us.

Someone rapped on the front door and opened it. Ginger glided in, carrying a platter bearing a large brown mound with a holly sprig perched on top.

"My, doesn't that look delicious!" raved Bonnie. She placed her hand on my arm and whispered, "Think about it and get back to me."

"Steamed plum pudding, just like the Cratchits ate," declared Ginger.

Edward stuck out his tongue and pretended to insert his forefinger into his mouth. I gathered he hated it.

On seeing Jen's gift, Ginger let out a small cry. "A vintage doll! Is it German? How beautiful!"

Bonnie beamed and the two of them launched into a conversation about dolls and antiques. Forrest and Edward seemed as uninterested as the rest of us. Forrest had wandered over to the window and appeared to be keeping an eye on the street. I joined him to see what he was watching.

"It's nice to see the kids having fun in the snow. Do you think it's just adults who are so miserable at Christmas?" Bags hung under Forrest's sad eyes and his lips pulled tight.

"I'm sorry," I said. "I guess Christmas is never quite as magical when we grow up."

Forrest stared into his drink. "You can't imagine what it's like to get up on Christmas morning knowing there's nothing under the tree for your kid. I know Edward is old enough to understand, but it's still a disappointment for all of us. Next year, I'm getting involved with one of the drives for gifts for underprivileged children. No one should have to go through this." He looked up at me. "You've been involved with crimes before. Do you think it's true that the culprit returns to the scene of the crime?"

"Is that why you're watching the street?"

Forrest grinned. "Partly. It can't hurt."

He was right about that. But the thief would have to be incredibly stupid to show up on Christmas Day.

"It's the Thorpe boy."

I turned to find Ginger standing behind us.

"Who?" I asked.

"Walter Thorpe. The kids call him Dasher."

"Like the reindeer?" I joked.

"He was a nightmare as a child." Ginger's tone left no doubt about her dislike of Dasher. "He was like a bee on legs, dashing every which way, bumping into things and knocking them over. His father finally put him on a leash, but the name stuck. Too bad he's not on a leash anymore — we'd have our Christmas gifts."

An angry tinge laced Forrest's tone when he said, "Why can't you ever give anyone a break? The kid made a mistake. That doesn't mean he's responsible for every crime forever after."

To me, she said, "Dasher vandalized the high school and had to be sent away to reform school."

"It was a military academy. He graduated last summer."

"And he's home for Christmas. Unemployed, I hear. Figures. What would you expect from a child whose father has the garish taste to blow up a Grinch big enough to be seen from planes landing at Dulles Airport?"

"At least *he* came home for the holidays," Forrest snarled.

Clearly in the middle of a private squabble between Forrest and Ginger that I didn't understand, my skin crawled and I wanted to slink away.

Thankfully, Marnie finally made an appearance. She wore enough makeup to cover an eight-day crying jag. Holding her head high, she announced, "Dessert is now served. Please come and help yourselves."

Someone had changed the tablecloth to a bright red weave with green trim. Highly polished red and green apples formed a pyramid on a silver platter in the center of the table. A stack of elegant Spode Christmas Tree dessert plates waited for use, next to red and green napkins, folded on the diagonal and layered decoratively, so they overlapped. A bowl of vanilla sauce sat next to Ginger's Steamed Pudding. Cookies of all shapes and types nearly overflowed on their platters, and at the far end of the table was a glamorous Red Velvet Cake. A piece had already been cut, showing off the red cake inside.

The twelve-year-old sophisticate's eyes nearly bugged out. She and Edward wasted no time loading plates and popping cookies into their mouths. A hopeful Daisy followed them, wagging her tail, and waiting for crumbs to fall. I held my breath as Phil and Bonnie approached the dining room, where Marnie stood.

Cool and distant, Marnie said, "Hello, Philip. How nice that you could bring your little friend."

I thought Bonnie might lash out but she said calmly, "So nice to meet you, Marnie. Are you responsible for the lovely centerpiece?"

"Laci made it, inspired by Natasha's show."

Bonnie acted like she was chatting with a new friend, not the woman whose husband she was dating. "Natasha is so talented. No wonder she has such a loyal following." She helped herself to a thumbprint cookie.

"I so envy you living in Old Town." Ginger glanced over her shoulder and whispered, "I've looked at a house for sale one block away from Natasha's house! Some old professor died, so they have to sell it. It's overpriced if you ask me, but it's my dream house. I'm hoping Forrest might get a promotion so we can swing it."

"I know that house. It's gorgeous. Well! I'm the envious one if you can afford that place."

Shawna sidled up next to Bonnie and helped herself to a generous piece of Red Velvet Cake. "Do you need a hand with anything for your party tomorrow, Bonnie?"

I squelched a snort. Would Shawna be more helpful to her potential future mother-in-law than she had been to her sister?

Bonnie flashed a broad smile at Shawna. "You're an honored guest. You don't have to do a thing but show up in a pretty outfit. I'm just so pleased that you and Beau will be there."

Marnie shifted from one foot to the other, and what I thought was meant as a smile wrinkled her lips like she'd licked a lemon. Who could blame her? Clearly she hadn't anticipated attending a party for her daughter in which her husband would be the date of the hostess.

The doorbell rang, and even though it wasn't my home, to be helpful, I answered the door. A young woman with a ring hanging in her nose and wild hair the color of coal said, "I was told my dad might be here?"

I didn't think so, but before I could say anything, she cried, "Daddy!" and launched herself at Forrest.

"Pumpkin! You came!" He embraced her in his arms like he might never let go.

Edward walked by and punched her in the arm.

"When'd you get so tall, rug rat?" she asked.

"Emma?" Ginger held her dessert plate in one hand and a cup of coffee in the other. "How nice of you to join us after all." She regarded Emma stiffly. "Honestly, I hate these modern fashions. You look positively pregnant. Maybe we can go shopping at the sales tomorrow and get you something a little nicer."

Mom whispered into my ear, "The next time I say something about your weight, I want you to remind me of this."

I was glad Mom realized how awful Ginger was being to her daughter, but Emma *did* look pregnant.

"Shopping for little teeny clothes might be more appropriate, Mom."

"You mean . . . ?" Forrest beamed and hugged his daughter again.

But a shadow crossed over Ginger's face. "I know you like to torture me, Emma. Never mind all the things I've done for you, beginning with hours of painful labor, but that's not funny."

Emma placed a proud hand on the top of her tummy. "I'm not joking."

Ginger sat down and primly sipped coffee. "At least tell me that you have a husband and a job."

Emma borrowed her dad's fork and took a big bite of the slice of Red Velvet Cake on his plate. Her mouth full, she said, "We're selling our art at craft shows."

"We? My sister found a guy who didn't dump her after the first date?"

"Edward!" Sitting so straight it made *my* back hurt, Ginger daintily ate a bite of her steamed pudding.

Forrest raised his eyebrows in fatherly

alarm. "Emma," he said gently, "you're not traveling around to craft shows with some stranger?"

"Of course not. It's Dasher."

Ginger's plate of steamed pudding tumbled to her lap, and she grabbed her throat.

FIVE

From "Ask Natasha":

Dear Natasha,
I'm so inept at decorating for the holidays that my friends make fun of me. I can't afford life-size Santas, animated figures, or a forest of poinsettias, and small decorations just go unnoticed. Any easy decorating suggestions that won't leave me broke?
— No Partridges in Peartree, Tennessee

Dear No Partridges,
Do you have pears? Fruit makes beautiful Christmas decor. Especially pomegranates and rosy pears nestled among pine greens. If that's not your style, pop colorful Christmas candies into glass bowls and use them to decorate. Or take a walk to collect pinecones and nuts, spray paint them gold or silver, and cluster them in

glass bowls and vases for an understated elegant look.

— Natasha

Phil, Marnie's estranged husband, grabbed Ginger from behind, lifted her, and squeezed in a Heimlich-maneuver fashion. She coughed and waved a hand at Phil. Wheezing, she said, "I'm okay. Just can't get air." Beet red, she rasped, "I'd like to go home."

"Maybe you should rest a moment," my mom suggested, rather reasonably, I thought.

But Ginger shuffled toward the door, bent forward and coughing, with her husband on her heels. Their son, Edward, followed, but Emma calmly finished the piece of cake she'd been eating before trailing after them.

When the door shut, George said, "That was quite a scene."

"All families have problems, dear." Mom bustled off to the kitchen, and the rest of us were left facing the other problem — Marnie, Phil, and his love bunny, Bonnie.

When I cut a piece of Red Velvet Cake for my dessert, Mom was covering Ginger's steamed pudding with plastic wrap. "Sophie, would you take this next door to the Chadwicks? They'll want it later."

"Sure." I savored a dollop of cream cheese frosting on my fork and dipped my finger in a tiny bit of the sweet icing for Daisy to lick. "Marnie recovered from her shock fast."

Mom groaned. "Wait until Phil leaves. I bet we don't talk about anything else tonight. Poor Marnie. I don't know how I would react if your father pulled that kind of stunt."

Daisy wagged her tail, and I realized that Jen stood behind us. "Can I go home with you and Hannah tonight?" she asked. "I can walk Daisy for you."

"That's not a bad idea." Mom handed me the pudding. "Bonnie's Boxing Day party tomorrow is in Old Town anyway." She pursed her lips. "I wonder if Marnie and Laci will still want to attend?"

She handed me the plum pudding and fed Daisy a cookie crumb that had landed on the tablecloth.

Since I was only going next door, I didn't bother with a coat. But I wasn't wearing boots and didn't want to tromp through the snow, so I walked down George's driveway to the street and turned up the Chadwicks' drive. I could hear screaming before I reached their front walk. I stopped and debated whether I should return later. But before I could decide, the door opened and

Emma blasted out onto the porch. She turned and shouted into the house, "Why can't you be like other mothers? I will never be the perfect child you wanted. Why can't you ever be happy for me?"

She stomped down the sidewalk toward me. "Are you okay?" I asked.

Emma peered at the steamed pudding. "What's that? Oh no! Not the witch's Olde English Cratchit dessert." She laughed heartily. "We all hate it. Edward and Dad will spend the next couple of days trying to figure out how to get rid of it. Dad is such a fantastic baker, but the witch won't let him in the kitchen. She knows he'll show her up. It's so much more important to her to have something authentic that matches her Olde English Christmas theme. Never mind if it's edible. We had to pressure her for years to make a turkey. Can you imagine — one year she made a boar's head. The head, for heaven's sake!"

Emma appeared to have calmed down. "At least she won't be pushing that vile pudding at me. If I didn't hate it so much, I'd take it with me just to spite her."

"Emma!" Across the street and one house down, a young man waved at her. From a distance, he looked like he hadn't bathed in a while, but then I decided it might just be several days worth of beard growth.

Emma waved back at him. "Well, see you around. If my dad asks, we're staying with the Thorpes. Maybe she'll have to go out for a while, and he can bake Red Velvet Cupcakes for me — my favorite!" She flickered her fingers at me and glanced back at her parents' house before striding off.

As I walked up to the front door, I saw that Ginger peered out from behind a curtain, her eyes on Emma.

I rang the bell and Ginger answered the door, Edward and Forrest crowding behind her. Their crestfallen expressions told me they'd hoped Emma had returned. I held out the pudding to Ginger, who took it and coolly thanked me. The stress of the family turbulence showed on Edward and Forrest, but Ginger had composed herself, and if I hadn't seen and heard it, I would never have guessed she had just had a screaming match with her daughter.

An hour later, we had packed Jen's outfit for the party the next day and loaded the car with an odd assortment of leftovers. Hannah, Jen, Daisy, and I drove away, looking forward to a fun night of movies and girl talk. I didn't envy my parents or Laci and George. Marnie was sure to be obsessed with Phil and his new relationship with Bonnie.

The next day, instead of hitting post-Christmas sales, Hannah, Jen, and I took a long winter walk with Daisy. Then we enjoyed a leisurely brunch of crabmeat quiche at home before dressing for Bonnie's Boxing Day party and strolling down to The Laughing Hound. My friend, Bernie, ran the chic restaurant for an absentee owner and had turned the place into one of Old Town's most popular dining spots.

Bernie greeted us at the door, his sandy hair tousled as usual and his British accent charming. "Merry Christmas, Bauer ladies!" He hugged each of us. "Bonnie booked the conservatory room for the party. You know the way, don't you, Sophie?"

I assumed he meant the dining room with a glass roof and wall that overlooked a garden. I nodded, but he was already greeting more guests, so I motioned for Hannah and Jen to follow me.

Someone had decorated the restaurant with lavishly draped swags of pine, accented with plaid bows. Tiny white lights glittered in the deep green. It was tasteful and festive — until we stepped into the conservatory room, where someone had gone wild with candy.

All pretense of teen maturity melted from Jen. Her eyes huge, she floated into the room with the wonder of a four-year-old. Red, white, and green ribbon candy hung from Williamsburg-style brass chandeliers. A table along the wall, decked in a green flannel cloth, bore glass containers of every shape and size, full of candy, cookies, and assorted bars. More glass urns filled with red licorice, candy canes, and ribbon candies acted as a centerpiece down the long dining table. A stocking with a chocolate Santa poking out of the top hung from the back of each chair. A candy cane leaned in the goblet at each place setting, and each plate held a lacy paper cone filled with sugared nuts.

Laci snuck up behind her rapturous daughter. "And you didn't want to come . . ."

"Mom! Did you ever see anything like this?"

Laci chuckled. "I hate to say anything nice about Bonnie now that she has stolen Dad, but if I didn't know better, Sophie, I'd think she was competing with you and Natasha for diva status." Laci turned to Jen and said firmly, "Now, young lady, you're old enough to know you can't eat all these sweets . . ."

I tuned out her lecture and Hannah nudged me. "Who's the hunk?"

I followed her line of sight and guessed she meant a tall young man with a self-assured demeanor. A slight pudginess around his jaw suggested a fondness for good food. Thick eyebrows the color of coffee beans matched his hair. The top corners of his forehead had become prominent, framing his face like a square at the top, but it ended with a prominent and determined chin. The extra pounds softened his appearance, as did the warm brown eyes shaped like almonds. At ease with himself and the world, he chatted with a group of other people in their early thirties, his hands in his trouser pockets pushing back the navy blazer he wore.

"He's too young for you," I said.

"I'm not too old to admire good looks."

Laci returned her attention to us. "You'll have to fight Shawna for him. That's Beau, Shawna's intended and Bonnie's son. Unless you mean the guy next to him with the shaggy hair. That's Tyler, whom I personally like much better than Beau. Beau's a little bit arrogant if you ask me. He, Tyler, and Shawna have been an inseparable threesome since the day she waited on them and spilled an entire bowl of chili on Tyler. Who'd have thought something like that would lead to friendship?"

Hannah wrinkled her nose. "There's just something icky about Beau's mom dating Shawna's father. Why does that seem so wrong? *Eww*."

I had to agree. I didn't quite understand how Bonnie could throw a party for Shawna and Beau, even using the excuse of Boxing Day, and show up with Phil. Didn't she realize how upsetting it would be for Shawna and her family? I glanced around for Marnie and spotted her outside in the cold without a coat, standing on the shoveled walk in the middle of a dead winter garden blanketed with snow. Even from a distance, her makeup looked perfect, but she couldn't conceal her bloodshot eyes. She gazed inside, her mouth grim.

I supposed she'd had no choice about coming. After all, Shawna expected to be making the big announcement about her engagement. Which made it all the more cruel. Couldn't Bonnie have waited a week before revealing her new relationship with Marnie's husband?

Shawna appeared to be taking the situation in stride. She placed a package on a table, which caused me to wonder if we were supposed to bring gifts. White snow-flakes dotted the red gift wrap. A wide red ribbon with a white border circled the package and a felt snowman, which appeared to be handmade, hung from the ribbon. I had no idea Shawna was so adept at crafting.

A hand on my arm distracted me. Bonnie, dressed head to toe in a winter white knit dress adorned with sparkling silvery bugle beads, held out her arms and kissed the air next to my ear. "I'm so glad you could come. I just know we'll do great things together. Don't you adore my sugarplum decor?"

Sugarplum? I wasn't completely sure what a sugarplum was, but I had a feeling it wasn't candy canes or ribbon candy. "When did you find time to do it?"

"Phil and I came over early this morning with my assistant, Tyler." She glanced around. "Have you met my son, the lawyer? He's here somewhere. Why don't you drop around my place this evening for cocktails? Around six, maybe? We can put our heads together about the organizing videos. I have some great ideas."

My parents chose that moment to join us and gush about Bonnie's candy theme. Bonnie beamed. "I love throwing parties. I hope Sophie will bring you to my Auld Lang Syne

Auction."

"An auction? Is it in Old Town?" asked Mom. "Sophie didn't mention a thing!"

My father had momentarily forgotten all about the sweets and listened in. The only people I knew who liked auctions more than me were my parents.

Bonnie was in her element as she explained about the auction. "When I opened my shop, I realized that we all acquire new things at Christmas, but few of us clear out old items. So I organized the Auld Lang Syne Auction between Christmas and New Year's. We ask everyone to donate items they no longer use, and we auction them off, with the proceeds going to needy families. Sometimes it pays for a new roof or guttering, sometimes it helps defray medical expenses. It's a win-win situation. Everyone gets to start the year on the right foot. That's why I called it the Auld Lang Syne Auction. We're saying good-bye to something old and everyone gets a fresh start."

"Sophie, I can't believe you've never mentioned this to us. What fun!" My mom shook her head in mock dismay.

"And for a good cause, too," said Dad. "Do George and Laci know about the auction? There they are . . ." He didn't even finish speaking before he and Mom rushed over to tell George, whom I was quite certain couldn't care less.

"I love your parents' enthusiasm. They're just the kind of bidders we need. Oh! I see someone I must greet. Excuse me." Bonnie took off, in nude-colored heels that would have toppled me, but she bypassed the people who appeared to want her attention and made a beeline for Phil, who stared out the window at Marnie with a wistful expression.

"I hope Phil's wife isn't stupid enough to fight Bonnie for him." The man next to me sipped from a glass of wine, then held out his hand. "Tom Thorpe."

"I'm George Bauer's sister, Sophie. Are you the neighbor who played Santa for the kids?"

"It was the least I could do. I still can't believe that anyone could be so mean to little children that he would steal their toys."

He didn't look like Santa Claus. Although his hair had gone silver, he wore it short, which emphasized his masculine bone structure. He also maintained an athletic physique and needed a big pillow to achieve Santa's girth. His dark eyes glinted with mirth. No wonder my mother found him appealing.

"My wife and I started that tradition when

77

our sons were young. I just kept it up through the years. Honestly, I think I get as much out of it as the little ones do."

"You're married? You'd better tell my mom." I pointed in her direction. "She's determined to find someone for you."

He laughed aloud, with genuine joy. "The effervescent Inga. She's delightful. I look forward to meeting the woman she comes up with — I've been a widower for many years."

Finally! Someone who wasn't annoyed by my mother's constant matchmaking. "I'm sorry about your wife."

He took a deep breath. "You never quite get over losing a spouse. But my sons Tyler and Walter are adults now, old enough to be getting married themselves. In fact, I'm going to be a grandpa in the spring." He hoisted his glass in a toast to someone across the room. Forrest and Ginger's daughter, Emma, toasted back, but her wineglass appeared to contain milk or eggnog. Without her mother present, Emma was all smiles. I guessed the young man beside her, with the modern messy top haircut, was Dasher. The sides were cut short, but some kind of pomade helped it stand up on top. He'd shaved off the grungy beginnings of a beard, revealing a surprisingly handsome face. In spite of Ginger's opinion of him, I could understand Emma's attraction. He appeared quite respectable in a maroon turtleneck and crisply pressed trousers, almost dashing.

"Now that the kids are grown, I think it's time for me to enjoy the companionship of a woman again," said Tom.

A bell tinkled, and Bonnie asked everyone to take their seats. I found my name written in an elegant script on the cone of sugared nuts on my plate. No sooner had I sat down than the bell rang again. Bonnie stood and raised a wineglass. "To my friends and family, thank you for coming to my Boxing Day party. Merry Christmas to you all!" She sipped from her glass but made no move to be seated. "And now . . ." She paused for dramatic effect.

I glanced at Shawna, seated next to Beau. This must be the moment of the big engagement announcement. Shawna sat up straight and beamed, her face full of happy anticipation. She brushed hair behind her ear with her left hand, but I didn't see a ring — yet.

"I have an announcement to make." Bonnie motioned for Phil to stand next to her.

He struggled to his feet and smiled.

"I'm thrilled to share my news with you. I

will be giving up my organizing business, and Phil and I will be tying the knot!"

Six

From "Ask Natasha":

Dear Natasha,
I loathe Boxing Day because it signals the end of Christmas and the beginning of Christmas cleanup. Where do I begin?
— Vexed in Vixen, Louisiana

Dear Vexed,
Take a cue from the British and the origins of Boxing Day. The servants worked on Christmas and had the following day off. Their employers used that day to box up items to give to the poor.
— Natasha

In the moment of stunned silence that followed, I thought Phil seemed as surprised as everyone else. I looked around for Marnie, who stared at Phil, who was still as a stone statue. Amid the smattering of applause that broke the painful silence, Shawna burst into tears and ran from the table. Laci and Marnie followed her, and though I couldn't hear what was being said, after a brief exchange with Bonnie, Phil, who no longer smiled, followed his wife and daughters.

"Mom!" Beau rose from his seat and glared at her.

"Oh dear. I thought Shawna would be happy for her father." Bonnie didn't look too contrite when she sat down.

Beau took off after Shawna while his mother addressed her guests, but no one in particular. "I feel just terrible. Who would have thought an adult would react like that?"

Hannah poked me. "Should we go to help? We're on their side — right?"

I didn't know what we were expected to do. Most of the guests appeared uncomfortable. Bonnie had already moved on and was proudly showing off a diamond ring on her left hand. In the end, it was my brother who initiated the mass exodus of the Bauer family. He motioned to my mother, and our entire family excused ourselves and met in the restaurant foyer.

Jen immediately located her mother and aunt in the large bar area a few steps down.

Shawna stood by the oversized fireplace, wiping tears from her face while Beau comforted her. Laci and her parents clustered nearby. Before anyone could stop her, Jen rushed down the stairs to her mom. Like bewildered baby ducks, we trailed after George into the bar lounge.

Bernie stopped me and asked, "What happened?"

When I explained, he appeared puzzled. "That doesn't sound like Bonnie. She's always so considerate."

"Exactly. It's totally out of character for her," I said.

Mom leaned in to our conversation and whispered, "Did it occur to you that she may have done it on purpose to help Beau save face?"

"What?" Hannah wedged between Mom and me. "That makes no sense at all."

"People do a lot of things for their kids. Maybe Beau isn't ready to pop the question, and Bonnie wanted to provide another reason to celebrate."

"But Bonnie is already wearing a ring," I whispered. "It couldn't have come as a last-minute thing."

"Good point!" exclaimed Hannah.

And then, as though we had planned it, our little group turned and watched Phil,

Marnie, and Laci. Deep in conversation, no one bothered to lower their voices, and they were plenty agitated.

"You have your nerve waltzing into Christmas with a fiancée on your arm." Marnie's jaw twitched in anger.

"As I recall, you're the one who threw me out into the cold. What did you expect me to do? No loving wife, no family. Did you think I'd sit on the stoop and cry?"

"It's not like you to be so hurtful. Is this what that woman brings out in you?"

"In retrospect, I see that it may not have been the best idea to bring her to Laci's house yesterday."

"And just whose idea was that?"

Phil clenched his fist. "There's no point in blaming anyone. What's done is done."

"Just as I suspected. You're blindly going along with anything she says. Don't you see? She's trying to drive a wedge between us."

"That's not fair. Bonnie is a fine woman. You'd like her if you had met under other circumstances."

"Wake up, Phil. She could have waited a few days instead of ruining Christmas for our whole family. She invited us to this nightmare of a Boxing Day party, and I could have met her then, instead of under the worst possible circumstances."

"I'm not going to argue about this with you," said Phil. "We're separated. I haven't done anything wrong."

"*Argh.* You're impossible!" Marnie threw her hands in the air. "Then let's set your relationship aside. What kind of woman dates her son's girlfriend's father?"

"It's not like that. Besides, she's not the only woman I dated. Can I help it if Beau happens to have a lovely mother?"

Marnie clapped a hand against her chest and staggered backward. "There were others? You didn't waste any time, did you?"

"Good grief, Marnie. You expected me to curl up by myself and whither away? You were the one who wanted me out of the house. Surely you expected me to date."

"I thought you would live in a pigsty and eat nothing but fast food until you came to your senses and realized how good you had it with me."

"You were waiting for me to come home?"

"I didn't expect you to marry right away."

Phil massaged his forehead. "That came as a surprise to me, too."

Laci wrapped a hand across her eyes for a moment and sighed. When she removed it, she said, "Enough. You two are only making things worse for Shawna."

Her parents had the good sense to look

over at their younger daughter. Tears streaked her makeup but she had managed to compose herself.

Beau addressed us. "I'm going back to join my mother's party now. I'm sure you understand. I trust one of you will see Shawna safely home?"

I wondered what he could possibly have said to her to help her dry her eyes.

Phil toddled over to Shawna, hugged her, and murmured something in her ear. He clapped a hand on Beau's back and the two of them headed for the stairs.

"Where do you think you're going?" demanded Marnie.

Phil stopped briefly to look back at her, but he didn't say a word. He seemed sad, but he walked up the steps, away from his family.

My dad broke the tension when he said, "I'm starved."

Marnie and Mom shot him incredulous looks, but Jen saved him by piping up, "Me, too."

Shawna sniffled and declared, "I hate that woman. She ruined everything." Her tone rose with hysteria until it was a shriek that drew the attention of everyone in our vicinity. "First she stole Daddy and now Beau *can't* propose to me because it won't be special, and Christmas is over!"

Marnie embraced her daughter and walked her toward the door, past a shaggy-haired young man, who looked on, his expression troubled.

"It doesn't have to be Christmas, honey. He can propose anytime." Marnie shot my mother a helpless look, and I knew she didn't believe a proposal would be forthcoming.

Since I hadn't been to the grocery store, and I'd brought my leftovers to Laci's, we decided to get takeout from The Laughing Hound and left Hannah and Dad behind to carry it back to my place.

The rest of us trudged home, the picture of gloom and doom, instead of happy partygoers. After a couple of blocks, Shawna peeled off, claiming she needed time alone to think.

If it had been Hannah, I would have coaxed her to come home with us, but Shawna wasn't my sister, and Laci didn't intervene.

The rest of us hurried home, hungry and cold. But the second we entered my house, I knew something was wrong. Daisy didn't rush to the foyer to greet us, and Mochie hissed at us — which he'd never done before.

SEVEN

From "THE GOOD LIFE":

Dear Sophie,
My wife refuses to put up a Christmas tree because of our cats and dogs. I don't want my children missing out on the fun of a tree. Any suggestions on keeping the pets out of the Christmas tree?
— Troubled in Tannenbaum, Arkansas

Dear Troubled,
Put up your tree for two days before you decorate it. That will give them a chance to sniff it and get used to it. Set the tree on top of a small sturdy table so it's not at nose height. If it's a live tree, cover the water since it can be a toxic drink for animals. Protect or hide electric cords from animals likely to chew on them. Never use tinsel. Swallowed tinsel

can mean emergency surgery or death. Don't hang treats or toys (especially not catnip-scented) as ornaments. When decorating your tree, always use unbreakable ornaments around the bottom in case someone is tempted to take a swipe at one.

— Sophie

His tail erect, normally sweet Mochie stalked around us, not allowing anyone to touch him. We hung up our coats, and I found the problem in the kitchen. Daisy sprawled on the floor with two adorable kittens nestled next to her tummy for warmth. Their noses were coal black in stark contrast to their fluffy silvery fur. It almost appeared as though they wore grayish masks. The most startling thing about the two kittens were their vibrant blue eyes.

Mochie strode by them and hissed, prompting them to snuggle deeper into Daisy's fur. It wasn't hard to figure out that Daisy meant to protect them from Mochie. I scanned the kitchen in disbelief. Where could they have come from?

Jen threw herself at them. "Kittens! Is this my real Christmas gift?"

George looked at the ceiling like he was saying a quick prayer.

Laci glared at me, threw her hands in the air as though she blamed me for buying the kittens for Jen, and immediately said, "No, honey. Now, we've talked about this. I'm a working mom and we don't have time for pets. I'm sure your Aunt Sophie knows that."

I wasn't sure Laci would ever pry the kittens away from Jen. She lifted one in each hand and cuddled them to her. I'd heard Laci complain about the burdens of pets many times, and I would never dream of giving Jen a cat or dog without her parents' permission. "Sorry, Jen. I don't know where they came from or why they're here."

Laci edged away from Jen, as though she was afraid of liking the kittens. "You mean they're not yours?"

Surely no one in my family would have surprised me with kittens. I squinted at George. Was this some kind of trick to manipulate Laci into giving Jen the kittens? "I've never seen them before."

George sputtered, "Oh, come on. Like we're going to believe that?"

Mom scratched them under their chins. "I think they're Ragdoll kittens."

They were gorgeous. These kittens had never scrounged on the streets. They looked like fairy-tale kittens — born to be pampered. I bent to stroke Daisy's head, and she batted her tail against the hardwood floor. "Hannah and Jen can confirm that they weren't here last night or this morning." Merely uttering those words sent a shiver down my spine.

"Someone broke into your house?" Mom took one of the kittens from Jen but she looked worried.

If they hadn't been so cute, I probably would have been concerned about their sudden appearance in my house sooner. Somehow, fluffy kittens just didn't equate with anything malicious. I strode into the sunroom to be sure the back door was locked and found a fleece-lined basket with a tag on the handle. The door was secure, so I returned to the kitchen and read aloud from the tag. " 'Merry Christmas! We hope you love these babies as much as we do.' "

"Who signed it?" asked George.

I flipped it over. "No signature." Nothing seemed amiss, except for the presence of the cats and the basket.

George left the room abruptly and I could hear him tromping up the stairs to the second and third floors. He returned shortly. "I don't see any signs of a break-in. Whoever brought those kittens had a key."

Mochie sat on the window seat and

watched grumpily as my family passed the darling kittens around. I tried to pick him up to prove he was still loved, but he was having none of it. Determined not to let him see me with the kittens, I busied myself at the stove, putting on the kettle for tea and heating cider. I plopped cinnamon sticks into mugs and wondered who could have left kittens in my house.

"Maybe they're from Wolf," suggested Mom.

Wolf loved cats and dogs as much as I did, and swung by the shelter regularly to donate food. He was practical, though, and I couldn't imagine Wolf giving anyone an animal unless he knew they wanted one.

"He left town yesterday morning and won't be back for a few days."

"Sophie, who has keys to your house?" demanded George.

When did George become so protective? I almost resented the tone of his voice. "Not Wolf."

"Mars?" he asked.

I chose my words carefully so I wouldn't mislead anyone. If my mother thought my ex-husband had a key, but Wolf didn't, she would jump to all kinds of incorrect conclusions. "Mars and Natasha have a key. They have to since we share custody of Daisy."

Daisy flapped her tail at the mention of her name.

"Bernie still has a key from the time he stayed here, but he was at the restaurant." Then I thought of my best friend and across-the-street neighbor, Nina Reid Norwood, who was used to letting herself in and out of my house. "Nina has a key, too, but she's in North Carolina visiting relatives over the holidays."

"You've given a key to everyone in the neighborhood?" George scolded.

"Just a few people. Don't you have a key for some of your neighbors in case of emergency?"

Thankfully, Hannah and Dad arrived with the food. I set the dining room table while Dad struck a fire in the fireplace. "Sophie, I don't like this business about someone entering your home while we were out."

I wasn't very happy about it myself, but we'd had enough aggravation, and I desperately wanted to change the subject. I opened takeout containers heaped with rosy, sliced roast beef, Yorkshire pudding, gravy, garlic mashed potatoes that smelled heavenly, and a festive salad of corn and diced roasted red peppers atop greens. It stood to reason that an Englishman would serve traditional holiday fare on Boxing Day, but I wondered if Bernie had given us the meal we would have eaten had we stayed at Bonnie's party, and I said so aloud.

Dad shrugged. "Looks good."

The last container brought a smile to my face, since I didn't think Chinese eggplant with spicy curry was a British Boxing Day tradition. Bernie threw that in because he knew how much I liked it.

Our noisy bunch finally sat down to eat. Daisy planted herself at my feet, and Mochie paced in the foyer, where he could watch us and the invading kittens. Laci tried to convince Jen to put the kitten down during dinner, but Jen wasn't letting go. A compromise was reached when Marnie, who held the other kitten, suggested they were so small they would be very happy in Marnie's and Jen's laps. That appeared to satisfy everyone except Laci.

"Since the kittens are so mysterious, I think we should call them Agatha and Edgar," said Marnie.

"Mother! Please! No names," cried Laci. "Dear heaven, what have you done?"

Dad asked innocently, "What's the problem?"

George cut a piece of roast beef on his plate. "Once you name them, you're stuck with them."

"I think they should be Alice and Jasper," said Jen.

Mom smiled at her only grandchild. "Those are charming names, sweetheart."

George flashed Mom a look. "Don't get excited, they're from her favorite movie and they're vampires."

"Vampires! I never let my children watch movies about vampires."

Hannah laughed aloud. "So sad but true. We had to sneak to see them."

We were all chuckling when the knocker on my front door sounded. I rose and opened it to Shawna, whose face was stained from tears.

I showed her into the dining room.

"What's wrong, honey?" asked Marnie. "Did something else happen?"

"Since I knew Beau was at the restaurant, I walked by his apartment and let myself in."

"Shawna! You didn't!" It was Laci who scolded her sister. Marnie didn't seem at all disturbed by Shawna's behavior and waited to hear more.

"I have a key, Laci. It's not like I was breaking in."

"Then why bother doing it? You were up to no good and you know it." Laci shook a finger at Jen. "Don't ever do that. It's wrong. Do you understand?"

"In November, I accidentally found an engagement ring in Beau's sock drawer."

Marnie looked so sad for her daughter that I thought she might start crying.

"And now it's gone."

EIGHT

From "Ask Natasha":

Dear Natasha,
Every year I say I'm going to get a jump-start on Christmas so I won't be so far behind and have too much to do. Is it tacky to put up the tree before Thanksgiving?
— Pooped in Pilgrim, Texas

Dear Pooped,
The time to start is the day after Christmas! The very first thing to do on Boxing Day is start your shopping list for next Christmas and take advantage of the sales. If you follow my plan for organizing throughout the year, you'll have plenty of time to put up your tree after Thanksgiving.
— Natasha

"Gone?" said Marnie. "Did you search thoroughly?"

"Mom!" protested Laci. "You two are the worst examples for Jen!"

It was my mom who weighed in with a less agitated voice. "He could have had it with him today. Maybe he meant to pop the big question, but his mother's announcement got in the way."

"Do you really think so?" Color returned to Shawna's complexion. *"Aaugh."* She moaned and clapped her hands to her face. "I shouldn't have run out. I bet he was going to propose right after Bonnie's announcement. What a fool I was." She took a seat, reached for the potatoes, and heaped them on her plate. "That's a relief. I'm meeting him later today. I bet he'll propose then! It won't be the same as if he'd proposed at the party, but the important thing is to get that ring on my finger so we can plan a June wedding."

Marnie's spirits didn't appear to improve, and I had a feeling she wasn't buying that explanation. I had doubts, too. Somehow, I didn't think Shawna found the ring accidentally in the first place. She and Marnie didn't seem to have any qualms about snooping. I couldn't point fingers, though, since I came from a family of snoopers.

"Wonderful." Mom winked at Shawna. "As I recall, Laci and George wanted to buy a few Christmas gifts to make up for the ones that were stolen. I thought Grandpa and Jen might walk Daisy while the rest of us get groceries. Then we can have a cozy dinner here tonight."

"Fine by me, but I have a meeting at six." Under the circumstances, I didn't think I should reveal that it was with Bonnie.

"I need to do a little shopping, too. I'd like to go to the mall with the kids," said Marnie. "You don't mind if I skip the grocery expedition, do you?"

No one said anything in response, so I guessed that Mom and Hannah were stuck with the grocery run. Hannah would be less than thrilled about *that*.

Five o'clock rolled around before I knew it, and truth be told, I was delighted to stroll with Dad, Jen, and Daisy, at least for the first leg of their walk. We'd left the mysterious kittens safely confined to an upstairs bedroom, so we wouldn't have to worry about Mochie. He seemed much more relaxed when he was the king of the kitchen again, but I knew he would soon discover that the kittens hadn't gone far.

Dainty bits of snow drifted in the air as we walked. The wind had ceased entirely, but the temperature was dropping, making more snow likely. The crisp air stung my face, but I was too busy exclaiming over bright Christmas lights with Dad and Jen to care.

The ancient brick sidewalks and historic houses of Old Town simmered with a magical quality. Candles burned in nearly every window, especially in the high dormer windows in attic rooms. Tiny white lights sparkled in trees and on bushes, and snow dusted pines and evergreens that graced front doors, as though Mother Nature had added to the festivity.

I was sorry to have to leave my family and miss the boats on the Potomac that had been strung with Christmas lights, but I dutifully peeled off and headed east toward Bonnie's house.

I had walked only one block when I spied a strikingly familiar figure. Wrapped in a leather bomber jacket, with a muffler around his neck, and wearing a bulky Elmer Fudd–type hat, George's neighbor, Forrest Chadwick, stood outside an empty storefront.

"Well, hello!" I said. "What are you doing in Old Town?"

Forrest blinked a couple of times. I thought perhaps he didn't recognize me away from George's house. "Sophie Winston? George's sister. We ate Christmas dinner together yesterday."

"Of course! I'm sorry. I was deep in thought — elsewhere. You know?"

I understood completely.

He glanced up and down the street. "Pretty quiet out tonight."

"I guess people are still celebrating the holidays — and it *is* cold out."

He didn't reply, and a horrible, awkward moment passed. I finally blurted out, "Any word on the Christmas-gift thief?"

"They're still looking for him, them . . . whoever. I don't think they have the first clue, but that doesn't stop Ginger from calling the police every couple of hours to pester them." He forced a smile. "I'd better not hold you up. It's freezing out here."

I said good-bye and continued on my way, but when I reached the end of the block, I glanced back. Forrest hadn't moved on. He still stood in front of the building where I'd first seen him. I wondered if he was waiting for someone.

I walked on — another two blocks to Bonnie's house. One of the older homes like mine, it sported a historic plaque by the door. I could have picked it out simply by virtue of the holiday decor. Bonnie had been in candy mode with her Christmas decorations this year. Like her sugarplum decor at

101

the party, she'd attached ribbon candies to the wreaths on her doors and windows. I wondered if they wouldn't disintegrate in the wet weather. Could they be made of plastic?

Faux candles flickered in each window in true Old Town–style. I rang the bell and waited. The scent of wood burning in a fireplace drifted to me, and I longed to head home to my own cozy fireplace. A bit impatient, I rang the bell again and leaned sideways to peer inside her front window. Artfully swagged drapes prohibited me from seeing inside.

I stepped back and looked up at her house. Maybe with the party and the brouhaha over Phil and Shawna, she'd forgotten our appointment? Or maybe I was now persona non grata because my family had marched out of her party? I hadn't thought about it from her perspective, but we'd left a lot of embarrassingly empty seats.

I sighed and the mist from my breath drifted like a little cloud in the cold air.

Surely Bonnie separated business from her private life. Besides, even if she was angry with me or my family for making a scene, wouldn't she come to the door and tell me that she no longer had any interest in working with me? Everything I knew about her indicated that she was as sweet as the candy she used in her decorations. I couldn't imagine her snubbing me.

As I looked up toward the second floor of her house, I saw smoke coming from a chimney. A good clue that she was home. I rang her doorbell again, though I felt a bit guilty for ringing it a third time. She still didn't answer.

Although I was sorely tempted to give up and go home, I thought about the fact that she lived alone like I did — well, when Phil wasn't there with her — and that she might need help. I stood on her stoop and debated.

Caution won out and I tried the handle on the front door. It didn't budge. I checked around the side of her house to see if there was an alley that would provide access to the rear. I found a cute cranberry red gate, higher than I was tall, with an arched top and a pineapple, the symbol of hospitality, carved into the wood. The gate swung open easily, and in moments, I stood in her fenced backyard, where someone had converted what had most likely been a screened porch into a cozy room with paned windows all around, making it look like a cottage.

A fire blazed in a corner fireplace and wrapping paper was strewn across the coffee table and the floor. She must be home. I leaned closer to the glass for a better look, and rapped on it, in case she was close by and could hear.

As I scanned the room, I spotted a shoe — beige with a pointed toe and three-inch heel — lying on its side on the brick floor. I squinted and used my sleeve to wipe condensation from my breath off the little square of window. Surely that couldn't be her foot in the shoe. A piece of red and white wrapping paper had fallen, partially covering the shoe. The angle of the coffee table prevented me from seeing more. I squinted again and decided there was definitely a foot in the shoe.

I whipped out my cell phone and called 911. When I hung up, I decided I couldn't wait for them. Even a minute or two might make a difference if Bonnie was sick or bleeding. I tried the handle of the back door, but it was locked. Taking a cue from the Christmas-gift thief, I found a cast concrete kitten and smashed it into a glass panel in the door. The sound reverberated through the small garden. Careful to avoid the shards of glass that wrapped around the hole like teeth in a shark's mouth, I inserted my arm and felt for a latch. *Oh no!* Smart Bonnie installed a lock that required a key on both sides. "Bonnie!" I called. "Can you hear me?"

No answer.

I backed up and kicked the lower part of the door with the bottom of my foot. *Ouch!* That didn't work. Poor Bonnie. Panic rose in me. I had to get inside — now!

I gazed around the garden, heaved a large terra cotta pot out of the snow, and slung it at a window. Much better. It left a gaping hole and spidery lines crackled through the tempered glass. I hurried the breaking glass along by knocking the edges with the concrete kitten. With one last tap, the remaining glass rushed to the floor in bits. The windowpanes proved to be ornamental and gave easily when I yanked them.

I was able to step inside, glass crunching under my feet, freezing air gushing in through the huge opening. The faint smell of bleach mingled with pine and the smoky scent of fire. I rushed toward the shoe I'd seen, and found Bonnie sprawled on the floor between the sofa and the coffee table.

I shoved the coffee table aside and kneeled by her head. Tapping her cheeks gently, I called her name, but she didn't revive. Surely she couldn't be dead? There was no blood, no sign of a wound.

My throat contracted with fear as I reached for her wrist. She still wore the winter white outfit she'd worn to her party earlier. Her makeup was perfect. She looked like she ought to sit up and start talking.

I couldn't find a pulse. I felt her neck, hoping I was just being clumsy, and that she was alive. The doorbell rang, and I jumped at the sound. My heart beating like crazy, I ran through the adjoining kitchen in search of the front door. Fortunately, Bonnie's house wasn't very large. I twisted the deadbolt and threw the door open to emergency medical technicians. Thanking them for coming, I led the way to Bonnie.

They moved the coffee table for better access, revealing a music box and a fancy ribbon with a felt snowman attached to it, as well as a jewelry-sized box and a little Christmas gift-wrap bag that it must have come in. I picked them up to get them out of the EMTs way.

Old, probably an antique, the large music box was made of inlaid woods and featured string instruments. I'd never seen one quite like it. Judging from the size of the white box on the sofa, the music box must have been a gift she'd opened while waiting for me to arrive. If I wasn't mistaken about the wrapping — a gift from Shawna.

The small white box contained a pearl brooch in the shape of a flower. The tag on the bag read, "Can't wait for another romantic evening with you."

Ouch. That had to be from Phil.

"Is she diabetic?" one of the EMTs asked.

I had no idea. I rushed to the kitchen, where the acrid smell of bleach hung in the air, proving Bonnie's prowess as an immaculate housekeeper. Her refrigerator was spotless. I moved aside a bowl of what appeared to be ambrosia, judging from the mandarin orange slices. Bonnie stocked a fairly amazing assortment of cheeses, a boxed angel food cake, a store-bought roast chicken, a container of cornbread stuffing, and several cans of refrigerator biscuit dough. I checked the door of the fridge but didn't see any insulin among her condiments.

When I returned to the EMTs, they were administering CPR. "I don't see any insulin," I offered.

Her purse! Of course. Wouldn't a diabetic have some sort of medical card in her wallet? I found it on the console in the front hall. A small beaded purse in ecru with a tarnished metal strap. Vintage, perhaps? I snapped it open. On top I found a black velvet ring box.

NINE

From "Ask Natasha":

Dear Natasha,
I make my own wrapping paper (I love your show!), and I die a little each time someone crumples it and throws it to the floor. I sneak behind them and collect it, but the following year, it always looks so sad. How can I save my beautiful paper?
— Unwrapped in Gift, Mississippi

Dear Unwrapped,
Place a protective sheet over your ironing board and iron your wrapping paper on a very low heat with no steam. Either fit it into a large, flat box, or gently roll it and insert it inside a long, cardboard tube for the next year.

— Natasha

Curiosity got the better of me, and I took

two seconds to snap the box open. A fancy diamond engagement ring sparkled inside. It definitely wasn't the honker Bonnie flashed around at her party. Still, it was a decent-size pear-shaped stone, the sort of thing a young lawyer might give his fiancée. The one missing from Beau's sock drawer, perhaps? I set it aside and located her wallet easily, but it didn't contain any medical information that I could see.

Beau would know. I glanced around for a home office, where she would have his phone number. I found a tiny room upstairs with a desk piled high with papers and magazines. For an organizer, she wasn't very organized. Hoping she'd called Beau recently, I found a phone and hit the redial button.

Beau answered the phone, and I breathed a sigh of relief. "It's Sophie Winston, Beau. I'm at your mom's house and she's been taken ill. Can you tell me if she's diabetic or has some kind of medical condition?"

I heard his breath catch.

"No. She's not diabetic. I'm on my way." The phone clicked off.

The doorbell rang again. When I opened the door, Detective Kenner stood on the doorstep.

His cold black eyes flashed wide at the

sight of me. "Sophie?"

Honestly, I was equally shocked to see him. As a homicide detective, he wouldn't have been called unless Bonnie was dead and someone suspected foul play. "What are *you* doing here?" It wasn't nice of me, but I blurted out the words before I realized how hostile they sounded.

"That's what I was going to ask you. We were called to the scene of a suspicious death."

"We?"

A woman trotted up the steps behind him and nodded at me before she passed.

"The medical examiner and me."

"That was fast." Granted, I'd been racing around in a panicked search for insulin, but Kenner's presence meant the EMTs must have called in right away.

"We happened to be at the police station when the call came in."

At least he hadn't accused me of murder yet, as was his habit. I braced myself, though. With Wolf out of town, I didn't have a friend on the police force.

"Merry Christmas!" he uttered softly, as though he was afraid to say it. The taut skin on his face flushed, and he pushed past me.

I followed him to the EMTs.

He stopped abruptly, and I knew he was

taking in the glass on the floor and the broken window.

"I did that." I might as well admit it up front. He would question me about it anyway. "I could see her shoe, and I thought she might need help."

He didn't acknowledge what I said, just went about his business with the EMTs.

The rush of adrenaline that had coursed through me began to abate. With great sadness, I realized that revival efforts had come to a halt.

Bonnie had died, much too prematurely. Poor Beau had been considering a future with Shawna, and now he would face it without his doting mother. I glanced around, wondering where Phil was. Was he staying with Bonnie over the holidays? I shivered from the combination of horror at Bonnie's sudden death and the frosty air that filled the room through the huge hole I'd made.

Kenner rose from a squat next to Bonnie. He walked over to me and asked when I had arrived and what I had seen and done. I made it clear again that I had broken the glass to gain entry.

For once, Kenner didn't badger me. He didn't shout or threaten me. In fact, the beady-eyed guy whom I disliked so intensely had vanished. The prominent nose and sunken cheeks looked the same, but he treated me with such politeness and deference that I almost forgot how dreadful he'd been to me in the past.

"What were you doing here?" he asked.

"We had an appointment. She wanted to talk about making organizing videos."

"Is there anyone who can confirm that?"

"My family."

He nodded and stepped back to allow a gurney with Bonnie's body to pass.

"What do you think happened?"

Kenner spoke matter-of-factly. "We'll know more after the autopsy." He looked away as though he was uncomfortable. "There's no outward sign of violence. She may have died of natural causes."

"Then why were you called?"

"The broken window, I guess."

I studied him. He'd arrived awfully soon. Then again, maybe there wasn't a lot going on in town on the day after Christmas.

He followed the gurney out. I picked the wrapping paper up off the floor and folded the festive print of snowflakes on a red background. Bonnie wouldn't want it strewn about and crumpled. Her holiday cheer showed everywhere. A fat red pillar candle surrounded by holly sprigs decorated the coffee table. The only books in the room were three carefully stacked art books on a side table on which a trio of elves danced. The slender artificial tree decorated in a cheerful candy theme seemed out of place now.

Shouting at the front of the house drifted to me. I placed the paper on the table and hurried to the front door. On the sidewalk under the streetlights, Bonnie's handsome son, Beau, yelled at Shawna, "This is your fault!"

Kenner eyed Shawna with the same sharp look that he had used on me so many times.

Shawna didn't notice his scrutiny. She threw herself at Beau, trying to wrap her arms around his neck. "You can't mean that! You're upset and not thinking straight. Honey, you need me."

Beau untangled himself from her groping hands. "My mother was right. You and your crazy family are beneath us. I never should have gotten involved with you. She'd be alive right now if I'd listened to her."

I shot down the stairs and into the street to Shawna's side. In as calm a voice as I could muster, I said, "Beau, I'm so sorry about your mother's death, but Shawna had nothing to do with it."

I expected him to burst into tears and take

comfort in Shawna's open arms, but he glared at me, which reminded me that I was a stranger to him.

"She warned me about Shawna. She said you would ruin my life — and now you have!" He stormed to a blue BMW and slid into the driver's seat. The ambulance carrying Bonnie's body drove away, and Beau pulled into the street behind it. Poor Shawna gripped the car door and ran alongside, begging Beau to listen to her.

He sped up and left her — a lonely figure standing in the middle of the street.

Kenner sidled up to me. "You know her?"

"You probably do, too. Shawna waits on tables at The Laughing Hound."

"I don't go there much. I thought you might be related."

Because my family was beneath Bonnie and Beau? "By marriage. My brother's wife is Shawna's sister."

His jaw pulled tight, and I would have sworn he stood a hair more erect. "Given the circumstances, I don't think we should date just now. I can't compromise an investigation — not even for you."

Date!? Good heavens, I'd hoped that nonsense was behind us. As scary as it was to contemplate a date, the word *investigation* worried me more. "But there's nothing to investigate!" As soon as the words left my mouth, I wanted kick myself. *What was I thinking?* It was the perfect excuse not to go out with him. But I couldn't leave Shawna in a bad position. "You know perfectly well that there's no sign of foul play."

In spite of the darkness, I swear I saw a twinkle in his eye when he said, "And you know perfectly well that not all foul play means blood and gore. There are plenty of ways to kill a person." He paused, like he was assessing my reaction. "Women are more prone to killing with poison, slow and sinister. Much tidier that way."

Chills rippled across my back. "Shawna didn't murder Bonnie. Beau's reaction came from the stress of bad news — the heat of the moment. It's not uncommon for people to want to blame someone when a loved one dies. It doesn't mean anyone committed murder. It's just a psychological response to the situation."

His thin lips pulled into a smile. "You're not going to talk me into that date until I know for sure that she died of natural causes. But it's very flattering that you're so eager."

I was anything but eager. As much as I didn't want Shawna to be under suspicion, it did buy me a little time. When Wolf returned, we might have to finally admit that we were dating just to get Kenner off my back.

A uniformed cop I didn't know looked out the front door and asked, "Do you have anything personal in here, ma'am?"

"No." I shook my head, and he secured the door. I turned to Kenner and said, "Good night." It was abrupt and reflected my discomfort, but I didn't know what else to say. I walked away, toward Shawna.

Wind whipped her hair into her face but she made no effort to remove it. Her arms hugged her chest, as if she were cold.

"C'mon, Shawna. Let's go home." I wrapped an arm around her and began to walk in the direction of my house.

She toddled along, like a child who had no choice in the matter. The twinkling lights I had enjoyed so much on my way to Bonnie's seemed wrong. Her death had brought the festive feeling to an abrupt end.

"He loves me, you know," Shawna blurted.

"I'm sure he does." I wasn't at all certain that was the case, but it wouldn't help her to know that. Besides, I was an outsider. I didn't know much about their relationship.

"Do you think we're not good enough for them? It's not like they're rolling in dough or they arrived on the *Mayflower*," she sniffed.

"Don't be silly. Beau was . . . is lucky to have you." I couldn't help suspecting that Bonnie had indeed said something about Shawna's unworthiness to Beau. It came out of his mouth in the heat of the moment, not like a lie that he had to make up first. But if Shawna and her family weren't good enough for Beau, then why was Shawna's father good enough for Bonnie?

I opened the gate to the service alley that ran alongside my home. Through the window in the door, my kitchen looked warm and welcoming. I ushered Shawna inside. With a whimper, she hustled to Laci for a hug.

"Sophie!" cried my mom. "Thank goodness you're here. I was getting so worried about you, but your brother and father insisted I shouldn't interrupt your meeting by calling you on the cell phone. Have you had dinner? I hope you don't mind that we went ahead and ate." She bustled by me and whispered, "I had to do something to distract everyone."

I shrugged off my coat and tossed it over the back of a chair.

Laci held her sister, her eyes closed and her face wrinkled like she was trying not to sob. She seemed to be having trouble composing herself.

"I guess you've already heard the bad news," I said.

Laci whirled toward me and hissed, "Not so loud. We don't want Jen to know Mom is missing."

TEN

From "THE GOOD LIFE":

Dear Sophie,
Christmas decorations have become a nightmarish chore. Digging through all the boxes in search of things I can't find drives me batty. Other than hiring someone else to do it (fat chance), is there a way to make it easier?
— Grumpy in Garland, Nebraska

Dear Grumpy,
Instead of tossing things into boxes, take a cue from professional movers and box your Christmas decorations by room. Place all the mantel items in the same box or boxes, put the kitchen towels, pot holders, cookie containers, and decorations in another box. That way it's fast to put everything away, and when you take it all out, everything you need will

be together.

— Sophie

Shawna shrieked, "Mom's missing?"

My mother grimaced. "*Shh.* Jen's in the next room." To me she said, "Thank goodness for those kittens. George took them into the family room to distract Jen."

"I thought Marnie went shopping with you," I said to Laci.

"When we got to the mall, she said she'd meet us back here." Laci tucked an errant lock of hair behind her ear. "I thought . . . I thought she was planning to meet my dad and didn't want us to know about it. But I called him and he hasn't seen her."

Shawna collapsed into a chair by the fire. "Not Mom, too," she moaned. She jumped up, grabbed Laci by the arms, and shook her. "It's all Dad's fault. Where is he? He killed them both and ruined my life."

"Killed? No one said Mom was dead. What are you talking about?" Laci's scared eyes never wavered from her sister's face.

"I don't mean with an ax. He left Mom and broke her heart, then he toyed with Bonnie and she couldn't take it and died."

"Bonnie's dead?"

Shawna launched into an explanation that bordered on hysteria, ending with, "And

now Beau despises me and blames me —
me! — for his mother's death."

Laci swallowed hard. "Then why do you
think Mom is dead?"

"She's not here. There isn't any other logical explanation."

"Well, I can't find Wolf's cell number
anywhere." Hannah marched into the
kitchen carrying Mochie. The second she
saw me, she did an about-face to leave.

"Hold it! Why do you want to call Wolf?"
Had everyone in my house lost their minds?

"Sophiieee. Maybe you've forgotten but
New Year's Eve is only five days away and I
don't want to spend it alone. I thought Wolf
could give me the lowdown on Zack, that
cute cop, and maybe invite him for New
Year's."

"You won't be alone. The whole family
will be here for fondue and our traditional
walk down to the river to watch the fireworks."

Hannah tossed her hair like an impatient
mare. "Kissing you 'Happy New Year' is not
the same as kissing a dreamily handsome
man in a romantic moment . . ."

"How can you be so shallow?" Shawna
turned on Hannah with a vengeance. "Bonnie is dead, and Mom is probably lying in a
ditch somewhere freezing to death — and

all you can think about is getting a date?"

"Stop it," I said. "Turning on each other isn't going to do anyone any good. Have you reported the fact that Marnie is missing to the police?"

Laci's shoulders froze. "I was trying to avoid that. I called but they said we have to go down there to fill out a missing person's report."

"Have you called Marnie's cell phone?" I asked.

"All I get is her voice mail." Laci paced the kitchen. "This can't be happening. She was so distraught about Dad. You don't think she did anything awful, do you?"

"Like murder Bonnie?" muttered Hannah.

I thought Mom's angry stare might burn a hole right into Hannah's forehead, but I noticed that George stifled a laugh.

"No, I mean like jumping off a bridge," said Laci.

"Now, now," Mom cautioned. "Marnie had a few shocks over the last days, but surely she hasn't gone over the edge."

Laci nibbled at a fingernail. "You don't know my mother like I do."

"Too bad you can't reach Marnie by phone. She might feel better once she hears Bonnie is dead."

"I raised you better than that, George Bauer!" scolded Mom.

"Give me a break," said George. "It's true. Bonnie's death is very convenient for Marnie."

Shawna screamed and pointed at the bay window. A palm hit the glass, compelling Mochie to spring to the top of the table, where he pranced like a Halloween cat. The palm slid down the window with a loud screeching noise.

I bolted out the kitchen door and around to the bay window.

At least Marnie wasn't dead — but Shawna hadn't been too far off when she imagined her mother lying in a ditch. She was now sprawled on the ground, wearing a Santa jacket and matching hat, complete with white fringe and a pom on the end. She giggled, but couldn't pick herself up. I reached for her, but she couldn't grab hold of my hands.

"Step aside, Sophie." George and Dad hauled her to her feet and walked her to the door between them.

"What's that jingling sound?" asked Hannah.

Jen pointed to Marnie's feet. She wore green elf shoes with toes that curled up and ended in jingling bells.

"Jen, honey, you'd better check on the kittens. They're all alone. Scoot now!" Laci held a hand to her cheek. "I never wanted her to see her Nana this way."

Mom leaned over and whispered, "I didn't know Marnie had a drinking problem."

"For heaven's sake, Inga, she doesn't," said Laci. "She's just been under such stress with the separation and the holidays without Dad, and now the whole thing with Bonnie and the engagement."

Mom motioned to me to follow her into the foyer. "Do you think we can take her back to George's house? I'm afraid the motion of the car . . . Marnie needs to sleep it off, but I hate to stick you with the job of taking care of her."

It was petty of me, but I didn't exactly relish that job. "The beds are all made. Under the circumstances, maybe everyone should spend the night here." I did some quick calculations. Shawna lived on the outskirts of Old Town, but she might want to stick around to help Laci care for their mom. If Hannah and Shawna took the third-floor bedrooms, Mom and Dad, and Laci and George, could sleep in the second-floor guest rooms. Laci probably ought to be near Marnie, though, and Marnie needed to be close to a bathroom. Which meant giving my bedroom to Marnie for the night. No biggie. "I think we can fit everyone if Jen and I sleep in the family room."

"Jen will love that!" Mom kissed me on the cheek and hurried back into the kitchen. I could hear her making up a story about wanting to stay overnight so she could bake a dish to take over to Beau in the morning. Trust Mom to help Laci save face by giving her an excuse to stay that was unrelated to Marnie.

After a brief scene moving Marnie upstairs to bed, Shawna, George, and all the women in my family scattered to bedrooms, leaving me alone in the kitchen, dog-tired and hungry.

I opened the refrigerator door hoping I might find delicious leftovers that only needed warming. No such luck, though an entire raw turkey, still in the wrapper, had appeared.

"If you're making a snack, I'll have some, too." Dad had wisely stayed out of the Marnie chaos upstairs. "Your mom and Laci served leftovers from our take-out lunch for dinner."

"Sounds like I missed quite a drama. How do ham and cheese sandwiches sound?"

"Great! You went through quite a drama yourself, bunnikins. Are you okay?"

Bunnikins. How we change. Only a decade ago I bristled when Dad called me that silly baby name. But now, surrounded by Christmas lights, with a fire crackling in the fireplace, after finding someone dead, it warmed me and brought tears to my eyes. "I'm fine." I pulled a jar of pickles from the fridge, picked one out to chew on, and handed the jar to Dad.

"No, uh, sign of foul play?" he asked.

"Not to look at her." I sliced a fresh loaf of sourdough bread and doctored the slices with mayonnaise and horseradish mustard. "Why do you ask?"

"Because a lot of Laci's family hated Bonnie, and that Detective Kenner is walking up to the door."

Oh no! Would this day never end? "What now?" I muttered on my way to the front door. I opened it before he had a chance to bang the knocker, which would have brought everyone downstairs again.

"Yes?" I demanded.

"Sorry, I know it's late."

A gust of snow flurries blew into the foyer. I debated shutting the door and leaving him outside, but then he would bang the knocker. "Come on in." I led him to the kitchen and sliced baby Gouda cheese.

"Would you care to join us, Detective?"

asked Dad.

My throat tightened in fear that he would take Dad up on his offer.

"Thank you, Mr. Bauer." His thin lips twitched to a Mona Lisa smile. "I've been trying to take out your daughter for months, but I believe joining you tonight would give the appearance of impropriety."

"No it won't." It was little Jen who appeared and spilled the beans. "Aunt Sophie is dating Wolf."

Where did she come from so suddenly?

I could feel my face flush. Thankfully, Dad asked, "What can we do for you, Detective?"

"I'm sorry to interrupt your dinner. Smells great, better than the turkey TV dinner I made for myself yesterday."

That was a low blow! How sad was that? I didn't even like the guy, but now I felt terrible for him.

"You don't have any family?" asked Jen.

Stop! Stop that line of thought right now! Kenner wasn't like a kitten that I could take in or find a home for.

"I'm afraid my parents have passed on. I won't keep you any longer. Enjoy your meal. Sophie, could I have a word with you?"

I hurried him into the foyer before Dad could ask him to join us again. I felt a little bit guilty for not asking him to sit down, but I wanted to get the interrogation over with as quickly as possible.

"How are you feeling, Sophie?"

"Feeling?" He came by to see if I was upset? He had to be kidding. Was this some kind of new police touchy-feely policy or just Kenner's method of getting in the door and throwing me off guard? "I'm fine. Thank you." For that he needed to speak to me privately? Why couldn't he have asked in front of Dad and Jen?

He bobbed his head. "Now that Wolf is out of town, you need me. And for the record, don't go hard on the little girl — I knew you were still seeing him. But I'm not afraid of the big, bad Wolf."

He turned and walked out of my house, leaving me with a pit of dread in my stomach. When I returned to the kitchen, Jen was busy inserting Dad's sandwich into the panini maker under his close supervision. The two of them laughed about something, but Jen stopped giggling when she saw me.

"Sophie, please don't be mad at me."

Mad at Jen? I couldn't imagine that. "What is it, honey? Did something break?"

"I want to sleep upstairs with Hannah tonight."

"Okay." I tried to smile reassuringly,

though I was surprised that Jen was turning down the chance to watch TV until the wee hours in the family room.

"See, if I sleep with Hannah, Alice and Jasper can sleep with us."

Dumped for kittens! I laughed aloud. "I can't blame you one bit." Though I did suspect that George and Laci were going to have a devil of a time getting her to leave Alice and Jasper behind when they went home.

Satisfied, she bounded out of the kitchen, leaving Dad and me to enjoy our snack. Although my mother would be horrified, I stacked the dirty dishes in the sink when Dad bade me good night. The day's events had taken their toll on me and all I wanted to do was crawl into bed — or at least stretch out on the sofa in the family room. Mochie and Daisy snuggled up with me, and I fell dead asleep until two in the morning. When I woke, Mochie and Daisy were gone, and I could hear someone crying in the kitchen.

ELEVEN

From "THE GOOD LIFE":

Dear Sophie,

My husband thinks we should leave the Christmas tree up and just scoot it into the basement and cover it with a drop cloth. I have a feeling that's a very bad idea. Please side with me.

— Apprehensive in Evergreen, Louisiana

Dear Apprehensive,

I've heard this advice before and I disagree. Scooting a Christmas tree is sure to result in broken ornaments. It's not easy to move a tree through a doorway. Even if you take off the ornaments, do you have enough space to devote to the tree all year? And how much will you enjoy the decorative spiderwebs when you take it out again? You win, Apprehensive!

— Sophie

My hand was on the kitchen light switch when Laci's teary voice said, "Please don't turn on the lights." In the near darkness, I could make out a shape in a chair by the dying embers of the fire. Daisy sat before Laci, her head in Laci's lap.

"How about the Christmas lights?" I turned on the little white lights in the pine greenery.

"That's nice," she sniffled.

"Are you okay?"

"Oh, Sophie. I wanted to have the Christmas I've always dreamed of — with all the relatives in good cheer, the house beautifully decorated, fabulous food, with us all singing Christmas carols — not stolen gifts, a cobbled-together dinner, a father announcing his engagement to his mistress, a drunk mother, and certainly no deaths!"

I poured eggnog into glasses embellished with white snowflakes, and added generous dollops of coffee liqueur and rum. "Everyone has a family, Laci, and there are no perfect families. Everything that happened was outside of your control."

"You know the worst part?"

I cringed. *The falling-down drunk mother?*

She exhaled, her breath ragged from crying. "Bonnie is dead and that's horrible. Just the worst possible thing that could happen. Yet, there's this teeny part of me that's relieved because she's not a threat to my parents' relationship anymore. I'm so ashamed!"

I handed Laci an eggnog and sat down in the chair on the other side of the fireplace. "Don't you think that's only natural? Bonnie brought major problems and heartache to your family."

"I still feel guilty. What a heartless person I must be."

"You can't beat yourself up over it. How could you possibly have embraced Bonnie given what she did? Bonnie brought your antipathy on herself through her actions. You're not actually glad that she died — you just wanted her out of the way. You wanted to protect the people you love."

Laci sniffled but sounded a little stronger when she asked, "Do you think your mother will ever agree to letting me host Christmas again?"

I leaned in her direction. "As long as you promise Jen will be there, Mom will agree to anything."

Even in the low light, I saw her smile.

"Besides, the holidays aren't over yet. Jen

wanted to go ice-skating, and we have New Year's Eve to look forward to. There are plenty of days of fun ahead of us."

I thought Laci felt a little bit better when we shuffled off to bed, but it was very likely that the liqueur in her drink had simply tired her.

On the morning of December twenty-seventh, I woke to my parents whispering.

"We have to wake her. It's the police, for pity's sake. Sophie was sort of a witness or something, wasn't she?"

"Maybe we could ask him to come back later."

They tiptoed out, but I could hear their muffled conversation in the kitchen.

I groaned and sat up, rubbing my eyes. That stupid Kenner. Did he think he'd get breakfast if he dropped by in the morning to ask how I was feeling again?

I flung on a ginormous red bathrobe made of fleece and tromped into the kitchen. "Where is he?"

Mom pointed. "In the living room."

The hardwood floors were cold on my bare feet, but I marched into my living room, prepared to tell Kenner off. Except he wasn't there. A fair-haired cop in uniform sat on my sofa next to the Christmas tree, playing I-got-your-nose with Daisy, whose tail wagged joyfully.

"I'm so sorry to get you up," he said. "It's just that we have a problem."

Jen, adorable in my Christmas cat print nightshirt that hung on her little frame, ran in, a kitten in each hand, and leaned against me. "Sophie didn't do it!"

At that moment, Hannah staggered in and came to a stop beside us. She'd borrowed an old blue bathrobe that had seen better days. Her hair clumped up on one side of her head where she'd undoubtedly slept on it, and the makeup she hadn't removed the night before clung to the skin under her eyes in unfortunate black crescents.

"Wha's going on?" Hannah yawned and sputtered like a horse. Her expression changed to horror. "Zack!" She left faster than I'd known she could move, and we could hear her dashing up the stairs.

Zack grinned. A hopeful sign, I thought.

"I'm so sorry to interrupt your holiday, but as I said, we have a crisis on our hands."

I swallowed hard. What could he want with me? Did he think I'd stolen the Christmas gifts?

"I believe you've already heard the sad news of Bonnie Scarborough's death."

My heart pounded. Did he think I had

something to do with her demise?

"You may be familiar with the Auld Lang Syne Auction that Bonnie ran every year. It has something of a reputation and lots of people look forward to it. Well" — he shifted uncomfortably — "it's only two days away but now, we don't have Bonnie to run the show. We'd rather not cancel it at this point because we can't retract the advertising, and so many people have already donated items to be auctioned. It would be a logistical nightmare to store it all or try to return everything."

Uh-oh. I might not be fully awake, but I knew where this was going.

Mom floated over to Zack and offered him steaming coffee in a bright red mug that featured a Christmas tree. She sat next to him on the sofa. The scent of nutmeg floated to me.

"Thank you." He sipped the coffee. "This is so much better than the swill they have at the station. So, Sophie, we were hoping you might find it in your heart to step in and help us."

"Us?" asked Mom.

"Several law enforcement agencies partici-pate. But we're not on the organizing end. Bonnie did all that. I'm in charge of Fairfax County's involvement."

I was mulling it over when Hannah flounced back into the living room. Dressed in a cerise shirt with one too many buttons unbuttoned to show cleavage, and a pair of my jeans that I couldn't fit into, she looked like a casual bombshell. Her hair hung loose and long, and her makeup concealed every hint of exhaustion.

Zack nearly spilled his coffee.

"We would love to help," purred Hannah. "The whole family will pitch in!"

Mom oh-so-subtly tapped her wedding ring. "Will your wife be helping, too, Zack?"

"Uh, no. I'm divorced."

I thought Mom and Hannah might swoon and break into applause. They controlled themselves, though, and immediately invited him to breakfast.

Zack appeared to thrive on their attention. Walking between Mom and Hannah, he was ushered into the kitchen.

Dad placed a hand on my shoulder. "I'm proud of you, bunnikins. Sounds like a lot of people depend on the proceeds from that auction. It would be a shame if they had to cancel it."

I wanted to point out that I hadn't agreed — it was Hannah who volunteered us all — but the truth was that I would have done it anyway. Bonnie's auction benefitted needy people. After the chaos of our holiday, it would do us good to help those less fortunate. Our turkey and gifts might have been stolen, but they weren't things we couldn't replace or do without.

As I walked up the stairs to my bedroom to change clothes, it occurred to me that the auction might help get Laci's mind off her troubles. I opened the bedroom door and found Marnie sitting up in my bed, holding a wet washcloth against her forehead.

"I'm sorry, I just came to get some clothes. Won't take me a minute."

"I'm the one who should apologize." She spoke softly, her eyes closed. "I've been such a fool. And now I've gone and made things worse."

I retrieved a soft green turtleneck and jean shirt while I pondered what to say. I'd been through a divorce, but it had been fairly civil. I never felt the need to go on a drinking binge or wear elf shoes. Folding the clothes over my arm, I decided she probably needed to vent. "He said you threw him out. Did you think he was seeing someone else?"

Marnie's laugh sounded like a croak before it warped to a moan. She opened her eyes and held her head between her hands as though she wanted to steady it. "I certainly didn't think so at the time, but now I have to wonder. Phil wasn't the type to fool around with other women. He was a good dad, and a loyal husband."

"Then why did you throw him out?"

"That's a bit of dramatic license by Phil. I imagine he meant to make me feel responsible, which I suppose I am. You don't have children, do you?"

I shook my head and found the jeans with the hidden elastic waist.

"Laci and Shawna were the center of our lives. When they left home, Phil was promoted to vice president in charge of personnel at the brewery, and I became the principal of our elementary school. Life was good, but it was all about work. We retired within a month of each other and it seemed like life screeched to a sudden halt. Phil and I were left staring at each other with nothing to say."

I didn't dare jostle the bed by sitting on the corner, so I perched on the edge of a chair and listened to her.

"I tried to talk him into ballroom dancing classes, but he refused. I suggested we buy a camper and hit the road, see the country. He couldn't leave his precious supersized TV behind. He didn't want me to join a book club or get a dog to take to visit kids in hospitals."

A note of irritation crept into her voice. "Then at Thanksgiving, after the kids left, it was just Phil and me and the TV and leftover pecan pie. I thought — is this all there is? Am I going to spend the rest of my days handing Phil pie and washing dishes while he watches TV?" Marnie sat up, her face full of fury, but she promptly groaned and carefully leaned back against the headboard. "So I suggested a separation and told him I intended to stay in the house. I had to! He wouldn't have lifted a finger. The place would have fallen down around him while he was glued to that TV set."

She applied the damp washcloth to her head again. "I thought it would be good for him to get out. To be forced to live again. I never thought the fat old fool would find another woman."

I hardly dared ask, but I did anyway. "Do you still love him?"

She sat up straight. "Yes. Yes, I do. And I'm going to get him back if it's the last thing I do!" She winced and spoke more softly. "But first I think I need a nap to sleep off this headache."

I tiptoed out, closed the door, and took my clothes into the bathroom.

After a shower, I dressed in the green turtleneck, jeans, and an oversized denim shirt embroidered with snowy pine trees, and returned to the kitchen, where Mom was cutting juicy cantaloupe and shimmering kiwis for fruit salad.

She'd laid round loaves of sourdough bread on the kitchen island. "Baked eggs with smoked salmon?" I asked.

"Do you mind? You know how much your dad and I like it."

I listened to Hannah flirt with Zack as I chopped dried rosemary and fresh parsley and slid the sliced bread into the oven to toast a bit. The aroma of dried rosemary soon wafted through the kitchen.

Mochie sat on the seat in the bay window, his tail twitching angrily at the sight of Jen and Zack playing with the kittens.

I poured cream into a baking dish, dotted it with butter, and shoved it under the broiler. In minutes, the butter had melted and bubbled. I slid two eggs per person on top, sprinkled them with the herbs, and slid the baking dish under the broiler again.

While they cooked, I laid slices of smoked salmon across the warm bread.

Since there were too many of us to comfortably fit around the kitchen table, Laci and Dad set the dining room table with a red and white tablecloth adorned with Christmas trees around the edge and set it with festive red earthenware plates. I carefully spooned the baked eggs on top of the salmon and carried a tray of them into the dining room.

Dad had built a fire, and Laci had whipped together a charming cascading centerpiece of rosy pears, red apples, and assorted Christmas cookies.

"How clever of you," I said. "We can eat the centerpiece for dessert."

Laci beamed, and George gave her a little peck on the cheek. He whispered, but I heard him say, "We'll get through this, too, babe."

Our spirits had lightened considerably, maybe because we knew we were going to do something good for other people? Shawna was the only one dragging. Hollow-eyed from a sleepless night, her shoulders sagged, and she looked so morose I feared she might burst into tears. Apparently Beau still wasn't taking her calls. Mom and Laci convinced Shawna that the trick would be to bake something to bring to him.

After breakfast, the three of them set to work making a chicken cheese casserole and a streusel cake. I used Daisy as an excuse to get out of the house and away from the chaos in my kitchen.

I slipped into a down jacket and clipped Daisy's leash onto her harness. We left by the kitchen door and found the street to be eerily quiet. Leftover snowflakes still floated in the air, which added to the Christmas charm of the historic houses. Daisy happily trotted ahead of me, sniffing every gate and lamp post. Meanwhile, I wondered how I could obtain more information on Bonnie's death. Wolf had always kept quiet about details, but my friends Humphrey and Nina had connections and dug up the best information. They were away for the holidays, though, and I was on my own.

Daisy turned the corner and I followed, deep in thought. She paused to smell an urn that contained lighted branches, and I realized that we stood exactly where I had seen Forrest the day before.

I peered into the store window but couldn't see much — just a dark, empty storefront. A FOR RENT sign rested in the window. I gazed around. There wasn't much to see. Forrest must have been meeting someone. Why else would he dally in front of an empty building?

There was no good reason to stroll over to Bonnie's house, but Daisy kept walking like she had a destination. She finally stopped to sniff around an adorable display of a green-clad Santa's elf peering into a red sleigh. I was so absorbed in my thoughts about Bonnie that it took me a few seconds to register that the darling elf who perched on the sleigh was wearing high heels.

Suddenly, I had a feeling I knew where Marnie's path had taken her the night before. Hoping no one noticed, I slid the shoes off the elf's feet, promising him I would return his shoes the first chance I got.

Bonnie's house was only a block away. I tried to convince myself that we were headed in that direction by Daisy's choice. *Right. I could blame it on Daisy, but I was the one itching to see what was going on.*

In the overcast haze of snow-laden skies, so many lights glowed in the windows of Bonnie's house, that it stood out from its neighbors long before we neared it. Figures hurried in and out, like busy giant ants. Police cars crowded the street, and a terrible suspicion sent a shiver creeping up my back — the autopsy must have revealed that Bonnie had been murdered.

Daisy pulled at the leash. Every dog owner in the neighborhood had used walking as an excuse to linger outside Bonnie's house and be nosy. I'm ashamed to say that I readily joined them.

Polite sniffing ensued as Daisy greeted the other dogs, and I brazenly listened to the gossip.

"The son is devastated."

"Did you hear she was planning to remarry? At *her* age!"

"Her killer broke into the house through a window in the back. This used to be such a safe neighborhood."

"Excuse me." I addressed the woman who spoke last. "I broke the window to get in when she didn't answer the door. I don't think you have to worry about your safety or the neighborhood."

As though rehearsed, everyone took a step away from me. "They're saying she was murdered," said the woman.

"Well, I didn't do it! I just found her."

A man holding the leash of a Rhodesian ridgeback laughed with too much joy given the situation. "Too bad you didn't do her in. You'd have been a heroine."

"What an awful thing to say!" A woman snatched her Chihuahua off the sidewalk and into her arms as though she was afraid the laughing man would harm it. "Bonnie was warm and generous, and about the sweetest person I know."

"Then you didn't know the real Bonnie

Scarborough." The man's Rhodesian ridge-back snuffled Daisy's muzzle. "A whole lot of people are going to sleep better now that she's gone. I'm not surprised that someone finally knocked her off. She was bound to torture the wrong person someday."

"Torture!" said someone in the crowd. "I'm confused. Are you saying Bonnie hurt people or blackmailed them?"

"Blackmail is a strong word, and it implies financial gain. Manipulation was more Bonnie's style. She got people to do her bidding, but they rarely realized she had manipulated them into it. Not until it was too late."

I left the crowd to their speculation and turned to leave, but before I'd taken two steps, a hand gently touched my elbow.

"How are you, Sophie?" The muted lighting didn't do anything kind to Kenner's sharp features.

It was a simple question — the same one that every polite person asked but didn't really want answered, yet there was something about the way he looked at me that creeped me out.

I was about to respond when a person in a large, unwieldy suit and a gas mask appeared on Bonnie's front stoop. "Is that a

Hazardous Materials Unit combing the house?"

Twelve

Kenner squirmed, like he didn't want to confirm anything. "Are you experiencing any upper respiratory problems?"

"No." I said it cautiously, taking a long breath.

147

"No coughing, wheezing, difficulty swallowing, or inhaling?"

"What's going on, Kenner?"

"Don't worry, I feel okay so far, too."

"So far?!" *Was he kidding?* "If my health is at risk, I think I have a right to know what you've discovered."

He chewed his lip. "Her upper respiratory tract swelled shut."

"That's why the EMTs gave up on CPR so fast."

"At first blush, they thought the swelling was from an allergy, but now they think she inhaled some kind of chemical."

"She died from some kind of weird chemical leak in her home?"

"That's what they're trying to rule out."

I swallowed as a test. Was my throat sore? "Do you feel anything? What about the EMTs?"

"So far everyone is fine. It's just that . . . you were the first one on the scene."

He left the implication hanging, but I knew what he was getting at. If there was toxic air in the house, I would have inhaled more than any of the responders.

"What do they think it is? Should I be worried?"

"I don't know much yet, but I'll keep you apprised."

So that was why he stopped by the house last night to see how I felt. He really wanted to know if I was having any adverse reactions. "Thanks, Kenner. C'mon, Daisy, we'd better be getting back."

He reached down to pet her, but she snarled. Kenner snatched his hand away.

"I'm so sorry. She must be agitated because of all the people and other dogs." I didn't really think that, though. She'd been a perfect lady up until Kenner tried to pet her. Daisy just plain didn't like the guy.

He kept his eyes on her as though he didn't trust her. "If you have any trouble breathing, go straight to the emergency room. Okay?"

Daisy and I walked away. I sucked in a deep breath. Everything still worked. No burning sensation or trouble inhaling. *Whew!*

I thought back to finding Bonnie on the floor. The house had smelled of pine, which I assumed came from Christmas decorations or some kind of pine-scented air infuser. The only other smell I'd noticed was bleach — not exactly an uncommon household odor.

We walked home, Daisy prancing happily in the cold weather, and me breathing erratically, making sure everything was functioning.

When someone called my name, I paused at the service gate to my house.

Natasha again.

"Sophie! Wait up."

Wearing robin's egg blue leggings that accentuated her long, slender legs, Natasha strode toward me with a young girl in tow.

"Did you hear about Bonnie Scarborough?" asked Natasha. The girl with her looked on in awkward boredom.

"Yes," I said.

"Do you know what happened? Car accident?"

"They don't know the cause yet." I smiled at the girl. "It's cold out here. Come on in."

A fire snapped and crackled in my kitchen fireplace, and the warmth was a welcome relief. The scent of cheddar cheese baking hung in the air. Hannah and Mom relaxed at the kitchen table.

Mochie leapt from his position, paraded by Natasha holding his tail high, and hissed at her.

"A drive-by hissing," giggled Hannah.

Natasha drew back. "What's wrong with him? He usually ignores me."

"He's put out because someone dropped off a couple of kittens. Sorry." I tried to pick him up, but he raced under the table, then bounded back onto the chair and resumed his mission of guarding the kitchen from the interlopers.

"He's a cat, they're cats — why wouldn't they like each other?" Natasha sounded puzzled.

"It's a territorial thing. How would you feel if another woman moved into your house?"

Natasha stiffened at the thought. "Don't be silly. Surely you're not comparing me to an animal."

I let it go. Natasha wouldn't appreciate cats or dogs until she finally loved one. Besides, if I really had a mind to compare her to an animal, it wouldn't be to a sweet feline or canine.

"They're absolutely adorable," said Mom. "It's the most peculiar thing, the way they showed up. I think they're purebred Ragdolls."

"Ragdolls?" Natasha looked at Mom quizzically.

"A lovely breed of cat. They're gorgeous and known for their loving and easygoing personalities."

"Can I see them?" asked the girl with Natasha.

Natasha introduced the girl with her as Vegas.

My mother recoiled at the name but recovered quickly.

"Vegas is my cousin — second cousin, we think," said Natasha. "She and her father are spending the holidays with us. I was hoping Jen might be around because I believe darling Vegas is getting a little tired of boring adults."

Vegas made a show of sighing and turning her eyes toward the ceiling. Her cute face suggested she was around Jen's age, but I thought I spied a spark of mischief in those big eyes. She stood nearly as tall as me, which wasn't saying much, and when she handed me her jacket, I saw that she wore the latest teen trend, which displayed her bare stomach.

Mom took her to the family room to meet Jen, who was watching a movie with my dad and the kittens. Mochie perched on a chair by the fireplace, near the passage that led to the family room, ready to pounce should a kitten dare show its face.

I hung all the coats in the bathroom so the dusting of snow could melt onto tile, and when I returned, Shawna sat in the other chair by the fire, her teeth chattering.

I spooned my favorite gourmet hot chocolate powder into a large pot, added a little water, and stirred it with a whisk to dissolve it. I poured milk on top and set the pot on the stove to warm. While Natasha chattered with Hannah and Mom, I fetched a soft throw from the family room, where Jen and Vegas each clutched an adorable Ragdoll kitten. The kittens nestled against them, amazingly content to be held.

Daisy followed me back to the kitchen. I draped the throw over Shawna's shoulders, and fed Daisy a dog cookie for being such a good girl to the kittens.

I returned to my pot of hot chocolate, and the others finally noticed Shawna's distress.

Natasha blurted, "When did Bonnie die? Not on Christmas Day, I hope?"

I filled Natasha in on the details, trying to be as considerate as possible of Shawna, who had begun to rock back and forth ever so slightly.

Natasha patted Shawna's arm. "I didn't realize you were so close to Bonnie. I'm sorry, honey."

I brought Shawna steaming cocoa in a mug with a Santa on it, hoping it would help her warm up.

She clutched it with both hands. "I don't understand why Beau won't take my calls. I walked over to his apartment but he's not there."

"Where are Laci and George?" I asked. Shawna could use comfort from her sister right about now.

Mom's mouth twitched. "I talked George into taking Laci shopping again. The poor girl is still so upset about everything. I thought he should try to distract her a bit."

As I poured hot chocolate into Christmas mugs for everyone, Natasha sidled over to me. "No cocoa for me, thanks. It makes me bloat." She leaned toward me and whispered, "Shawna's taking this awfully hard."

I'd seen Natasha play the drama queen when someone she barely knew had died. I shot her an exasperated look and whispered back, "Beau was ugly to her."

"Oh! Well, that's understandable if he just lost his mother." Natasha smiled gently in Shawna's direction. "I'm sure Beau didn't mean anything he said."

A jingle played and Shawna hurriedly withdrew a phone from her pocket. The disappointment in her voice was obvious when she reported, "It's just Tyler." Still, she stood up and walked outside to speak with him privately.

The second the door shut, Hannah asked, "Bonnie wasn't, uh, murdered, was she?"

Natasha's eyes widened and she gasped.

"It's not a dumb question." Mom sipped her cocoa. "Bonnie upset a lot of people over the last two days. Almost like she didn't care whom she hurt."

Natasha sat down at the table and leaned toward Mom and Hannah. "Since we're among friends — I couldn't *stand* that woman. She was a cheat and a liar. She would smile in your face, pretty as could be, and stab you in the back at the same time. It wouldn't surprise me one bit if she finally crossed the wrong person."

I settled into the chair next to the fire that Shawna had vacated. Natasha alienated a lot of people who worked with her. Her loyal viewers thought she was marvelous, but she'd ticked me off plenty of times with her superior I-am-always-right attitude. She had a habit of plowing ahead, oblivious to everyone else's wishes. "Everyone I know loved Bonnie. She was always very nice to me."

Natasha glanced through the door window at Shawna, who didn't seem to mind the cold. "Bonnie wanted to be me."

I bit my upper lip to keep from laughing. Would my mother and sister, who adored Natasha, finally see her true colors?

"She found out I was doing a series of

shows on organizing and wanted me to feature her. When I refused, she had the nerve to contact *my* videographer about shooting organizing videos to put online. Rumor has it that she lined up someone else with an audience to help her. Woe be to that person! Bonnie would have climbed on her back to get where she wanted to be and then push her under. Trust me."

I didn't feel quite so much like laughing anymore. Surely I hadn't been so wrong about Bonnie, but too much of Natasha's rumor rang true. I should have given more thought to Bonnie's motivation for wanting to make the videos with me, but I hadn't had any reason to be suspicious of her.

Shawna burst back inside. Snow covered the throw on her shoulders. She whipped it off, paying no attention to the watery mess that landed on the floor. Her malaise had vanished. She stood in front of the fire and rubbed her hands together. "Man, but it's cold out! Tyler is coming over to pick me up, and we're going to find Beau. I'm sure he's at a complete loss. There will be so much to do — he'll need me. I'll show him that I'm good enough for him."

Very gently, Mom said, "Go easy on him, Shawna. Remember, he lost his mom."

"Oh, sure, Inga!" She flashed a happy

smile at Mom. "But he'll have to pick out a casket, find a burial plot, write an obituary, notify relatives — all things I can do for him."

I understood Mom's concern. Shawna looked all too pleased at the prospect of such dreaded and sad tasks.

"Tyler will be here any minute. Do you have a bathroom on this floor, Sophie? I must look a mess."

I walked Shawna to the foyer and pointed out the powder room, neatly tucked under the stairs.

When I returned to the kitchen, Natasha had changed the subject to herself, as usual. "Didn't you adore the pink peacocks I used? George's neighbor, Ginger Chadwick, headed up the committee. She wanted so badly to build the decor around a Dickens Christmas theme, but that's been done to death. Pink and turquoise are the new red and green, you know. They're so much fresher, don't you think?" She gazed around my kitchen, at the fresh pine wreaths hanging from red ribbons in the picture window, the festive fir garland that ran along the tops of the cabinets, the three nutcrackers nestled in a corner on the kitchen counter, and the needlepoint pillows of birds in snow on the chairs flanking the fireplace.

"You really ought to choose a theme to bring everything together, Sophie." Turning to my mother and Hannah, Natasha added, "I did a show on this very topic. Pine, berries, apples, and angels are so passé. Imagine how much fun it would be to bring turquoise Christmas decor into this kitchen."

The picture of Mars's Aunt Fay that hung near the fireplace swung to a slant. There were those, namely Mars's mother, June, who thought her sister's spirit resided in my kitchen. We hadn't let Natasha in on that little detail, but her own mother, an ardent believer in the paranormal, had announced that she felt a ghost in my kitchen.

Natasha eyed the picture of Fay. "It seems like that happens every time I'm here. You really ought to secure it better."

I had some choice words for Natasha given her criticism of my holiday decor, but the door knocker sounded. I hurried to the front door, Daisy loping along, and opened it to a young man whom I had seen at Bonnie's party the day before.

"I'm here to pick up Shawna?"

Close to six feet tall, he wore his plain brown hair in a shaggy style and his ready smile reminded me of someone. Certainly not as polished as Beau, but he had a comfortable casual charm.

I invited him in and showed him to the kitchen. Daisy sniffed him cautiously from behind.

Natasha sprang from her chair. "Tyler! I didn't know Shawna was talking about you." She planted a kiss on his cheek but Tyler cringed as though embarrassed by it.

"I gather you know each other?" I asked.

As though I was too dumb to live, Natasha sighed and explained, "His father is Tom Thorpe."

"Of course! George's handsome neighbor across the street," said Mom. "You have your father's smile."

Hannah emitted a little snort. "You're not the one they call Dasher, are you?"

"That would be my younger brother."

"We met his . . ." Mom stopped, at a rare loss for words. ". . . the mother of his child yesterday. Your family must be very excited about the baby."

Tyler didn't look excited. He seemed ill at ease, like a boy ten years younger who'd landed in a knitting class. He brightened up at the sound of Shawna's voice.

"Do I look okay? I want Beau to see me as being totally together. My eyes are still puffy, though. Maybe he'll think I was crying about his mom." Shawna already wore her coat, which had been drying in the bathroom. She cocked her head at Tyler. "C'mon. Do you know where he is?"

They let themselves out. Hannah stared out the bay window and watched them walk to Tyler's car. "There's something odd about that boy. Did anyone else notice?"

Mom rinsed out her mug. "He grew up without a mother. Maybe he's shy around women."

"Hardly." Natasha flicked her hand. "He worked for Bonnie. She liked everyone to think she was the driving force behind that organizing business, but Tyler did all the clever installations. If there was anyone who would benefit from her death, I suspect it would be Tyler."

THIRTEEN

From "Ask Natasha":

Dear Natasha,
My husband is kind enough to take down the outdoor decorations each year. I hate to criticize since I'm grateful that I don't have to unplug everything in freezing weather, but he jams some of it willy-nilly into the storage shed and other parts in the basement, and sometimes we have to look at Santa's sleigh in the garage the whole year. When he takes it out, he's always crabby because he can't find what he needs and half the lights don't work.
— Usually Happy in Donner, Nevada

Dear Usually Happy,
Brave the weather long enough to take a tour around the yard with hubby and make a decoration inventory each year after Christmas. Note which lights need to be

replaced, and what needs to be fixed. Repair those things now, when you're not in a hurry, and you can avoid seeing Mr. Crabby in December. Store items together and make a list of where you put the items that don't fit.

— Natasha

"Natasha! That's so unlike you." Mom looked at her in disbelief.

"You have no idea how wicked that woman was. Sweet as molasses on the outside, but underneath, she was conniving and manipulative. Like biting into a luscious truffle and finding it filled with a worm. A thick, nasty, snickering worm."

"So much for not speaking ill of the dead," muttered Hannah.

Natasha rose. "Goodness! I'll have to bake something to take over there."

"Are you kidding?" I cried. "You just said you hated her."

"It's still the right thing to do. Do you mind if Vegas sticks around for a while? You can send her home whenever you're ready." She lowered her voice to the tiniest whisper. "I could use a little time away from her, if you know what I mean."

I didn't know what she meant, but Vegas was more than welcome to stay. Jen was probably equally bored with all the adults and would appreciate someone her age to hang with for a while.

Mom saw Natasha out, gabbing about whether pound cake or ham biscuits were the better option to bring to Beau.

Mochie, still guarding the kitchen from the vicious kitten intruders, turned his head and focused on something in the other direction. Seconds later, I heard muffled voices, and Daisy trotted to the kitchen door, wagging her tail.

George opened the kitchen door and stepped aside for Laci, who scolded, "Don't you knock first?" She staggered in, her arms loaded with shopping bags, followed by George, who carried just as many.

"It's my sister's house. I don't knock for family." George set the bags down and fell backward into a chair by the fire. "I'm beat. Shopping is murder."

Laci lifted her eyebrows as though she thought it ridiculous that George was tired. "How's Mom?" she asked my mother, who had returned from the foyer.

My mother responded in a matter-of-fact tone, "She got up, drank a cup of coffee, ate a piece of dry toast, took aspirin, and headed straight back to bed."

"I'm so sorry about all this. Please don't

think ill of her. She's not usually like this."

Unfortunately, George chose that moment to snort.

"She . . . she's just had such a hard time dealing with the separation."

Mom swooped down on Laci. "Honey, nothing could change how we feel about you. Now, what bargains did you find today?"

"The burglar may have done us a favor. I'm tempted to move Christmas down a couple of days every year. You wouldn't believe the great buys we got. Everyone else was standing in line to return things, and we just dashed right in and found unbelievable deals. Fifty percent off on Jen's camera!"

"Did you leave anything for the other shoppers?" asked Hannah.

Laci shed her coat and was pulling a purple top from a bag when Mom laid a hand over hers. "Have you spoken with your dad? Bonnie's death must have come as a big shock."

Apparently, it was the wrong thing to ask. Laci's head drooped. Behind her, George waved his hands frantically, his eyes huge with alarm, he shook his head — *no!*

"I called his cell phone yesterday when we were looking for Mom. He was . . . agitated.

I think he feels we all sided with Mom and ganged up against him."

"He must feel very alone right now," said Mom.

She was right, but George slapped his palms against his forehead. Clearly, the issue of Laci's father was a sore spot.

A joyous look came over my mother's face. An expression I had seen enough times in my life to know that I should run in fear. I glanced at George, who'd sat up straight in alarm.

Mom clasped her hands together under her chin, probably appearing angelic to anyone who didn't know better. Hannah jumped out of her seat, shoving the table in her eagerness to leave the room.

But it was too late.

Mom's words floated out of her mouth, almost in slow motion, like watching a car wreck. "We'll invite Phil to dinner tonight so we can reignite the spark between him and Marnie."

George leaped to his feet. "Mom, we should stay out of their relationship. Besides, I don't think Laci is up to pulling off another family dinner on such short notice."

"Don't be silly, George. We wouldn't put all that pressure on Laci. We'll do it here. Everyone can pitch in."

Now I love my family. I accept their quirks and their enthusiasm for some things that aren't quite kosher — like snooping. Sometimes, though, they had higher expectations of me than I was willing to embrace.

I had to be rational. Point out the folly of this plan in a logical way. It was past noon. Not much time for lunch plus a trip to the store. "What were you planning to serve?" I asked it as sweetly as I could.

"The turkey we bought yesterday."

Turkey? I'd forgotten that they'd bought another turkey.

Mom acted like it was the most natural thing in the world. "Hannah and your dad love turkey sandwiches so much and it's just not the same with deli meat."

I happened to be a fan of turkey leftovers myself. "Did you get ingredients for stuffing?"

"Of course!"

Laci burst into tears. "I feel like this is all my fault. I tried so hard but nothing turned out right," she blubbered.

"That's not true." Mom flashed her an indulgent smile. "Your Red Velvet Cake was the best I've ever tasted."

Laci sniffled. "It was good, wasn't it? But look" — she held up her palms — "my hands are permanently pink from the red

166

food coloring."

I took a closer look. "That will wash off eventually, won't it?"

"It hasn't yet." She looked completely miserable.

George chuckled — but in a nice way. He hugged his wife from behind. "The things that went wrong were outside of your control, Lace. Christmas dinner was great. You had fun shopping today, didn't you?"

"I'm sorry to be such a mess."

My mother, the micromanager, started issuing orders. "Laci, call your father and invite him. Then wake Marnie. After lunch take her to a beauty parlor or one of those day spas. She'll feel much better."

Aha! Finally. A chink in Mom's plans. "If you recall, Marnie came home last night in a Santa coat and elf shoes."

Laci covered her eyes with her hands. "I'm so embarrassed."

"The shoes would have been tough," Mom conceded. "But you and Daisy found them. You don't mind lending her clothes, do you, sweetie?"

Actually, I didn't mind at all, though I was a good bit shorter and rounder than Marnie, so I had my doubts that she'd find much that fit her in my closet.

"George, you and your father take Jen and

Vegas ice-skating this afternoon, and Laci will make a list of clothes for you to pick up at your house on the way back. There!" She dusted her hands off, clearly pleased with herself.

"Have you completely forgotten that you and Hannah volunteered me to take over Bonnie's auction in two days? I'm sorry, Laci, but I have no idea how much work is involved. I really need to focus on that instead of a dinner party."

Laci's disappointed expression reminded me of Jen when she was told she couldn't have something she wanted, like an ice-cream cone. I felt totally heartless.

Mom intervened quickly. "Sophie, hon, you can roast a turkey in your sleep. I'll handle the stuffing, Hannah can be in charge of cocktails. It won't be a problem at all."

My mother had made up her mind, and to be perfectly honest, she was right. Roasting a turkey was almost a no-brainer. It was all the side dishes that required so much time.

After lunch, I took a mug of cinnamon-spiced tea back to the tiny study that served as my office. Daisy sprawled at my feet and Mochie curled up on the sofa, both probably fearful that if they stuck around the kitchen, they, too, would soon be assigned a task by Mom.

I didn't have a lot of information about the Auld Lang Syne Auction, but I found the website, which filled me in on details. The only contact information was for Bonnie. It appeared she'd kept the business end of things close to the vest. I made a few phone calls to allay fears of cancellation. Bonnie had booked a well-known local venue for the auction. Long a cultural center in Alexandria, it had served as a hospital during the Civil War. Now a museum, the elegant building was still popular for lectures and weddings. Word of Bonnie's untimely death had reached the facility coordinator, who expressed relief on hearing from me.

She had the name of the auctioneer, so I phoned him next. Within an hour, I had my bearings and confirmation from most of the significant people involved — but I had no idea where Bonnie kept the items being offered for auction. I was betting on a spare bedroom in her house or a storage room in her organizing business.

Whether I liked it or not, I would have to bring up the delicate topic with Beau. He didn't answer his phone when I called.

I snapped a leash on Daisy and told Mom I was headed for Beau's condo. She and Hannah packed up the cake and casserole they'd made for Beau, and readily walked over to his place with me.

Located near the waterfront, in the heart of Old Town, Beau's condo must have cost him a small fortune. The new building combined the typical redbrick exterior of colonial buildings with sleek, modern lines.

Shawna answered the door when I rang the bell and she accepted the food graciously. If I hadn't known better, I'd have thought she was Beau's wife. We followed her through a cluster of people that crowded the tiny apartment. She placed the food on a dining table and thanked us for coming.

"How is Beau holding up?" I asked.

"I think he's numb. Everyone has been so kind, but there's a lot to do, and he's a little off his stride."

Mom, Hannah, and I moseyed over to Beau to express our condolences. He said the same thing to each of us, "Thank you for coming." His eyes blank, I didn't think he saw any of us.

"Beau," I said gently. "In honor of Bonnie's memory, the Auld Lang Syne Auction will go on as scheduled. I'm stepping in to help, but I don't know where Bonnie stored the auction items."

His eyes met mine and showed a flicker of recognition. "I forgot all about that. I guess she has them at her office. If you could leave your address with Tyler, I'll find a key and have it delivered to you."

I thanked him, and though I wanted to urge him to hurry, it didn't seem the right thing to do.

I wrote my address on a slip of paper and handed it to Tyler, who hovered at the dining table, helping himself to the vast assortment of foods Bonnie's friends had brought. "It's the house where you picked up Shawna. Beau's going to have a key to Bonnie's shop delivered to me so I'll have access to the auction items. Were you involved with the auction?"

He popped a miniature ham biscuit into his mouth and spoke before he finished eating it. "Not much. I used to lug things around for her."

Hannah tapped my arm. "I've had about enough."

We left, much more somber than we had been when we arrived. Fortunately, it wasn't a long walk home. I tried to brighten our spirits by encouraging Mom and Hannah to keep an eye out for a Santa Claus who was missing a jacket and a hat.

Unfortunately, we didn't see him. The house was quiet when we got home and the three of us knocked out dinner in no time. I wasn't used to having my sister and mother helping in the kitchen, but it went very well, maybe because we gossiped about Bonnie, Phil, and Marnie.

Hannah appointed herself official chopper, which sped up everything. I scooped up handfuls of diced carrots, crisp slices of celery, and pungent onions and spread them in the bottom of the turkey roaster, along with a cup of water. After I rubbed the turkey skin with sea salt, the turkey went on the rack breast-side down and into a 425-degree oven.

Done with my share of the cooking, I pulled a couple of homemade frozen pie crusts from the freezer and let them come to room temperature while I mixed the fillings for First Murder Bourbon Pecan Pie.

An hour later, the pies had baked, the turkey and stuffing were still in the oven, and we had set the table with an elegant green holly jacquard tablecloth and red napkins. Laci and Marnie returned first, looking well rested and pampered. The rest of the crew, including Phil, arrived shortly thereafter.

We sat down to dinner in the dining room,

with almost everyone in good spirits. Laci was a bit miffed that Shawna hadn't shown up, but the point was to throw Phil and Marnie together, so Shawna's absence didn't make much difference. As we began eating, the knocker on the door sounded and Jen jumped from her chair. "I'll get it!" Alice clung to her shoulder, no doubt purring.

Jen returned with Detective Kenner. I wasn't sure if my mother remembered him, so I made quick introductions.

Kenner interrupted me. "I'm sorry. I'm not here for social reasons. I have a warrant for the arrest of Shawna Lane for the murder of Bonnie Scarborough."

FOURTEEN

Dear Sophie,
I love to send home leftovers with my guests. Some of them live a good distance away, so I don't like to use plates or pricy containers that I'll never get back. Any suggestions?
— Noelle in Holiday Hills, Illinois

Dear Noelle,
I'm fond of using disposable aluminum baking tins available at the grocery store. They usually come in sets of three. Pie and cake pans are great for holding the equivalent of another dinner, and the deep loaf pans work well for larger amounts. Cover with aluminum foil or plastic wrap and secure with a rubber band. Too utilitarian? Pop a ribbon

around it or a bow on the top!

— Sophie

Laci shrieked and placed her hands over her mouth like a tent.

Marnie's perfectly coiffed head rolled back and her entire body slumped lifelessly in her chair. I ran to her side and tapped her cheeks.

Phil bolted to his feet. "Let me see that!"

Kenner willingly handed him the warrant in his hand. "Is Shawna here?"

I shook my head. "We don't know where she is." I almost asked if he had tried Beau's condo, but thought better of giving Kenner any leads.

"There must be a mistake," Laci cried.

Clutching Alice and Jasper, a bewildered Jen ran to her mother's side and leaned against her, but Laci bounded to her feet and dashed to the kitchen, Jen on her heels.

From the look on Kenner's face, I gathered he thought Shawna might be there. He whirled and followed Laci. I left Marnie to my dad and hurried to the kitchen.

A horrified Laci clutched Jen to her, much like Jen held on to the precious kittens. In her other hand, Laci held a cell phone.

Kenner's eyes reduced to evil slits. "Mind if I look around?"

Ouch. About the last thing I wanted was Kenner poking through my house, or even knowing the layout, for that matter. "Actually, I do mind." I tried to sound like I knew what I was talking about. "Shawna is not here. Unless that warrant of yours gives you the right to search my house, I'm afraid I have to ask you to leave."

His expression morphed to the angry Kenner I had known in the past. "Harboring a criminal is a crime, you know. You don't want to go to jail with Shawna, do you?"

Laci clapped her hands over Jen's ears. "My sister is not a criminal."

"Your sister," he sneered, "is a diabolical, devious murderess. So clever that she almost got away with it. I've never seen anything so nefarious."

"Nefarious?" sputtered Laci. "Are you sure we're talking about the same Shawna? My sister is a kind, generous person — anything but nefarious!"

I couldn't help thinking of Shawna's surreptitious trips through Beau's dresser in search of a certain diamond ring. Maybe Laci didn't want to see her sister's less becoming side?

"I don't understand," I said. "You told me Bonnie died from a chemical she inhaled.

Has that changed?"

"Only in that it wasn't accidental."

"What? What was it? Should I be checked out?"

"If you haven't felt any ill effects by now, you're in the clear."

Laci's cell phone jingled "Grandma Got Run Over by a Reindeer." Her cheeks blazed Christmas red when she answered the call. After listening for a moment, she said, "I'm sorry, I can't talk right now. The police are here to arrest my sister for murder."

Kenner's eyes blazed and he lunged for Laci's phone.

She snapped it shut and slid it into her pocket. "One more thing I don't believe you have a warrant for."

The old Kenner appeared to be back, angrier than ever. "The next warrant will be for you — for helping a killer escape."

Jen burst into tears.

"I think you've done enough damage here." With icy politeness, I showed him to the front door.

A gust of frigid air blew in when I opened it. Kenner turned to me. "I'm sorry to ruin your holiday, but there's no doubt that Shawna murdered Bonnie."

"There was a time when you were equally

177

convinced that I killed someone," I spat back.

He shook his head. "This is different. She planned ahead. This was no heat-of-the-moment crime of anger. She wanted to be rid of Beau's mother, and she went to great lengths to accomplish her mission." With a last glance at me, he strode off into the night.

In spite of the cold, I watched him walk along the sidewalk, amid the magical Christmas lights — a lonely, bitter man, who probably didn't even notice the gaiety of the season around him.

When I returned to the kitchen, Jen had stopped crying, and my entire family clustered together, praising Laci for warning Shawna.

"So that was Shawna who called you just now, right?" I asked.

Laci nodded her head, pushed a button on her cell phone, and lifted it to her ear.

George squeezed Laci's shoulder affectionately. "You bet it was. Do I have a clever wife, or what?"

"I don't want them to arrest Mommy!" protested Jen.

George cupped her cheek. "Don't worry. That was just an idle threat."

Laci snapped her phone shut. "Rats!

Shawna's not answering."

"Do you think she ditched the phone?" asked Hannah. "That's what I would do. Plant it in bushes where it couldn't be easily seen — just to mislead the authorities if they used the ping to track me."

Laci tried calling again. "I bet that's exactly what she did." She looked to George. "What do we do now? Shawna needs help. It's cold and dark and she can't go home or to Beau's."

George gazed around at us and sucked in a deep breath of air. "Okay, here's the plan. Mom, Marnie, and Laci are going to take Jen home."

"No!" wailed Jen.

"Honey, don't you think we should be there waiting for Shawna?" said Laci.

Jen snuffled and wiped her nose with the back of her wrist. "I guess so."

George continued. "Dad and I will take my car, Phil will drive his, and we'll check out logical places where Shawna might go. Soph, do you think you could call Wolf?"

"He's in Maine with his parents and sister. What can he do?"

"He could make some phone calls. We need to know what's going on," said Dad.

I sighed, but Laci's and Jen's distraught faces tugged at my heart. "I'll do my best."

Hannah flicked her hair over her shoulder. "I could call Zack. Maybe he could help."

Sarcasm dripped from George's tone when he said, "Gee, thanks. Don't put yourself out, Hannah. Actually, I was hoping you and Sophie could take Daisy and set out on foot. I know it's cold out, but Shawna might be wandering the streets right now, wondering where to go."

I nodded. "I bet she's afraid to take her car. The police probably know her license number."

"Is everyone's mission clear?" asked Dad.

"Give me five minutes to wrap up the turkey," said Mom. "I'll slice off a nice chunk to leave for you girls. Such a shame our lovely meal was ruined. It can't be helped, I suppose."

Laci shooed Jen away with an admonition to pack fast. The second Jen left the kitchen, Laci pulled aluminum foil from the box. "We have to hurry before it dawns on Jen that she'll have to leave the kittens here. Sophie, do you mind that we're taking so much of the food? I feel like we're stealing your dinner."

In a normal family, mere knowledge that the police were hunting a family member might spoil appetites. I'd learned long ago that my family could eat their way through any crisis. "Don't be silly. You'll have a house full of people to feed as soon as they find Shawna."

Phil, Dad, and George pulled on heavy jackets and took off. I wondered exactly what we were supposed to do with Shawna once we found her — a major chink in the big plan.

I never would have believed that the women in my family could vacate a kitchen in five minutes — but they did. Amid protests from Jen about leaving Alice and Jasper, they shuffled out to the car and were gone in a flash, leaving Hannah and me to phone Wolf and Zack.

I could do little more than leave a message for Wolf on his cell phone — a very apologetic message for bothering him during his holiday.

I collected Alice and Jasper and was shutting the doors to the study, so they would be safe from Mochie during our absence, when Hannah bounded in.

"Zack is going to make some calls and meet me at The Laughing Hound."

"Terrific! If Bernie is there, see if he knows anything. He always has the latest news."

She took off up the stairs to freshen her makeup and don a more alluring outfit.

Meanwhile, I wrapped up in boots, muffler, gloves, and a bulky down jacket with a hood. I jammed the elf shoes into my pocket in case we went in that direction. Daisy hated wearing a coat. I hoped that her long fur would keep her warm enough. With a sigh, I slipped a harness over her head and clicked her leash onto the loop. She waited at the front door, wagging her tail at the notion of an adventure in the dark.

We stepped out into a starless night. A cruel wind blew. I wrapped the muffler up around my mouth, but Daisy seemed to thrive on the cold weather and pranced merrily under the glittering holiday lights. She led the way, her long-haired tail like a happy plume in the breeze.

She paused occasionally to investigate an interesting scent, giving me the opportunity to gaze around in case Shawna was hiding somewhere in the shadows. Several blocks later, Daisy turned down a street full of storefronts and offices. At the end of the block, in the show window of the building second from the corner, hard candies hung from ribbons in empty closet setups. A fancy script in the shape of a half-moon arc announced *Clutter Busters* — Bonnie's organizing business.

What would happen to her shop now?

Would Beau want to leave his lawyer job and take over Bonnie's business or work with Tyler? Maybe Tyler could buy out Beau. Was Shawna organized like Laci? Maybe she would take over Bonnie's position — once the mistake of her murder arrest was cleared up.

"C'mon, Daisy." I gave her leash a little twitch, but she pressed her nose against the store window. Did Bonnie have a resident cat to declutter mice?

There certainly wasn't a cat in the lighted window display. Cupping my hands around my eyes, I tried to focus on the interior behind the window. A light glowed briefly far in the back — so briefly that I wondered if I had imagined it. Daisy pawed at the window, confirming that she'd seen something, too. I leaned against the window to look again.

A small orb of light flashed briefly in our direction. I thought we might have been seen and my heart pounded. Fortunately, the light moved on. Barely visible in the dark interior of the store, the obscure shadow of a person moved about.

FIFTEEN

From "THE GOOD LIFE":

Dear Sophie,
My mother-in-law, a woman who lectures me endlessly about organizing my house, is visiting and nagging me to take down my Christmas tree. I hate it each year when all the ornaments are rolling around, and it looks like the tree exploded. Other than buying her a one-way ticket out of town, how can I take down the tree so she won't see the chaos?
— Disorganized Daughter-in-law in
Spruce, Michigan

Dear Disorganized,
Don't explode the tree! Take off ornaments first, placing them in the boxes in which they came. Tuck those boxes into a bigger box and stash away. Then remove the ornaments that don't have

boxes. Wine boxes are excellent for storing them. Next tackle the garlands and finally the lights. If you take the tree down one step at a time, nothing will explode into a mess.

— Sophie

I patted Daisy and praised her for seeing the intruder. For a long moment, I debated calling the police. I loathed the idea of another encounter with Kenner. Anyone creeping around with a flashlight had to be up to no good, though. In case the intruder happened to look toward the street, I thought it prudent to move to the corner before I phoned 911.

While I waited for the police to arrive, Daisy and I peeked into the alley behind the stores. Tiny mounds of previously cleared snow gleamed against the darkness. The rear hatch was open on a large SUV parked behind Bonnie's store. I pulled Daisy back and, glad I was wearing pants, straddled her to keep her close while I spied. I leaned forward and watched as someone loaded a box into the SUV. He returned to the store and, seconds later, pushed another box into the car.

A police siren howled in the distance, and Daisy, a hound mix, joined in. I tried to quiet her, but as the siren came closer and grew louder, so did Daisy.

The dark figure in the alley slammed the SUV hatch shut, hopped into the car, and spun his tires in his eagerness to depart. He drove out in the other direction without his lights on, so I never got a good look at the driver or the license plate.

Daisy and I returned to the front of the store, and the police car came to a halt. A young officer stepped out, and I explained what had happened. He tried the front door, then walked around to the rear entrance. Daisy and I accompanied him.

I expected to find a broken lock or window but everything appeared intact. The officer waved a strong flashlight beam over the rear of the building. "I don't see any sign of breaking and entering, do you?"

I had to admit that I didn't.

He pulled a cloth from his pocket and tested the doorknob. "If someone was in there, either he had a key or he's an ace locksmith. This door is locked tight."

"May I borrow your flashlight?"

"Sure."

He handed it to me and I trained it on the paved alley. "There. See it? Right there." I let the light play along the surface of the road. "Those are the marks his tires made when he left so fast."

The young officer seemed doubtful. "We'll have to locate the owners. They'll know if anything has been stolen."

I'd seen the guy carrying boxes out. What more did he need? It was a bit peculiar to imagine that a talented locksmith chose the day after Bonnie died to rip her off. Though he could have seen her obituary in the paper and jumped at the opportunity. "You can probably cut through a lot of effort by calling Detective Kenner."

"Kenner? He's in homicide. Is he a friend of yours or something?"

"The owner of the store — or maybe the half-owner, I don't know — died yesterday. Kenner is" — I sought an appropriate phrase — "on the case."

The officer jumped back and studied the ground. "Are you kidding? This could all be a crime scene." His voice rose to a shrill pitch. "You couldn't have mentioned this before? We've probably contaminated something."

Waving his arm, he motioned for me to follow him out of the alley. When we reached the sidewalk, he strode away from me, but I could hear him calling the dispatcher. When he returned, he said, "Who burglarizes a store *after* Christmas? They didn't get enough gifts, so they thought they'd just help themselves to more?" He wrinkled his nose. "A closet store? What would anyone want in a closet store? I understand breaking into a jewelry store, not that I condone it, but this is nuts. Who steals coat hangers?"

It was a rhetorical question, confirmed by the fact that he kept muttering about it until Kenner arrived. Even though they spoke privately, I could hear him telling Kenner that I'd concealed the owner's death from him.

Kenner kept his eyes on me the whole time the young officer pleaded his case. He finally nodded and, without a word, strode over to me. "A burglar? That was the best you could do?"

Huh? "I beg your pardon?"

"It's fairly obvious you made up this burglar so you'd have a reason to see me again."

"Why, you obnoxious, conceited, pompous blowhard!"

Daisy punctuated my ire with a vicious growl, and I took that opportunity to turn on my heel and walk away, hoping I hadn't just made him so angry that he would turn into the old monster Kenner I'd known before.

"Sophie," Kenner said gently, "you don't have to be embarrassed by your desire."

Desire!? Ugh. At that very moment, the only desire I had was to go home and snuggle up in a warm house — *without Kenner!* I kept walking and made no sign that I'd heard him. If he needed information, well, much as I hated to admit it, he knew where he could find me. Besides, I'd told that whiny young officer everything I saw. It was their turn to pick up the ball and run with it.

It grated on me that Kenner managed to twist my report of a crime into an attempt at an assignation. One thing was certain — I wouldn't be calling the police for anything until Wolf returned. I didn't need Kenner hanging around, imagining I had designs on him.

Every inch of me longed to go home, to get out of the lousy weather, to finally eat dinner, and snuggle up with a warm drink by a blazing fire. I couldn't, though. I couldn't do that to Laci and Jen, who loved Shawna so dearly.

I could, however, stroll by The Laughing Hound, to see if Bernie or Hannah would take pity on me and bring a hot chocolate out to the sidewalk. I steered Daisy in that direction, pondering where I would go if I

189

were Shawna.

She would expect the police at her apartment. She could hide at Beau's condo, but if the police thought she murdered Bonnie, Beau surely knew about their theory. He'd already tried to blame Bonnie's death on Shawna. Could he have changed his mind about that and be protecting her now?

Where would I go under those circumstances? I guessed I would turn myself in, but not until I had consulted an attorney. Had she met some of Old Town's legal eagles while she waitressed? Probably. Daisy and I hoofed it over to Bernie's restaurant. I felt a little like Tiny Tim, standing out in the cold and staring in at the fancy people having a good time. I poked my head in the door and asked the seating host if he could send Bernie out. He gave me an annoyed look, but through the glass doors, I watched him walk toward the back and hoped he was fetching Bernie.

Minutes later, Bernie shot out the door. "Why aren't you coming inside?" Daisy pawed at him, her head down. "Ohhh." He squatted to rub her head. "Your sister is here with a good-looking guy. Bring Daisy around to the garden gate. I'll get a jacket."

Daisy and I let ourselves into the garden area where I'd watched Marnie only the day before. As though he could read my mind, Bernie joined us minutes later with two Irish Monks — hot chocolate with Bailey's Irish Cream and Frangelico. Steam wafted from the mugs and whipped cream melted into the liquid. Thoughtful Bernie hadn't forgotten Daisy. He handed her an aluminum take-out tin of leftover prime rib.

"Hannah and her new beau seem to be getting fairly close," Bernie said.

"We're supposed to be out looking for Shawna. She didn't come here, I suppose?" I sipped at the rich, hot liquid.

Bernie exhaled. "Kenner came by looking for her. You don't think she really killed Bonnie, do you?"

"You know her better than I do. All I know is that she was obsessed with getting a Christmas proposal from Beau. It was all she thought of."

"Yeah, we heard about it nonstop here, too. It doesn't follow, though. Even if she was upset with Bonnie for announcing her own engagement, it wouldn't make sense to kill her. That wouldn't have changed the situation."

"Unless she thought Bonnie stood in the way."

"Nah." Bernie held his mug with ungloved hands. "Shawna is a sweetheart. She remembers everyone's birthday, she's always cheery — I don't see it. Don't get me wrong, I like Shawna, but I'm not sure she's the type to plan a complex murder. Bashing Bonnie over the head in front of everyone at the party in a fit of anger would have been more her style. Planning? Not Shawna's forte."

Planning? "What did Kenner tell you?"

"Not much. The man is irritatingly coy. But the local rumor mill has it that the killer managed to pipe some sort of gas into her house. Doesn't sound like anything Shawna would figure out on her own."

I gulped the warm liquid while watching Daisy push the aluminum tin around with her nose to be sure she got every last morsel of meat. "Are you saying you think someone helped her?"

Bernie shot me an exasperated glance. "No. In the bluntest, but not nicest, way, just between us, I'm saying Shawna isn't bright enough to have thought of something so devious, much less executed it."

Laci did strike me as the smarter sister. "It's hard to imagine anyone would do that. Would you know how?"

The cold had pinked Bernie's fair cheeks, but a blush rose up his neck. "Actually, I would. But don't spread that around. I don't want Kenner after me."

I should have known. Bernie, whose nose had been broken at some point and left a bit askew, whose sandy hair always appeared as though he'd just gotten out of bed, who looked more like Dennis the Menace than a restauranteur, was something of a Renaissance man. His unending array of talents never failed to amaze me.

A light snow began to drift down again. I finished my drink and handed him the empty mug, thanking him. Bernie leaned over and kissed my cheek. "Merry Christmas, Sophie."

"Thanks for Daisy's treat, too." We headed for the gate.

"Keep me posted about Shawna!" he called after us.

As we walked away, snow floated around us, lights twinkled, and brisk air nipped at my warm cheeks. I decided to head home, yet felt a little bit guilty about that decision. I wanted to think about what Bernie had told me, and I clearly wasn't doing Shawna any good by wandering aimlessly. The short walk would have been completely romantic if the specter of Shawna's imminent arrest hadn't overshadowed the holiday joy.

Daisy and I walked up to my front door. A dusting of snow clung to the pine wreath

I had adorned with holly leaves, fresh red berries, and pinecones. I slid my key into the lock and opened the door.

Without my noisy family hanging out, my house had become eerily still. I lit the fire in the kitchen fireplace and turned on the Christmas lights to cozy it up. I was about to make myself a turkey sandwich when the phone rang.

"I'm out of town for three days and you're already in trouble?" asked Wolf. His voice resonated with depth and warmth, and suddenly, I wished he weren't so far away.

"I miss you." *Ugh.* Why did I say that? He would surely misinterpret it.

He chuckled. "Me, too. It's great to see my folks, though. Have they found Shawna yet?"

"How did you know about that?"

"I know my Sophie. She would never call unless something was very wrong. I placed a couple of calls to my pals and got the scoop. The victim's son told the police that Shawna killed Bonnie because she was against their marriage."

"That's odd. I'm under the impression that Shawna didn't know about Bonnie's feelings until after she was dead. But I did find an engagement ring in Bonnie's purse. Do you think she pinched it so Beau wouldn't have it to propose to Shawna?"

"In her purse?" Wolf chuckled. "Snooping already, Sophie?"

"I was *not* snooping! I just got back from looking for Shawna. Get this — someone broke into Bonnie's store tonight and was removing things."

Wolf was silent for a moment. "It wouldn't be the first time someone saw an obituary and took advantage of the situation. On the other hand, it certainly is suspicious timing. Do you have any reason to think someone was cleaning up some sort of evidence?"

"Only the fact that the burglar had a key. There was no sign of forced entry."

"Kenner on the case?"

"Of course."

I heard Wolf sigh. "Stay away from him, okay?"

"Wolf? Did you find out how Bonnie died? Kenner won't tell me."

"Looks like Shawna gave Bonnie a Christmas gift that spewed poisonous gas when she opened it."

I staggered backward and fell into a chair by the fire. What was that phrase — malice aforethought. Shawna hadn't killed Bonnie because of the way she acted at the party. She had to have planned the murder well in advance. "Where do you buy poisonous gas?"

"Good question. Isn't that the craziest thing? Plus, it had to be rigged to go off somehow. Man, I wish I was there for this one."

"When are you coming back?"

"I still have to drive my folks home to Pennsylvania, and they're having a blast, so I hate to cut the trip short. Soph, keep me posted, okay?"

I promised to keep him in the loop, though frankly, he had connections who could tell him more in an instant. I hung up and stretched my bare toes toward the flickering warmth of the flames. Mochie jumped into my lap, probably wondering why I hadn't diced any turkey for him yet, and head-butted me.

I stroked him absently. I had been the first person on the scene, so the gift in question must have been the music box that I found on the floor. It made some degree of sense in the abstract. Bonnie had brought the gift home from her party, opened it, and died when she inhaled poison.

But if Bernie was right, and as Shawna's boss, he was certainly in a position to gauge her abilities, Shawna wasn't the brightest bulb. Just because I wouldn't know how to go about creating a poisonous music box didn't mean she couldn't, though. A person could find instructions for just about anything on the Internet these days. Maybe she really had planned to get rid of Beau's mother.

I didn't have to look far for motives. Everyone in Laci's family wished Bonnie would drop dead. Shawna could have thought Bonnie would come between her and Beau, or she could have lost it when her father showed up with Bonnie as his date. I held Mochie close and exhaled a long breath. Poor Laci. As if they hadn't had enough problems, it looked to me like Shawna would be doing time.

Daisy nudged me with her nose, a gentle reminder that her dinner was late. "Bernie's treat was only an appetizer?" I asked.

She wagged her tail in response and pawed at me gently.

At least we'd roasted the turkey earlier in the day. Mochie and Daisy would enjoy it as much as I would. I made their dinners and added diced turkey to their food before making my sandwich.

I heated a mini-baguette in the oven and cut thin slices of turkey breast. With relief, I found Mom had left a good bit of cranberry sauce behind. My mouth practically watered at the treat of turkey and cranberry sauce.

I slid the bread out of the oven, halved it, added a bit of mayonnaise to both sides, layered the slices of turkey breast on one side, and added a generous dollop of the burst berries. I had just placed the top on my sandwich when Daisy growled and raced for the sunroom. *Oh no!* The only person she'd been growling at lately was Kenner. I hoped he wasn't back, imagining some sort of romantic connection. I turned off all the overhead lights and crept into the sunroom.

A shadowy figure lurked outside the door.

Sixteen

From "The Good Life":

Dear Sophie,
I'm addicted to wreaths. I hang them on each window, on the front and back doors, and over the fireplaces. Storing one or two wasn't a problem, but how do I store so many without squashing them?
— Going in Circles in Advent,
West Virginia

Dear Going in Circles,
Look up — in a closet, that is. A lot of walk-in closets and utility closets have plenty of empty space around the top. Hang your wreaths high, out of the way. If you have a basement or attic, use threaded rod hangers to hang a long, removable rod parallel to the ceiling. Slide your wreaths onto the rod, drape

with an old sheet, and they'll be ready for next year.

— Sophie

The shadow knocked tentatively. "Sophie!" It was a desperate whisper.

Shawna?

She knocked again, ever so softly.

I neared the door and recognized Shawna peering through the glass. Quickly, I unlocked the door to let her in.

She trembled with fear. "Thank you! Thank you, Sophie," she whispered. "Is anyone else here?"

Normally I wouldn't have let a killer into my house, nor would I have admitted to being alone, but something about Shawna struck a chord with me. She seemed pathetic and frightened. If Hannah were in the same situation, I hoped Laci would help her.

"No one is here but me. They're all out looking for you." I switched on a small lamp.

She pressed bloodless fingers against her face. "I don't know what to do, where to go. I didn't kill Bonnie. Honest, I didn't. That horrible Detective Kenner has me in the electric chair already. You believe me, don't you?"

I was searching for a vaguely reassuring but noncommittal response when I realized that I did believe her. I had run up against Kenner before and knew how stubborn he could be when he thought he had figured out a crime — even if he was dead wrong. I also trusted Bernie's judgment, and had doubts about Shawna's ability to conceive and construct the devious method of killing Bonnie.

She rubbed her hands together to warm them. "He convinced Beau that I murdered his mother."

Far be it from me to defend Kenner, but I had been there when Beau found out his mother died, and he'd blamed it on Shawna without any help from Kenner, or anyone else for that matter.

"I've lost everything, Sophie. My life is over. They're saying I poisoned her with some kind of gas. I don't even understand how a person would do that."

Either she was being honest and I was right about her being innocent, or she was a talented actress.

I reached for her jacket. "You're sopping wet!"

"I've been out in the snow, dodging through alleys."

"Go upstairs and take a hot shower. You're taller than I am, but maybe you can find some dry sweats in my closet? Meanwhile,

I'll try to reach your dad. Okay?"

She nodded, handed me her jacket, and shuffled toward the stairs.

While she showered, I made her piping hot chocolate, carried it upstairs, and left it next to the sink. If she didn't warm up, she would get sick. I heard the water stop as I returned to the kitchen.

I phoned Phil on his cell phone number. Maybe he would be able to hire an attorney who could smooth the way if Shawna turned herself in.

When Phil answered his phone, I tried to convey the message in code in case anyone was listening. "We're reconvening at my house."

He promised to be there soon. As I hung up, Daisy headed to the front door. Moments later, I heard a clatter. Not Kenner! Oh, please, not Kenner! He would toss us both in jail if he found Shawna at my house.

I peered through the peephole in the door, wondering if I dared not open it. Was it illegal not to open the door for a cop? I tried to still my hammering heart. I couldn't make out anything through the peep hole. Was Shawna dressed yet? Could she escape out the back before Kenner figured out that she was here? Had he followed her? What if he had listened to my phone call?

Kenner had warned Laci and me about harboring a criminal. Had he come back with a search warrant for my house? *Argh.* I beat my head gently against the door. What now?

I peered through the peephole again. Why hadn't the person knocked on the door yet? Shawna was upstairs, and I couldn't imagine who else would dally at my door.

Leaving the safety chain in place, I eased the door open for a better look. There, under the romantic glow of the Christmas lights surrounding my door, Hannah had locked lips with Zack.

My initial relief faded as I gently closed the door. He was still a cop. Hannah had surely told him about Shawna. He may have even made some phone calls to find out more. What would he do if he found her in my house?

I stood with my back against the door, as though it would send some sort of psychic message to Hannah to get rid of Zack.

It didn't work. I could feel the door handle turn against my back. Hannah barged in, holding Zack's hand.

They shook snow off their coats, laughing about a branch that had deposited its snowy load onto them. I gently shooed them into the living room and suggested Zack light a fire. I eyed Hannah. Should I risk telling her Shawna was upstairs? Or was she so deep in the throes of new love that she would blab?

I scurried around the living room, turning on the lights on the tree and on boughs of pine decorating the mantel. It turned out they'd eaten at Bernie's, so I offered to whip up after-dinner drinks for them — anything to keep them in the living room, where they'd be least likely to see Shawna.

To cover up the sound of Shawna's footsteps upstairs, I turned on lively Christmas music and was immediately rewarded with "It's Cold Outside." Not the noisiest song, but Hannah and Zack would relate to it tonight.

I rushed into the kitchen to make their drinks and saw a car cruising slowly down my block, as though the driver sought a parking space. Crossing my fingers, I hoped it was Phil and that we could get Shawna squared away before any of the rest of us got into trouble.

My stomach rumbled, out of nervousness as much as hunger. I reached for my sandwich. A few crumbs dotted the plate but the sandwich was gone. Daisy looked up at me innocently. I was about to scold her, but realized she wouldn't have left crumbs. She wasn't licking her chops, either. But if she didn't take it, then where did it go? Shawna!

I sped to the sunroom and gazed into my backyard. The gate to the alley closed behind someone. Hoping I'd been right about the car cruising the street, I ran through the house and out the front door, in search of Phil's car.

Someone was trying to parallel park a boat-size car in a spot far too small for it. I sped up and knocked on the window. Thank goodness I'd been right — it was Phil. "She's in the alley." I pointed to help him understand.

"Is she okay?"

"Fine, but confused. She needs your help."

"This is all my fault," he moaned. "I just wanted to make Marnie jealous, but now I wish I had never met Bonnie. I needed to prove to Marnie, and maybe to myself, too, that I was attractive to other women. I guess I'm not. I lied about seeing other women. Bonnie was the only one, and now I think she was using me to break up Shawna and Beau. Who knew that Bonnie would be crazy enough to announce our engagement at her party?"

"But you were engaged?"

"No! I have no idea where she got that ring she flashed around. Never in my wildest dreams did I think anything like this would happen."

I peered through the window at him. Could I believe what he was saying? He seemed sincere. But if Phil hadn't been engaged to Bonnie, what would have possessed her to make such an announcement? She'd obviously planned it since she brought along a ring.

"Why didn't you say something then?"

"She took me by surprise. Plus, I would never embarrass a lady in front her friends and family like that. I figured I'd deal with it later, but then Shawna ran out of the room and the whole thing just spiraled out of control. Now Bonnie's dead and the cops are after Shawna. I've been driving around in circles, looking for my little girl and chastising myself for bringing this horrible situation on my family."

I appreciated his grief, but he didn't have time to linger. Shawna could turn down another alley and be lost in the shadows in seconds. Besides, I'd noticed a movement in a nearby car. It was too cold to just hang out in a car — I had a bad feeling Kenner had charged someone with the unenviable duty of watching my house.

"Phil, I think we're being watched. I'm going to act like I'm wishing you a nice holiday, okay? You need to find Shawna while she's still in the neighborhood."

Phil put the car in gear, and I backed away from the driver's window, shouting, "Happy Holidays! It was great seeing you."

I stood in the middle of the street hoping to prevent Kenner's henchman from pulling out immediately behind Phil. Fortunately, there wasn't much traffic, but the cold had permeated my turtleneck and snow collected on my shoulders and head. I shook it off and used the motion as a pretense to get a better look at the person in the other car. To my complete surprise, Kenner sat behind the wheel watching me.

Phil's taillights disappeared around the corner at the far end of the street. I said a little prayer that he would find Shawna. I couldn't imagine being alone on the streets on a frigid night like this.

Although I thought I would drop any second from the cold, I decided I'd better stall Kenner. I rushed over to his car and he rolled down the window.

"Awfully cold to sit out here," I said.

"Are you inviting me in?"

"Look, Kenner — Shawna is not in my house. You can sit here all night and freeze your nose off for all I care."

He held out a hand. "I swung by to bring you this."

Seventeen

From "The Good Life":

Dear Sophie,
I try so hard to be organized, but papers accumulate in piles until I can't stand it. What's worse, then I can't find the things I need — like bills that have to be paid.
— Overpapered in Piper, California

Dear Overpapered,
Buy a shredder and a basket. The key is to place them where you open your mail. If you stand at the kitchen counter, find a spot for them in the kitchen. Don't put the paper down once it's in your hands. If it's trash, shred it. If it's important, put it in the basket. Be sure to clean out the basket regularly so you won't overlook those bills.
— Sophie

Guilt saddled me for a moment, but only a moment. There was no doubt he'd been spying on my house. "What's that?"

"The key to Bonnie's office. You'll need access for the auction."

"How did you know about that?"

He grinned, his horsey teeth gleaming in the semidark. "I'm in charge of the auction for the Alexandria Police. Beau asked me to give you the keys."

Argh. How did I get myself into these messes? The last thing I needed was more contact with Kenner. I sighed and took the key from his palm, but he closed his fingers over mine and pressed. A shiver sparked down my back, and it was *not* from the cold air.

I tried to jerk my hand away, but Kenner held fast. There just wasn't any good way around this. As sweetly as I could, I said, "I'm sorry, Kenner. The truth is that I'm seeing Wolf." There. It was out in the open, plain as it could be, clear enough for anyone to understand.

Kenner didn't release my fingers. "Married?"

I tilted my head in irritation. "No."

"Engaged?"

"No."

"Then consider this my declaration of a

good old-fashioned fight for your affections. He leaned forward and kissed the back of my hand.

Ugh! I was so horrified that I jerked it out of his firm grip. Fortunately, the key was in my possession.

I should have said something clever. Should have shot back a retort, but he left me speechless, and I marched to my house without so much as a glance back at him.

I did, however, continue to surreptitiously spy from my windows. His car remained in place, even after I fed the kittens, Mochie and Daisy, ate a turkey sandwich, and went up to bed.

I rose early the next morning, thoughts of the Auld Lang Syne Auction hammering me. Heaven only knew what remained to be done by tomorrow. I donned jeans with an elastic waist and an oversized sweater the color of celery. Grateful that I could call on my entire family to pitch in, I made a big pot of coffee and poured half of it into a carafe to take with me to Bonnie's office. Mochie rubbed against me, reminding me that the kittens needed to be fed.

The door to my study was open and the kittens nowhere to be seen, so I assumed Hannah had taken them upstairs to sleep with her. Life had been so crazy after Bonnie's murder that I hadn't given the kittens much thought. Who would have left them here? They were adorable, but Mochie had first dibs and he clearly didn't care for them in his territory.

After he ate, Mochie curled up on the window seat in the kitchen. I slid Daisy's harness over her head, bundled up, and left Mochie and Hannah to doze.

The hazy clouds had lifted, and for the first time in days, the sun glistened on ice crystals and sparkling decorations. The brisk air felt good against my face. Daisy trotted with her tail high, and I felt like I could think clearly.

I unlocked the front door of Clutter Busters. It was eerily silent and the far corners seemed dark and sinister. I didn't let Daisy loose until I'd located light switches. The shop came alive when overhead lights beamed. I snapped off Daisy's leash and locked the front door, so no one would catch us unaware if we were in the back.

Daisy explored eagerly, and after a brief look around at the many closet and storage displays, I wandered to the office in the back, set down the coffee on a chair, took off my jacket and muffler, and stared at the desk of a dead woman.

It was a frightening mess. Heaps of paper threatened to tumble off. Bits of wrapping paper and craft projects clung precariously to stacks of boxes and organizing folders. Boxes upon boxes lined the walls, two and three deep in places. The organizing diva had been a sham. Maybe Natasha and the man with the Rhodesian ridgeback had been right about her. She presented a sweet, organized image to the public, but underneath lurked someone entirely different.

Thankful that I didn't have to clean up the mess on her desk, I set about exploring the little rooms in the back, in search of anything auction related. A storeroom in the back overflowed with boxes. So much so that I couldn't reach the light switch. I opened an unsealed box and found a small table and a footstool. They had to be auction items. I groaned aloud at the thought of having to go through every single box.

If I had been running the show, I would have kept a list of donated items. Surely she must have kept some kind of log. I drifted back to Bonnie's office and stared at her overburdened desk. With enormous dread at the prospect of having to dig through that pile, I plopped into her desk chair. The sharp corner of something dug into my hip. I reached back and pulled out a receipt book. I held my breath when I opened it. Bingo! The names and addresses of donors, along with itemizations of what they'd donated. I sang aloud, "Hallelujah."

Now that I had a clue about the donations, what I needed was a team of Santa's elves to help me find it all and cart it over to the auction site. I pulled out my cell phone and called George's house.

He answered his phone with a gruff, "Yeah?"

"Very nice. Is that how we answer the phone now?"

"C'mon, Soph. We're in total chaos here. What do you want?"

"What happened? What are you talking about?"

"Hannah didn't tell you? I just got off the phone with her. Know any good lawyers? Shawna and Phil are both in jail."

EIGHTEEN

From "Ask Natasha":

Dear Natasha,
My husband keeps everything that is remotely computer related. We have seven boxes of disks that no longer work in today's computers. We have boxes of cords, plugs, scanning items, memory devices — until I want to scream. Not to mention all the old computers and keyboards. Hubby is convinced that they will all be "worth something someday." How do I get rid of them?
— One Computer Woman in
North Pole, Idaho

Dear One Computer Woman,
I have learned the hard way that there are some things that cannot be wrenched away from men, no matter how useless, filthy, broken, or outdated. I recommend

giving up a closet or a storage cabinet in the garage to hubby for his computer clutter. Mark it with a piece of straw in the door, so that it will fall to the ground if the door is opened. If he doesn't open it for two years, have the contents hauled away.

— Natasha

I jumped to my feet. "When did this happen?"

"Early this morning. Shawna was arrested for murder and Phil was taken in for helping her — an accomplice after the fact or something. Now we're worried that they think Phil was involved in the murder all along."

Oh no. It made sense that the police might think someone more clever had rigged up the gas. Phil had seemed perfectly happy with Bonnie on Christmas Day, though. He didn't have a reason to kill her. Well, not until she announced their engagement anyway. "So what now?"

"We're coming to town in the hope we can find a lawyer who can spring them." He lowered his voice. "Do you have something to keep Laci occupied? She and Marnie are beside themselves."

Did I have something to keep them busy?

"You bet! Come straight to Bonnie's business."

The second I hung up, my phone rang. Hannah was calling to relay the message from George. "I thought you were home until I found your note in the kitchen."

"Feel like calling Zack?" I asked.

"Isn't he fabulous? Sophie, I'm dreamily in love."

"Call your dreamboat and tell him we need help organizing and transporting items for the auction. Then drive my SUV over here so we can fill it up, okay? Oh, Hannah? Stop at a bakery and pick up croissants or doughnuts or whatever they have that looks good — and get lots of it."

I poured myself coffee and revved up Bonnie's computer and printer, both nearly buried under papers. Please, please let her have kept a running list of all the items as they came in. That would save an enormous amount of time. I felt a little bit guilty going through her computer files, but someone had to do it.

When I didn't find anything that sounded quite right, I gave up and made a list of what needed to be done. I'd just finished when Daisy barked in the front of the store. I raced to the door and unlocked it. My family piled in, along with a bunch of strangers who seemed to be there with Zack.

He helped Hannah carry in the baked goods, grinning like a lovesick fool the whole time.

I found a chair to stand on, and explained my plan to everyone. Half an hour later, we had an unbelievable assembly line going. Cops took turns opening the boxes and calling out the contents. Laci found the corresponding listing in the receipt book, and Hannah, the computer wizard, transferred the information to a spreadsheet. Zack then marked the boxes, and the cops moved them out to a troop of SUVs and vans that waited to transport them all.

I put Jen in charge of Daisy, and George quietly slipped off to spring Shawna and Phil. Marnie seemed completely hopeless, and drifted aimlessly until I told her to find a coffeemaker and disposable cups, and brew coffee for our team of elves.

I drove Dad over to the auction site and arrived just in time to receive the first load of items the cops were driving over.

Surprisingly, the process went smoothly for two hours, and then Hannah called me. "Houston, we have a problem. Better come back to Bonnie's shop."

NINETEEN

From "THE GOOD LIFE":

Dear Sophie,
I have some expensive heirloom ornaments that I would like to pass along to my grandchildren someday. Should I store them in a special way to be sure they last?
— Doting Gramma in Silver Bell,
Arizona

Dear Doting Gramma,
Ornaments, Christmas houses, and other collectibles should be stored in the boxes in which they came. The boxes are usually made to fit the exact dimensions of the items, which cushions and protects them. In addition, because boxes are so often thrown out, the value of collectibles is usually higher if the original box is still available and in good condi-

tion. Never store them where the temperature will exceed eighty degrees or be less than forty degrees.

— Sophie

I left Dad with a couple of the cop elves so they could continue to receive the items en route while I drove back to Bonnie's shop.

The second I entered the store, Daisy dashed to me for petting, and Jen ran along behind her, waving a Christmas ornament in the air.

"Here." She shoved it in my face.

I squatted to Daisy's level and stroked my wriggling mutt with one hand, while accepting the ornament with the other. Handmade, it appeared to be a hard foam ball covered with glittery beads attached with pins. "Very pretty."

Zack walked up behind Jen, his mouth grim. "That ornament is one of the items stolen from your brother's home on Christmas Eve."

"What?" I stood up.

Jen reached for the ornament. "I made this for Grandma but the thief stole it. Daisy found it behind a bunch of boxes in the back."

I blinked at her, trying to absorb the implication. How could it have gotten here?

"Honey," I said as gently as I could, "did you make this from a kit? Maybe it just looks like the one you made."

"Kit? I bought all the beads and made it myself. Look, see how some of the beads are a different shade of silver? They spell out Grandma's name, Inga."

So they did. I looked to Zack, bewildered.

"I've got three officers phoning the donors to be sure they donated the goods and that they weren't stolen. So far, everything checks out. This is the only item we've found that corresponds to the list of stolen items. I'm not sure what to make of it."

"The Christmas Eve thief donated something to the auction and included this little bauble? How else could it possibly have gotten here?"

"That's what I'm thinking." Zack ruffled his hair by running a hand through it. "I can't quite wrap my head around it, though. The timing is a little bit weird. It wasn't stolen until Christmas Eve, and Bonnie was murdered on the day after Christmas, so she would have had to accept the donation on Christmas Day or before her party."

A chorus of laughter broke out near the pastries. "Is that Tyler?" I asked. "Could he have accepted the donation?"

"Isn't he cute!" said Jen. "I'm so crushing

on him."

Zack shot me a look of amusement.

"He is very cute," I assured her. And he was. The shaggy hair in need of a good cut made him seem boyish, and far younger than his years.

"He told me the police called him about a break-in here last night." Zack massaged his eyes. "Says nothing is missing."

I bristled a little. "I'm the one who reported it. I saw someone loading a car in the back. No question about it."

Zack's concerned cop expression returned. "But there was no sign of a break-in, right? Could you have confused this building with one of the other stores that back to the alley? They look a lot alike in the rear."

"I suppose so, but I don't think so." I thought back. "No! I'm certain of it. I looked through the show window right there and could see someone moving about in the back with a flashlight."

"Hey, Tyler!" called Zack.

Tyler ambled over, and Jen blushed. "I think my Aunt Shawna should be in love with you instead of Beau."

Tyler laughed aloud. "You tell her that."

"Okay. As soon as Dad springs her from the slammer."

Tyler's expression changed fast. "Slammer?"

"Shawna and Phil were arrested early this morning. My brother is trying to get them out of jail," I explained.

"No!" Tyler shouted it so loud that everyone turned to look. "Not Shawna. I'm sorry, I have to go. Maybe I can help."

"Just a couple quick things before you leave." Zack issued that very polite request in a no-nonsense voice. "There were a lot of boxes when we arrived today. How did you know nothing was missing?"

Tyler seemed taken aback. "Nothing had been moved. I didn't do an inventory, if that's what you mean. Everything was exactly as I last saw it."

"And there was no sign of a forced entry?" Zack asked.

Tyler's mouth pulled to the side. "I checked my coat at Bonnie's party — you were there," he said, pointing at me. "Stupidly, I left my keys in the pocket, and when the coat was returned to me, the keys were gone. Initially, I thought I'd just misplaced them, but now it seems apparent that someone took them on purpose." Tyler jingled coins in his pocket.

Zack fixed him with a cold stare. "Did you accept any donations to the auction?"

"Sure." Tyler shrugged. "I brought them to Bonnie."

"Did you receive any between Christmas Eve and the time of Bonnie's death?"

"No. The shop was closed. If that's all, I'd like to go see what I can do to help Shawna."

Zack flicked his hand in approval, but seemed deep in thought.

Tyler hurried out as Hannah floated toward us. She slid an arm around Zack's waist, and they grinned at each other in that giddy new love sort of way.

"You looked so serious!" she said.

He couldn't stop the silly grin. "I was just thinking that it has to be more than coincidence that Bonnie was murdered and someone stole the key to get into her office." He glanced around. "Do you suppose they got what they wanted?"

I drifted over to the coffee and pastries, poured a cup of java, and selected a croissant. I bit into it. Something didn't seem quite right. It made sense that the killer might have stolen the key to Bonnie's office, killed her to silence her, then paid a nighttime visit to the office to find whatever she possessed that troubled the killer. If that desk was any indication, though, he might not have found an incriminating document, if that was what he was looking for.

If viewed from that perspective, Shawna might be off the hook. I doubted Bonnie had anything Shawna needed back.

Instinctively, I glanced at the door from which Tyler had left. Had Shawna been involved with Tyler at some point? Did she have something to hide? He certainly had been eager to help her.

"Last box!" called Laci, which caused whooping and high-fiving in the back. She ambled toward me and poured herself a cup of coffee. "I know you needed help to do all this, but it couldn't have come at a better time. I would have worried about Shawna and Dad nonstop."

"Have you heard anything?" I was almost afraid to ask.

She shook her head. "I'm going to call George now."

She pulled out her cell phone and dialed. I debated walking away to give her privacy, but I wanted to know what was going on. Unfortunately, I didn't get much from her side of the conversation. When she hung up, she said, "He'll meet us at Bernie's in an hour."

"What about Shawna and Phil?"

She swallowed hard. "He didn't say." She stared into her coffee cup for a moment. "Sometimes I get upset with George because he keeps things from me. The truth is that he knows me really well and tries to protect me. He knows how agitated I can get, so I try to see his 'no news' as good news."

Couples have odd rituals, and Laci and George were no exception. I would have interpreted his lack of information as some kind of silly power play, but the women in Laci's family were capable of overreacting, so maybe George had learned this as a coping mechanism.

"One hour? We'd better wrap up here." I thanked all my helper elves, especially the police, and trusted Hannah and Zack to lock up. I collected Daisy and Jen, deposited Daisy at my house, and headed back to the auction site to pick up Dad. He and his helpers had done an admirable job of arranging all the items on tables around the room for viewing before the auction.

By the time we arrived at The Laughing Hound, it was well past anyone's idea of lunchtime and heading toward mid-afternoon. I apologized to Bernie for our slightly grubby appearance, but in his typical easygoing way, he didn't seem to care.

We'd just been seated when George and Phil walked in. A cheer rose from our table, and a few chairs landed on their backs in the big scramble to embrace Phil. Laci, Marnie, and Jen beamed, and for a few minutes, it looked as if they would never let him go.

Eventually, we made room for Phil to join us at the table, between Laci and Jen. When he sat down, Shawna's absence became horribly overwhelming.

George spoke and everyone stopped talking to listen. "Shawna's attorney did his best, but they see Shawna as a flight risk because they caught her with Phil, and they're convinced Phil was going to transport her out of state."

I glanced over at Phil, who lifted his brows and made a face.

"Phil hasn't been charged with murder . . . yet," continued George. "He's not completely off the hook, though. Here's what we know. The deadly gas was inside a music box, which Shawna gave Bonnie as a gift. There's not much doubt about that. Shawna admits giving it to her, and her name was on the gift tag."

Laci frowned at him. "I love my sister, but she nearly flunked high school chemistry. Even if she meant to kill Bonnie, which I don't think was the case, where would she get deadly gas?"

George sighed. "We have it in our house."

TWENTY

From "THE GOOD LIFE ONLINE":
SOPHIE'S TIP

Don't forget to remove batteries from animated decorations, candles, and Christmas toys before storing them. Batteries can corrode, damaging the items permanently.

Laci's eyes sprang wide. "Impossible!"

George nodded. "I'm willing to bet we all do. It seems that if you combine ammonia, which most people have for window washing, with bleach, it makes an unbelievably deadly chlorine gas. People innocently make it at home all the time, thinking they're getting a better and stronger cleaning agent."

"I don't get it," I said. "How could the gas be contained in the box? Wouldn't it have leeched out?"

"The two ingredients were in separate

228

plastic bags in the lined movement compartment. The cops are saying when Bonnie wound it up to play its song, the winding action broke the bags, the ammonia and bleach combined and wafted out. If Bonnie had been farther away from the box, she might have survived, but she probably held it on her lap and inhaled it before she realized what was happening."

"I thought I smelled chlorine in her house, but chalked it up to Bonnie being a cleaning fiend," I said.

George raised his eyebrows. "It's a good thing you broke that big window so fresh air could blow into the house."

No wonder Kenner called it devious. What kind of person would do anything so heinous? As we bit into an assortment of Bernie's fabulous oversized sandwiches, I tuned out the conversation and entertained serious doubts about my judgment. I'd thought Bonnie was lovely, but she'd pulled a fast one on Phil with that engagement business. Beau had said Bonnie thought Shawna and her family were beneath them. Had she tried to break them up? Had she stolen Beau's engagement ring and ruined his proposal by making her own announcement of an engagement? What a contrast to the thoughtful, caring person who came up with the Auld Lang Syne Auction. Had I misjudged Shawna, too? The police had to be wrong. I didn't know her all that well, but I never would have expected her to be capable of such a clever murder. The killer didn't need to be at the scene of the crime, and the murder weapon — the gas — would have dissipated into thin air before the police arrived.

I bit into my veggie-surprise sandwich. Creamy avocado contrasted with the fresh crispness of julienned cucumber. Red delicious apples and an occasional spark of lingonberry provided the surprise.

Meanwhile, Laci's family speculated about the poison gas and Shawna. I forced myself to pay attention.

"Then someone has to talk with Shawna," said Mom. "Someone she would confide in." I couldn't help noticing that Mom stared at Laci when she said that.

There was one other person at our table who'd been very quiet. Zack chewed on an onion ring and listened attentively. "I don't know Shawna. Could she be protecting someone? Who would she be willing to go to jail for?"

He'd honed in on the right question.

"Do you think they'd let me talk to her this afternoon?" Laci asked George.

"We'll take Jen home. I've been wanting to play Cat-opoly." Mom winked at Jen.

Weariness overcame me as we finished our late lunch, and even a strong cup of tea did nothing to reenergize me.

Hannah and Zack, now in the hand-holding stage of their romance, chose to go to a movie, so for the first time in days, I would be home alone.

When we were collecting our coats, Hannah pulled me aside. "Guess what I found out. The kid who lives next door to George and Laci — Edward Chadwick — he wasn't at the pageant like he said he was."

"He's the thief?" I hated to think that. He'd loaned his camera to Jen. Surely a thief wouldn't do that. Or had he offered it out of guilt? "Are they going to arrest him?"

"They don't have evidence yet, just the fact that he lied about where he was." She raised her eyebrows at me and slipped into her coat.

Everyone scattered to their appointed destinations. Early darkness fell as I drove home. I found a parking space a block away and trudged toward my house. The automatic candles in the windows had already clicked on. I let myself in, shared a mini-lovefest with Daisy and Mochie, and snapped a leash on Daisy for her evening walk.

We hadn't reached the sidewalk when I heard, "Yoo-hoo, Sophie!"

Natasha strode toward us and handed me a gift.

"What's this?"

"It's really for Daisy, and somehow in the commotion of Christmas, we overlooked it. Daisy will forgive me" — she bent her head ever so slightly in Daisy's direction — "won't you?"

"Thanks!" We walked under a streetlight. I ripped open the elegant wrapping paper and did a double take. The halter and leash with Daisy's name on the fabric was exactly like the one I'd given Mars for Christmas.

"I don't understand."

"What's to understand? It's a special leash with Daisy's name on it."

"It's exactly like the one Mars said he wanted. It's made for running with special give in the leash so the dog can move ahead or slow down."

"Oh?" Her tone changed as though she recognized her blunder. "Oh! Well, now Daisy has one."

"You're regifting this, aren't you?"

Natasha laughed. "Don't be silly."

"I gave this to Mars for Christmas."

Natasha inhaled noisily. She composed herself quickly and giggled. "It had to happen someday, I suppose. I thought it was from Bernie."

"I can't believe you regift! Does Mars even know about the halter and leash?"

"Oh, don't play innocent. Everyone regifts."

"I don't!" I protested.

"Then your friends and family must have better taste than mine. I can't have all that *stuff* cluttering up the house. You just keep the halter at your place, okay?"

I wanted to shove it into her face and demand she take it home to Mars, but I had a bad feeling it might land in the trash. It would be better if I handed it to him personally.

A little miffed that my gift had bypassed Mars entirely, I wondered how many other gifts I'd given them that landed elsewhere. "You're always so proper. I can't believe you regift."

"Everyone does, Sophie. Once a gift is given, it's the property of the recipient, and he or she has every right to give it to someone else."

I shook my head. Nothing like the spirit of the holiday. I always took such joy in picking out something special and hoping the person would love it. That was more fun than getting gifts as far as I was concerned. "C'mon, Daisy, let's find a spot for your new harness."

Natasha smiled sweetly, and I figured she thought she'd won, but she wasn't through with Daisy's harness just yet . . . I was just too beat to tangle with Natasha.

Poor Daisy got a short walk. Too tired to do anything requiring mental acuity, I switched on a movie. Leaving the rest of the lights off, I turned on the lights in the little Christmas village Jen had helped me set up. Grabbing a throw, I snuggled up on the sofa with Mochie and drifted off.

I jerked upright out of a dead sleep thirty minutes later. The kittens! Where were the kittens?

I ran to the study and through the living room and dining room. No sign of kittens. Were they asleep upstairs on Hannah's bed? I chugged up the two flights of stairs and staggered into the attic bedroom. No kittens. This couldn't be happening. Had they found some chink in the wall of my old house and crawled inside it?

I stood completely still and listened for mewing but only heard silence. "Jasper! Alice! Here, kitties!" I didn't hear a thing. Dread that they might be in trouble weighed on me. I walked down to my bedroom on the second floor to retrieve a flashlight from my nightstand. The closet door stood ajar, and Daisy poked her nose into the depths, wagging her tail. I looked more carefully and found Alice and Jasper curled up together, asleep in my laundry basket. They yawned and blinked their bright eyes at me. Laughing, I scooped them up and carried them downstairs to feed them before I hunkered down on the sofa again.

Dawn struggled to cut through heavy clouds on the day of the auction. I showered and pinned my hair up in a loose version of a French twist so I wouldn't have to worry about it all day.

As soon as I opened my closet door, little balls of fur zoomed past me and jumped into my laundry basket again. I giggled about their fondness for the laundry and heaved them out.

The Christmas season would soon be over, so I dressed in a deep green sweater with white angora sleeves and shoulders, and matching green trousers. The waistband was tight. Achingly tight. After promising myself that I would lose weight in the new year — *sure I would* — I relented and used the old rubber band through the button hole method to close the top of the pants. The sweater hung over the waistband, so no one would be the wiser.

I convinced myself that I needed a hearty breakfast, though. After a cold stroll with Daisy under leaden skies that threatened more snow, I made a bowl of oatmeal to fortify myself and shared it with Daisy. Mochie, Alice, and Jasper preferred kitty salmon.

I left a note for Hannah, lectured Mochie about being polite to the kittens, and donned a cozy hooded jacket for the walk to the auction site.

To my surprise, Laci was sitting in a folding chair in the middle of the auction room.

TWENTY-ONE

From "Ask Natasha":

Dear Natasha,
I hate to sound ungrateful, but we receive so many gifts from family and friends that our house overflows after Christmas. I don't have enough room for all this stuff. Is there a nice way to tell them to give us less?

— Stuffed to the Gills in Turkey,
North Carolina

Dear Stuffed to the Gills,
My rule is that for every one item you receive, two similar items should be given away. Think of it as renewing and recycling. Someone else will appreciate the items you can't use anymore.

— Natasha

I whipped off my coat. "Good morning!"

Laci glanced up from the pad of paper on her lap. "Tyler called us. Shawna's not doing well. We *have* to get her out of jail. I'm so angry with Beau. If he really loved her, he would have stood by her."

Even if he thought she murdered his mother? That would be asking a lot of him. "Are you all alone?"

She nodded. "It's terrible of me, but the noise level and drama at my house was getting on my nerves." Her shoulders sagged. "I'm sorry, Sophie. I've been a basket case. I needed a little quiet time to get my thoughts together. The rest of them will be along later. Right now, I have to concentrate on my sister." She thunked a pen against her thigh. "Will there be a food vendor? I could use some coffee and a nosh."

Like magic, Bernie backed through the glass door, holding take-out coffees and a box of pastries. "I thought the early birds might need some sustenance."

Laci jumped from her chair and cleared a spot for him. "You're an angel. Now if you could just wave your magic wand and spring Shawna."

Bernie shrugged off an elegant loden coat. "Got some time, Soph? Maybe if the three of us put our heads together . . ."

Laci pulled the top off a coffee and added

sugar. "I'm making a list of facts. Someone else did this and framed Shawna. I'm sure of it. She was an easy target because she's so nice."

I wanted to believe Laci. She was right about Shawna being an easy target for framing, but the facts didn't bear that theory out.

"Laci," I said gently, "I saw Shawna bring that package to Bonnie's party and leave it on the gift table. I remember because of the cute felt snowman decoration. I didn't realize that Shawna was adept at crafts."

Laci pointed at me with her pen. "*Aha!* Another fact. I'll start a list of inconsistencies. Shawna isn't a crafter."

"What are you saying? That someone else wrapped the package for Shawna?" I asked.

"A lot of stores wrap gifts when you buy them," offered Bernie.

It was a nice try but it didn't fly. "So she bought a music box that already had poisonous gas in it and the store wrapped it?" I didn't think so.

Bernie bit into a bear claw. "Do we know where she bought it?"

Laci flipped the page on her pad and said as she wrote, "Questions to ask Shawna."

"It looked antique, or at least vintage," I offered.

Bernie sighed and said sarcastically, "Like there aren't any antiques stores in Old Town."

He was right. It seemed like there was an antiques store, if not two, on every block.

"I'm sorry, Laci," I said, "but I think Shawna wrapped it herself. There was a huge fancy bow and the paper coordinated perfectly."

Laci flipped back to another list. "That's evidence, too. Shawna is a lousy wrapper."

"You don't think she would have taken extra time on the wrapping for a future mother-in-law she wanted to impress?" I asked.

Laci scowled. "Then we're back to someone else wanting to murder Bonnie, and convincing Shawna to give her the music box. From what I'd heard, there was a huge field of contenders. Bonnie wasn't the sweet, thoughtful person she pretended to be." At that moment, the food vendor arrived to set up, and our little discussion came to an abrupt end.

People began to straggle in to view the items before the auction. I'd been to the auction in prior years, but I suspected that news of Bonnie's demise had brought more people than ever. I saw my family arrive, and gave them a quick wave, but didn't have time to chat.

Tom Thorpe glad-handed his way through the crowd, with Dasher and a very pregnant Emma following along. Tom extended a hand to me. "Thank you so much for pulling off my sister-in-law's auction. The whole family is grateful. We were shocked by her sudden death."

"Bonnie was your sister-in-law?"

"My late wife's sister. She was such a help to us when my wife died. The boys were small and I had trouble coping. We're all devastated by her death."

Aha. So Tyler was Bonnie's nephew. Not that it mattered, but it did make sense that he worked for his aunt. I smiled at Emma. "You look positively radiant." She did, too. Her hair was still wild, but she'd removed the ring from her nose. She wore a chic new maternity outfit, and she played with a couple of elegant gold bracelets dotted with what appeared to be diamonds.

"Thanks! The Witch will be here today, and I want her to see that we're doing great. If she ever wants to see her grandchild, she needs to accept us. I've done everything I can. I gave her a beautiful Christmas gift —"

Dasher interrupted her, "That nearly bankrupted us."

She gave him a friendly shove. "I knew she would adore it. Haven't you ever done that? Spent more than you should have on a special gift? It was my way of trying to reconcile with her."

Tom hugged her. "Your mother is a difficult woman." To me, he said, "You should have seen the fight she had with Natasha over the Christmas decorations for our community center and the Christmas pageant. Like two cats in an alley."

I hoped Ginger would come around and be the mom Emma so desperately wanted. They moved on to talk with Mars and Natasha, and it was time for me to open the auction. I thanked everyone for coming and gave a tribute to Bonnie for her generosity over the years. The audience was an odd mixture of people who didn't seem to care and others who dabbed at their eyes when Bonnie was mentioned.

The auctioneer had a lively style and got the crowd going with a few deals that were so incredible I wished I could bid. Kenner had shown up, not a huge surprise. He kept an eye on me that made me uneasy. I tried to put him out of my mind, which wasn't hard since I had a lot to do.

Lamps, statues, paintings, small tables, china, and crystal fairly flew out. Forrest engaged in heavy bidding for a gorgeous crib with fancy carving. Emma sat next to him, wearing an excited grin, eagerly awaiting the result. I scanned the crowd for Ginger. She watched with interest and a sour expression.

Poor Emma. At least her father shared her delight about the baby. I tried to give Ginger the benefit of the doubt. After all, the bidding had gotten a bit high. Maybe she thought they shouldn't spend so much on a crib. When Forrest won the crib, Emma threw her arms around her father's neck and planted a major kiss on his cheek. He embraced his daughter, laughing and clearly delighted by his win.

Ginger didn't join in their happiness. From her position several rows away, she bid aggressively on the next item, an antique Staffordshire bowl and pitcher. Apparently, money wasn't the issue.

"Sophie," whispered Natasha, "do you think Vegas could sleep over with Jen tonight?"

"Jen's not staying with me. You'll have to ask Laci."

Apparently that was the wrong thing to say, because she returned minutes later with Laci in tow.

"If you don't mind, I think it would be

great for Jen. She needs to get away from the drama like I did this morning," said Laci.

"Hello? I've been on my feet all day. I love Jen, but I'm fairly sure I'm not going to want to host a slumber party tonight."

"George will get some movies and you can order in pizza," said Laci.

"Order in?" Natasha's nostrils flared like she smelled rotten eggs. "I'll make you pizzas. We're having a big meeting about Vegas tonight, and I don't think she should be in the house. She might overhear too much."

"What do you mean?"

"Her father is home for the holidays from a military deployment. Her parents are divorced, but her mother agreed that Vegas could spend Christmas with him. He has to go back next week, and now her mother has vanished. Packed up and left her apartment without a word to anyone. Mom and I are her closest relatives, so we're trying to help her dad figure out what to do with her."

"That's awful!" Laci and I chimed simultaneously.

Natasha took a deep breath. "I don't think we should tell her the truth. When my father left me and my mother, it was devastating. Anyway, I don't think she should be in the house where she might overhear our discussion."

"Sure, drop the girls by." It was the least I could do for Vegas, poor kid. "Movies and pizza will be much appreciated, since I plan to collapse."

It was with enormous relief that I wrapped up the auction, and the icing on the cake was the phenomenal amount of money we collected for the donated items. Kenner and Zack expressed their gratitude and assured me that several families would receive much-needed help from the proceeds.

Hannah and Zack rushed back to my house, so Hannah could change for a holiday party with Zack's friends. The rest of my family took off with plans to try to visit Shawna, leaving Jen with me. When we emerged from the auction site, two inches of snow covered the ground. It came down heavily as Jen and I walked home. She skipped ahead, giggling and sticking out her tongue to catch the icy flakes.

Vegas met us at the gate, armed with videos and a makeup kit she'd received for Christmas. The girls bounded into the house, hugged an excited Daisy, and immediately chattered about the kittens, ignoring Mochie, who had raced to the foyer to greet us. I swooped him up, but he didn't care for the cold snow that clung to my jacket and wriggled to free himself.

"Look what I brought for the kittens! They'll flip." Vegas pulled off her jacket and handed Jen what appeared to be a little snowman. "I brought one for each of us."

I followed them into the family room, where Alice and Jasper snuggled in their basket like little angels. Vegas dangled a felt snowman over their heads.

Alice saw it first and snagged it with her tiny claws. The girls giggled.

I peered closer. The snowman looked an awful lot like the one that hung on Shawna's gift to Bonnie. "May I see yours?" I asked Jen.

"It won't hurt them," she protested.

"I'd just like to have a closer look."

She handed it over with preteen disdain. Had she already picked that up from Vegas?

Made of felt, the snowman was stitched around the edges with white yarn. He wore a black hat and a red muffler, and the longer I studied him, the more I thought he looked exactly like the snowman on Bonnie's deadly gift.

TWENTY-TWO

From "Ask Natasha":

Dear Natasha,
I loved your show on wrapping presents so much that I taped it. But now I have paper, ribbons, glitter, glue, felt, stamps, and ink all over my desk. How do you keep everything organized?
— Wrapping Wizard
in Rudolph, Wisconsin

Dear Wrapping Wizard,
The trick to a neat crafting area is boxes that are the exact same size. They stack easily and look neater. Choose two or three sizes that work best for you. Even better, don't buy them, make them your-self, and label them with calligraphy for that special touch!
— Natasha

"Where did you get these?" I asked Vegas.

"Natasha made them on her show. She used them on a lot of her Christmas packages this year. I can probably get you one if you want it."

Had Shawna watched Natasha's show and made the snowman? If she was as inept at crafting as Laci suggested, that seemed unlikely. Could Natasha have given Shawna a gift with a felt snowman on it that Shawna reused on Bonnie's package?

In spite of the long day, curiosity prickled me. "Before you take off all your outdoor stuff, how about we walk Daisy?"

The girls readily agreed, and flounced out with energy that I coveted. By the time I reached the front door, Jen held Daisy's leash and was racing around my teensy front yard with her. Vegas fell to her knees and began rolling a ball for a snowman.

"Stay right here, okay? I'm going over to Natasha's for a minute."

They were absorbed in snowy fun, and I thought they'd be fine since I wouldn't be far away. I crossed the street and walked to Natasha's home on the end of the block. She'd hung teal lights on the railing of the stairs that led to the entrance of her home. The wreath on her front door was square, and made of magnolia leaves that she'd painted pink and sprinkled liberally with iridescent glitter — another project from her TV show, no doubt.

I rang the bell and waited. Natasha didn't hide her surprise at seeing me. "The pizzas are almost ready. I'll bring them over."

"That's not why I'm here." I held up the felt snowman. "Did you make these?"

"Aren't they cute?"

I agreed that they were. "Did you by any chance give one to Shawna?"

"Did she love it? I got so many compliments. Next year I'm thinking about gingerbread men cut out of felt. Wouldn't they be darling?"

So Shawna had regifted the snowman Natasha gave her. "She used it on the package she gave Bonnie."

Natasha drew a sharp breath. "She regifted it!?"

Who was she kidding? I laughed. "You regifted what I gave Mars — and it was personalized! You're hardly in a position to criticize her for reusing your little snowman."

She waved a hand carelessly. "To be honest, I didn't plan to give her anything, but then Mars made a big fuss about how she waits on him and his business clients at the restaurant all the time. She's made sure he got a table when they were full — things like that."

"So you gave her a snowman?" I suspected she would have preferred a tip.

"Don't be silly. The snowman was part of the giftscape."

"Giftscape?"

"Don't you watch my show? First impressions are the most important thing about a gift. Just like food tastes better when it looks beautiful, a gift is more meaningful and fun to receive when it's wrapped in a gorgeous giftscape where everything matches harmoniously. You covet the gift because the wrap is so wonderful, without even knowing what's inside. I gave her a lovely music box, and the snowman was simply part of the giftscape."

Music box? A shudder ran through me. "You gave her a music box? What did it look like?"

"Not that it's any of your business, but it was an antique with musical instruments inlaid in wood."

I felt like the air had been knocked out of my lungs. Shawna had regifted Natasha's gift! "You have to tell Kenner."

"I can't imagine why."

Uh-oh. She didn't know yet. Would she confess to the police if she knew the music box was the instrument of death? "Bonnie died from inhaling poisonous gas that was in the music box. Shawna has been arrested."

Natasha stiffened, and I could see her going pale under her perfect makeup. She lifted a trembling hand and braced herself on the door frame. "Ginger!"

"What?"

Natasha gulped air, and for a moment, I thought she might collapse. "Ginger Chadwick gave it to me. I thought it was an apology for the spat we had over decorating the community center. She was determined to use an Olde English Dickens theme. She must have meant to kill *me!*"

I blinked at her. "Let me get this straight. Ginger Chadwick gave you the music box. You regifted it to Shawna, and Shawna regifted it to Bonnie."

"I guess so."

Anyone along the line could have rigged it with the gas. And who knew where Ginger got it? What if Natasha was right, and Bonnie was never the target?

"You have to tell Kenner. I'm no cop, but I think this puts the situation in a completely different light." My head spinning with the implications, I started down the stairs, but Natasha caught my sleeve.

"Ginger actually tried to kill me?!" Her mouth dropped open and she gulped air. "Why didn't I see it? She was so angry that they picked me to decorate the square. Just like Bonnie, Ginger wanted to be me."

Too bad Natasha had such a poor self-image. "You don't know that."

She clapped a hand to her chest and scanned the street. "What if she's still after me? I can't stand out here. Who knows where Ginger might lurk?" She shut the door, and I hurried down the street in blowing snow. Even though I'd wanted to pooh-pooh Natasha's immediate conclusion that Ginger intended to murder her, I was a little bit creeped out and couldn't help glancing around for a snow-frosted killer.

During my absence, Vegas and Jen had erected a small snowman, complete with twig arms and carrot nose. I recognized Jen's muffler around his neck.

The perfect symbol considering that an innocent snowman might have led to the very information we needed to spring Shawna. I praised their project and dashed into the house with them right behind me. Since they were so full of energy, I asked them to put our wet duds in the bathroom, and I sped to my study to phone George.

I spilled Natasha's story, and he promised

to call me back after he phoned Kenner. At least I didn't have to do that.

What a nightmare. It didn't really get Shawna off the hook, though. The poison could have been added at any time. Had one of these women hated another so much that she had to eliminate her? Ginger was certainly unpleasant and generally disgruntled, but would she really want to kill Natasha over Christmas decorations? Or had something else gone on between them?

I found it hard to imagine that Natasha would have any reason to murder Shawna, unless she thought Shawna had designs on Mars — but that was silly. Shawna only had eyes for Beau.

Oy. My head spun. I needed a drink to warm up from standing out in the cold, too. I ventured toward the kitchen. The girls had started a fire in the fireplace and turned on the Christmas lights. They kneeled on the seat in the bay window with the kittens, looking out at their snowman and the neighbors' festive lights.

"Have you tired of hot chocolate yet?" I asked.

"No!" they chimed.

"Natasha won't make hot chocolate," said Vegas. "She says it's too fattening."

That sounded like Natasha. There were

simply times when one deserved to indulge and the holidays certainly qualified.

I stirred milk into the pot, finding it hard to concentrate. Although I had my doubts about Shawna being clever enough to come up with the idea of gassing Bonnie, somehow the situation had seemed sort of simple. Natasha's new information had expanded the field of suspects and, even worse, the potential field of intended victims.

I poured the hot chocolate into three mugs decorated with snowmen, sprinkled minimarshmallows on top, and garnished each one with a candy cane.

When I handed them to the girls, Vegas said, "Wow. I don't know why Natasha pretends that you're not a domestic goddess like she is."

I bit back a grin. "Thanks, Vegas. Natasha and I have different styles." I resisted the urge to add — *and Natasha thinks her way is the only way.*

I settled into a chair by the crackling fire, and tried to lure Mochie onto my lap. He paced angrily, hissing at Daisy, who did nothing to deserve his ire. Otherwise, my warm kitchen in semidarkness evoked all the wonder of the holidays. Snow fell outside, but the neighbors' Christmas lights sparkled across the street. The girls, perhaps exhausted from their snowman building, had fallen silent.

My eyelids grew heavy, and I thought about setting up a movie for the girls to watch so I could sneak a nap.

But a strobing light flickered through the bay window and Vegas screamed, "Daddy!"

TWENTY-THREE

From "THE GOOD LIFE":

Dear Sophie,
I have four dogs. Between leashes and harnesses, I have a tangled mess filling a drawer and can never find what I need. How can I store them so they won't tangle?
— Dog Mom in Angel City, Florida

Dear Dog Mom,
I'm a big fan of peg rails, especially for leashes. Hang one on each peg and they won't tangle anymore. No room for a peg rail? Look for an expanding peg rail. They're also useful in the kitchen for mugs and hanging utensils.
— Sophie

I jumped up, spilling hot chocolate on my sleeve and pant leg. "What's wrong?" I looked out the window and saw a police car, but no one else.

Too late. Vegas had run to the foyer.

"What did you see?" I shouted, running to the foyer. "Your dad isn't out there."

Vegas turned toward me for all of a second. "I have to be sure he's okay. He's all I have left." She tore out the door. Jen raced after Vegas, and Daisy loped along in the street. I slammed the door behind me and dashed outside, grateful that there wasn't much traffic due to the snow. A police car was parked at the curb in front of Natasha's house. Teal Christmas lights still glowed along the handrail leading up stairs to the door. I still stood at the bottom, catching my breath, when the door opened and Vegas, Jen, and Daisy disappeared inside. I could hear Natasha yell, "What is that dog doing in my house?"

Kenner stood at the door, and I guessed he was confused about whether to enter. As far as I could tell, Natasha had chased after the girls and Daisy.

The girls would be fine, but I didn't want Natasha to be unkind to Daisy. I rushed up the stairs, panting, passed Kenner, and paused in the foyer, trying to hear where they'd all gone.

It wasn't hard to figure out. Natasha

shouted, "Have you lost your minds? You're tracking snow all over my hardwood floors!" I peeked in the room to my right.

My ex-husband, Mars, rubbed Daisy's ears, apparently unconcerned about Natasha's ire. Vegas clung to a younger man with a military haircut, who seemed extremely uncomfortable, and Jen looked on, cringing.

Still ranting, Natasha stormed toward me, fussing about the melting ice on the floor. She didn't get far, though. Kenner blocked the doorway to the foyer.

He flashed his badge, which I thought unnecessary, but given Natasha's state of mind, maybe he thought it would lend an official tone to his visit.

"I'd like to have a word with you," he said to Natasha.

"I have to get a mop," she growled.

"What's going on?" asked Mars.

Kenner ignored him. "Is there someplace we could speak privately?"

"*Excuuuse* me! I have to mop the floor." Natasha brushed past Kenner, and his face turned the shade of a candied apple. His nostrils flared and he waited, as frozen and motionless as the snowman the girls built.

"Won't you have a seat?" asked Mars, ever the diplomatic political consultant.

Natasha swept back into the room. "The dog is not allowed in my living room."

I thought Kenner might explode.

Cleaning is not my favorite thing. In fact, it's pretty much at the bottom of the list, but there are times when you have to do what's right. "Let me do that for you," I said gently, taking the mop.

Natasha held fast, and for one long, painful moment, we all stared at her in silence.

"Is there someplace we could speak privately?" Kenner asked again. It sounded like he was gritting his teeth when he spoke.

Natasha let loose of the mop. "What on earth for? Mars, get that dog out of my living room."

I swished the mop a bit to satisfy Natasha.

"Ma'am, I am here on official police business. You don't seem to understand that." The words pelted from Kenner's mouth.

Natasha flashed me an annoyed must-I-do-everything-myself look, seized the mop, and asked Kenner testily, "What do you want?"

"Did you give Shawna Lane a gift recently?"

"Yes."

"What was the nature of the gift?"

Natasha continued mopping and glared at me. "It was a music box that Ginger Chadwick gave me, evidently intending to kill me."

"Natasha!" cautioned Mars.

"Excuse me, I have to wring out the mop." She left the room and returned shortly. "Mars, what is it about 'the dog is not allowed in my living room' that you're finding so difficult to comprehend?" She mopped her way to Daisy's feet.

Kenner turned to me, eyes wide, cheeks gaunt, complexion purple. He swung back toward Natasha and barked, "Sit down!"

Natasha plunked onto the sofa next to Mars, and Jen scrambled in my direction. I placed a reassuring hand on her shoulder.

"Are you saying that this Ginger Chadwick intended to kill you?" asked Kenner.

"That's exactly what I'm saying."

"Oh, good heavens, Natasha," grumbled Mars.

"Has she made threats?" asked Kenner.

"I thought policemen were supposed to be bright. Isn't it obvious? I did not plant anything in the music box, and I hardly think Shawna has the IQ to pull it off. Ergo, it must have been Ginger."

Jen turned her face up to me and whispered, "The Ginger who lives next door to me tried to kill Natasha?"

As much as I hated to miss the rest of

Kenner's interview, the time had come for Jen and Vegas to leave. I borrowed a leash from Mars and coaxed the girls to come home with Daisy and me.

Vegas bit her top lip, looking like she might burst into tears. "You'll still be here in the morning, won't you, Daddy?"

Her father's face wrinkled with pain and worry. "You bet! You have fun now."

"Wait!" Natasha called out.

I thought Kenner's face might explode from high blood pressure when Natasha disappeared to the kitchen. She returned with a pizza packed in a robin's egg blue pizza box with NATASHA printed across it. "It's shiitake mushroom and venison burger with rosemary and Asiago cheese. Enjoy it, girls!"

Curious about what Kenner would do next, I wished I could stay, but the fire still blazed in my kitchen, and we had to get back. None of us had even worn our coats. We rushed through the blowing snow, relieved to reach the warmth of my foyer.

We hadn't been gone long. Still, I was relieved that the fire had dwindled substantially in the kitchen fireplace. I threw another log on and sent the girls up to my closet to find dry clothes to wear. They sprang up the stairs gossiping about Natasha and murder, with Alice and Jasper racing ahead of them and Mochie stalking the kittens from behind.

I set the table with a bright red and white tablecloth, and washed crisp Romaine lettuce for a salad. The tiredness I'd felt earlier had vanished, probably from the cold snow, or the scene between Kenner and Natasha. I chopped crunchy pecans to throw in the salad, along with apples and celery, and whisked together a vinaigrette with apple cider vinegar.

I was cutting the pizza when the girls pranced into the kitchen decked out in evening clothes. They'd hit Vegas's new makeup kit and my closet, and somewhere, they'd even found two boas that they threw around with pomp. Jen turned on funky Christmas music and the two of them paraded like they were models on a runway with all the enthusiasm of "almost thirteen-year-olds."

After dinner, they pulled out the sofa in the family room, fetched fresh sheets and down comforters, and settled in to watch movies. They changed into jammies but still wore their boas and flicked them around.

I ought to have gone up to bed, but some sense of duty compelled me to curl up under a throw in a big chair with my feet propped up on a hassock.

When I woke up a few hours later, the girls were asleep, looking as angelic as the kittens that nestled by their feet. I switched off the TV and the Christmas lights and dragged upstairs to my bed. Daisy and Mochie joined me, ready to settle down.

In the morning, the girls were still asleep when I tiptoed downstairs to make coffee. While it brewed, I threw on a winter coat and took Daisy outside at the exact time that Natasha marched along the sidewalk.

Snowplows had worked their magic during the night, but I noted that I needed to shovel the snow from the sidewalk in front of my house.

She thrust a foil-covered dish in my hands. "This is for Vegas. The girls will need a decent breakfast."

I almost laughed at her feeble attempt at a slight.

"I baked extra, in case your family is still around. Make no mistake, however, that I'm furious with you for reporting me to the police. I thought we were friends."

We were, in a weird way. "I did no such thing."

"Please, Sophie. I tell you about the music

box and less than an hour later a cop shows up to grill me? I'm not stupid."

That last part was debatable. "I did not call the police. In fact, if you paid any attention to me, you'd know that I loathe Kenner and wouldn't call him except under the most dire circumstances. I did, however, call George and Laci, because it puts Shawna's case in a new light."

"Honestly, I can't imagine who would have thought she was smart enough to create a poison gas in the first place. Of course, that just makes me appear to be the guilty one since I have skills and could have pulled it off." She scowled at me. "How do you get me mixed up in these things?"

Me? "I had nothing to do with it. If you hadn't regifted the music box, you wouldn't be in this pickle."

"I'd be dead." She placed three fingertips on her forehead like a drama queen. "Thank goodness I regifted it. It could have been me who inhaled the poison instead of Bonnie." She removed her hand from her face and cast her gaze toward my house. "I was saved for a reason."

Give me a break. "Because everyone wants to be you?"

"Face it, Sophie. They do. Bonnie and Ginger would love to be domestic divas like me. But I was saved because of Vegas. Mars and I have no choice, we have to take her in when her dad returns to the military."

My knees nearly buckled. No one I knew was less nurturing or maternal than Natasha. "She's going to live with you?"

"Can you believe it? The child has nowhere else to go, and you know Mars, he's a sucker for anyone in need. Oh, Sophie! What have we done? I know nothing about children."

I pitied Vegas. Life with a perfectionist like Natasha wouldn't be easy. All I could do was try to reassure her. "You're doing a generous and wonderful thing. Besides, Vegas isn't a baby . . ." I swallowed the rest of my thought — *she's almost a teenager.* Babies were probably easier than teens!

"Send her home after breakfast, okay? Does this mean I need to schedule play dates?"

It was a rhetorical question, muttered as she walked away. I watched her, proud she was going to care for Vegas, but worried, too, since Natasha never thought about anyone but herself.

I carried the breakfast into my kitchen, where Vegas was pouring herself a mug of coffee. Jen looked on, and I had a bad feeling she was experiencing extreme peer pressure to be mature. "Would you prefer tea or hot chocolate?" I asked.

"I adore coffee," said Vegas.

To help Jen save face, I zapped a little milk in the microwave. "I'm having café au lait. So much more decadent than plain old coffee." Before they could object, I diluted their coffees with generous quantities of hot milk and suggested they add sugar.

Hannah stumbled in wearing a bathrobe. Jen and Vegas tittered and whispered to each other. When Hannah sat at the table nursing a mug of coffee, Jen cried, "Oh, Zack!" Vegas and Jen immediately smooched the backs of their hands as though they were kissing boys.

Hannah smiled coyly. "I thought I heard some mice scurrying around last night when I came in."

The girls burst into giggles.

"Did you invite him to our New Year's Eve dinner tomorrow night?" I asked.

"Of course. I have such a great time with him."

That brought on a fresh bout of unmerciful teasing by the girls while we ate Natasha's rich ham and cheese brioches. Light and buttery dough encasing salty meat and melted cheese — heavenly! Even if Natasha wasn't the best mother type in the world, at least Vegas would eat well.

After breakfast, Vegas walked home, and Jen, Hannah, and I drove to George's house so we could return Jen to her parents. When we arrived, except for the fact that the sun shone, the scene was so reminiscent of Christmas Eve that Hannah and I simultaneously chanted, "Déjà vu!"

Neighbors mingled on their lawns, and spilled into the road. I pulled into a spot behind a parked police car. Jen jumped out and ran to Laci, George, Phil, and my dad, who stood in George's driveway with Tom Thorpe. They all held steaming mugs.

Hannah and I joined them. "What's going on?" I asked. "Not another theft?"

"It's Kenner," said George. "We think he's here to talk to Ginger about trying to poison Natasha."

"Great news for us." Phil lifted his mug like he was toasting Ginger. "They're more likely to let Shawna out of jail if they suspect Ginger."

"I feel terrible." Tom held his warm mug in both hands. "I was the one who suggested they work together on the Christmas decorations. Who would have thought someone would commit murder over something like that? And it was our Bonnie who died as a result. I'll never forgive myself."

"Where's Mom?" asked Hannah.

Laci's mouth twisted in disapproval. "Babysitting my mother. We don't want her out here. There's no telling what she might say to Kenner."

"Why is everyone standing around outside?" I asked. "It's not like you can hear what's going on between Ginger and Kenner."

George snorted. "Are you kidding? The meanest woman in the neighborhood accused of murder? This is high drama for our street."

Their patience paid off. The door to Ginger's house flew open, Kenner marched out, pale as the snow dusting the trees, and Ginger's husband Forrest ran after him shouting, "It's a lie. I'm telling you — my wife is lying."

Twenty-Four

From "The Good Life":

Dear Sophie,
I'm pregnant and my mother-in-law has already told me I can't put up a tree next year because of the baby. I think that's ridiculous, but she insists the tree will fall on him. What do other people do?
— Expecting in North Star, Michigan

Dear Expecting,
Congratulations! Don't worry about your mother-in-law's predictions. Protect the baby and the tree by placing the *tree* inside a baby or dog playpen!
— Sophie

A titter spread through the little crowd.

Kenner stopped in front of Tom Thorpe. "I need to speak to your son — the one they call Dasher."

"Has Ginger made allegations against him again? She has a vendetta against my boy, especially now that he's going to be the father of her grandchild. She'd like nothing more than to saddle some kind of blame on him."

Kenner appeared unmoved. "I need to speak with him and Emma."

Tom shook his head. "They left."

"Left?" sputtered Kenner. "For where?"

"They sell their artwork and crafts at fairs. I think they were headed south — to Florida."

"You see?" Forrest Chadwick preened. "Maybe now you'll believe me. I told you they weren't here."

"I wouldn't be so pleased if I were you. An abrupt departure can be a sign of guilt," sneered Kenner.

Forrest's Adam's apple bobbed. "My daughter is not a killer."

Emma? Why did Kenner suspect her?

"But your wife is?" asked Kenner.

The spunk left Forrest's voice. "I didn't say that, and you know it."

"Emma couldn't kill anybody," protested Jen. "She's too nice. She always comes outside to protect us when the school bully walks by on his way home. And when her dad bakes cookies and cupcakes, she shares them with the neighborhood kids."

The hint of a smile grazed Kenner's lips. "Kid, there's no such thing as someone too nice to murder."

Forrest's son, Edward, lingered near the side of the house, looking gawky and uncomfortable. Moving slowly, so Kenner might not notice me, I strolled over to him and asked softly, "How are you holding up?"

"Things have been better. I think I just sent my mom to jail."

Poor kid! "What happened?"

He plowed the snow on the ground with the toe of his shoe. "You remember Christmas Eve? I went to the pageant with my parents so Mom wouldn't make a big fuss, but when we got there, I doubled back and ran home because my girlfriend was coming over."

I tried to suppress a grin. It was hard to imagine this gangly young fellow being romantic.

"We were upstairs in my room when we heard someone enter the house."

"So you saw the Christmas-gift thief?"

"Not exactly. See, at first Emma didn't think she would make it home for Christmas, so a couple weeks ago she sent a big box of gifts to Mr. Thorpe. I guess she was afraid Mom would throw them all out if she sent them to us. So Mr. Thorpe brought over our presents. Talk about a scene. Dad opened his right away. Emma had sewn him an apron and hand embroidered it, which infuriated Mom because she can't stand that he's a better baker than she is. Then Mom unwrapped hers early because it didn't match her decor."

"Her decor? I don't understand."

He took a deep breath. "It's so stupid." His words dripped with teen disdain. "Every year, Mom announces a gift wrap color scheme that matches the tree decorations. This year all the packages had to be red and gold. Emma wrapped her gift to Mom in red and green, so Mom refused to put it under the tree and opened it early. Anyway, when I peered over the railing on Christmas Eve, Mom had come back from the pageant to get the gift Emma sent her — a music box."

My knees nearly buckled. "Music box?"

Edward nodded. "An old and fancy one."

I could see why he felt guilty for telling Kenner. "Did you see your mom putting anything into the music box?"

He seemed relieved for a second. "No. She was wrapping it. She took it with her. If you stand in the doorway to Emma's room, you can see over the railing into the foyer. I was lurking there so I could intercept her in case she came upstairs. When she left, I ran back to my room."

"And then the Christmas thieves came?"

"After she left, we heard somebody downstairs. I thought Mom came back because she figured out I wasn't at the pageant. My girlfriend and I hid under my bed. But nobody came upstairs to look for me, so I think it must have been the gift thieves." He averted his gaze and held his head down as though in shame. "My girlfriend should have left right after we heard the thieves leave. But . . . we, uh, kind of got caught up in saying good-bye, and before I knew it, my folks came home. Then things got worse when Mom called the cops."

"So you were necking with your girlfriend?"

A flush as bright as Rudolph's nose flooded his face.

"When the cops went to your house that night, you ran home ahead of them . . ." I left my question open-ended.

"Yeaaaah! My girlfriend was still hiding in my bedroom, and I had to get her out the back door before the cops and my mom found her! Can you imagine the kind of scene my mom would make? She threw Emma out of the house because of the ring in her nose. I didn't want her to do that to me. Where would I go?"

Edward had been living under more stress than any teen deserved. I felt guilty for prying but told myself it might be cathartic for him to talk about his feelings. "Your dad said your mom was lying."

He looked at me incredulously. "We're all lying. Don't you get it? Every single one of us is lying about something. I don't know what the truth is anymore. Mom told the cop that Emma and Dasher were trying to kill her, but as awful as Mom's been to them, Emma would never murder anybody. She won't even use a fly swatter — she catches wasps and takes them outside. Dad told the cop that Emma and Dasher left yesterday, but they didn't. When the cops got here, Dad snuck out the back way and went over to the Thorpes to tell them to leave." He wiped his eyes. "I hope Emma gets away, and they figure out who wanted to kill Mom before they catch up to Emma."

I reached out to hug him, and to my surprise, he didn't pull away. It seemed to me that his dad, Forrest, might have wanted to kill his mom. I hoped that wasn't the case. Edward needed a stable parent.

After a short visit with my family, I took off

for home. Zack was supposed to pick up Hannah at George's house, so I had the luxury of a day to myself. A few hours to straighten up and prepare some dishes in advance for a late New Year's Eve dinner the next night when they would all stay with me so they wouldn't have to drive home after Old Town's First Night celebration.

I swung by my favorite grocery store to replenish my cupboards. I planned to serve fondue before our trek down to the New Year's celebration. Fondue occupied guests and made for a fun leisurely dinner with lots of laughs. Gruyère, white wine, steak to cut into cubes, veggies, and the Sterno that I usually forgot went into my shopping basket. I stopped in front of the cat-food section. I'd been so absorbed in Bonnie's murder that I'd forgotten about Jasper and Alice. It was odd that no one had taken credit for giving them to me. If I had dropped kittens off, I would have called to check on them. As much as I would love to keep them, Mochie didn't seem to be adjusting to their presence. I plunked canned cat food into the cart and was selecting coffee and chocolate ice cream for my bombe when my phone rang.

"Sophie!" Laci sounded excited. "I need a favor. A huge favor. Anything you want, I'll do it — I promise."

Why did I suddenly find it difficult to swallow?

"In light of the new information about Ginger, Emma, and Dasher, the police are letting Shawna out on bond!"

"That's great news!" It was. Unless they expected me to put up money for her bond.

"There's a teensy provision, though. She can't leave Alexandria."

"Isn't her apartment in Alexandria?" I asked, afraid I knew what was coming.

"Just across the line in Arlington, actually. Could she stay with you? Please?"

What could I say? I didn't really mind, and if the shoes were on my feet, I'd be forever grateful if someone did the same for Hannah. It would be cruel to leave Shawna in jail. "Sure. Should I pick her up?"

Laci squealed and then said, "No, no, no. We'll arrange everything and bring her over."

She clicked off and I hurried through the grocery store, picking up extra supplies in case the whole family descended upon me a day early.

The car loaded with groceries, I drove home, past a Santa Claus who'd lost his hat. I pulled over and got out to have a closer look. Sure enough, someone had also removed his jacket. When Daisy and I walked tonight, we would have to bring Santa's clothes back. Next to him, Mrs. Claus had also been stripped of a few items. Her white locks were missing, as was her skirt. I grimaced. Looked like Marnie wasn't the only one out pilfering Santa's threads. The owner of the cute Claus display must be irate.

I took note of my location, and walked to the nearby intersection. To my left, Bonnie's house was only a couple of blocks away. Immediately to my right and two doors down was the empty building where I'd run into Forrest the day Bonnie died. The fact that Forrest and Marnie had both been in the vicinity of Bonnie's house around the time of her death seemed significant, but I couldn't tie the facts together in a way that made sense. They could have been there at different times, though I'd thought Forrest might be waiting for someone. Had he planned to meet Marnie? *Ohhh, I did not want to go there.* Surely there wasn't an affair brewing between the two of them.

Marnie had acted devastated by Phil's attraction to Bonnie. Could her odd behavior have been due to guilt over an affair with Forrest? What if he had tampered with the music box to kill Ginger so he could be with

Marnie? It was the perfect setup. He could have ditched the deadly music box before the police came and they never would have known the source of the poison gas. The mere thought made my head spin.

"Hi."

I looked up to find Forrest standing next to me, and shrieked like I'd seen a killer. "Oh! I'm so sorry. You surprised me."

"We have to stop meeting this way."

It was a joke, of course. Or was it? Could he mean it in a threatening way?

He carried a bulging environmentally friendly grocery bag. Biting the tip of the finger of a glove on the free hand, he pulled off his glove, unwound the muffler from his neck, and casually stuffed it on top of the bag as if he wanted to hide the groceries that peeked out of it. The palm of his hand glowed red — much as Laci's had from making the Red Velvet Cake.

"Thanks for being so nice to Edward today."

"I didn't do anything."

"Just taking the time to listen is something, especially since he feels like his entire life is falling apart. Having his mother and sister accused of murder will mar him for life, and I don't know how to make it any better for him." Forrest certainly seemed sincere. Rather abruptly, he said, "I'd better get going." He crossed the street, going back the way he came, away from the building where I'd seen him before.

That man was hiding something. I just hoped it wasn't murder.

I returned to my car and drove to the intersection where I'd spoken with Forrest. I stopped for the light behind another vehicle just in time to see Forrest, wearing a big cat-ate-the-canary smile, striding briskly across the street past the spot where we'd spoken, in the direction of the empty building where I'd seen him before.

TWENTY-FIVE

From "Ask Natasha":

Dear Natasha,
My wife watches your show faithfully and strives to do everything you suggest. Perhaps you could help me with her car. The passenger seat is piled with makeup and jewelry. The gearshift acts as a holder of necklaces and bracelets. The backseat is loaded with children's books, toys, assorted shoes, lost French Fries, and half-eaten chicken nuggets, not to mention the packets of ketchup that fly around.
— Wiseguy in Wiseman, Arkansas

Dear Wiseguy,
Cars are not moving closets. They should contain a flashlight, a small first aid kit, no more than three CDs, and a blanket in the winter. Anything else left in the car should go into a trash can — even if you have to

do it for her. She will soon learn to remove extraneous items each time she comes home and won't have a problem with clutter anymore.

— Natasha

The light took forever to change. By the time I turned right and cruised by the empty storefront, Forrest had disappeared. I didn't know what bothered me more — that he felt he needed to deceive me, or that he was clearly up to something.

I drove home and unloaded groceries, promising Daisy we would go for a walk very soon. I had to get my New Year's Bombe started first. A Bauer family favorite, the bombe featured a frozen raspberry interior covered with layers of coffee ice cream and chocolate ice cream. When sliced, the pink center surrounded by the café au lait color and then the deeper chocolate made for a beautiful presentation. I'd left the chocolate ice cream on the counter while I put away groceries. It had softened enough for me to run a knife around the edge of the containers and slide the cylindrical chunks of ice cream onto a cutting board. I sliced them into half-inch rounds and pressed the frosty chocolate into a bowl, starting with the bottom and working my way to the top, until the entire bowl was lined with a layer of ice cream. Working fast, I pressed a top onto the bowl and stashed it in the freezer to firm up.

Daisy sprawled on the floor, her eyes half-closed, so I took a few extra minutes to work out the path the music box had taken.

It appeared that Emma had bought it. There was the possibility that she had unwittingly purchased a music box that already contained poisonous gas. Unlikely, but still a possibility. While it was in Emma's possession, Dasher, who had every reason to dislike Ginger, could have installed the poison. I didn't know why I was so reluctant to imagine that Emma could have wanted to kill her mother. Maybe I felt sorry for her because of the way Ginger treated her. I had to face facts, though. Emma could have installed the poison herself.

Emma sent it to Tom Thorpe, who made no secret of his hatred for Ginger. Tyler could have had access to it during that time, too.

Tom delivered it to Ginger, after which Forrest and Edward could have tampered with it.

Ginger rewrapped it and gave it to Natasha, in spite of, or possibly because of, their disagreements about decorating the community center. While it was in Natasha's possession, Mars could have tinkered with it. But I felt certain I could scratch Mars off the suspect list. I knew my ex-husband well enough to know he couldn't hammer a nail in the wall, much less set up poisonous gas inside a music box.

Natasha gave it to Shawna, who rewrapped it with Natasha's snowman. Shawna left it on the table at Bonnie's party where anyone could have picked it up and fooled with it. Actually, wasn't that when Marnie went missing?

Soft mewing complaints attracted my attention. I followed the sound into the sunroom and caught Mochie in the act of carrying Jasper. Just like a mother cat, Mochie held Jasper by the scruff of fur on his neck and was depositing the kitten in the basket in which they'd arrived.

Utterly surprised, I waited to see what would happen. Mochie scampered away and returned with Alice, whom he also placed in the basket. When he was finished, he sat next to the basket, washed his front paws, and then stared at me.

I wished I could see inside his little cat head to know what he was thinking. I had the notion he thought he'd packed up his cat company and it was time for them to go home.

In any event, I didn't think I should leave him alone with them. I took the basket to the sofa in my den and left the kittens there, safely behind closed doors. Mochie rubbed against my ankles. I picked him up, and for the first time in days, he head-butted me and purred.

I wished our music-box problems could be solved as easily. I fed Mochie some leftover turkey and put on my coat. Grumbling about the number of people who could have arranged for the poison in the music box, I grabbed the Santa hat and jacket that Marnie had worn, latched a leash to Daisy's harness, and struck out for the Santa and Mrs. Claus who were missing clothing.

We had just crossed the street that ran along the side of my house when I pulled Daisy to a halt. No doubt about it — Ginger Chadwick was driving her vanilla latte–colored Cadillac along my street at a snail's pace. I didn't think she noticed me, even though she leaned forward and appeared to be scoping out the area. She'd mentioned an interest in a house for sale in Natasha's neighborhood. Had she turned her attention to moving in order to get her mind off her other troubles?

I gave the leash a little tug, and Daisy gladly resumed forward movement with occasional stops for particularly enticing scents.

To an outsider, the Chadwick family seemed to have everything. Forrest was employed and, from the looks of things, made a considerable income. They lived in a nice house and neighborhood. Yet trouble clearly brewed under the surface. Edward was a sweet kid, but saddled with the burden of hiding everyday activities from his mother so he wouldn't incur her wrath. Forrest didn't agree with his wife's tough-love attitude toward their daughter, and Emma suffered from her mother's contempt. And then there were Forrest's mysterious repeated appearances in Old Town.

Daisy and I reached Santa and Mrs. Claus. I stepped behind a small red sleigh. The Santas and their sleigh were neatly displayed in the curve of elegant stairs that led to the front door of a historic town house. Working fast, I stuffed Santa's arms into the sleeves of the jacket, pulled it up over his shoulders, and buttoned it. I slid the belt around his middle and fastened it, glancing at the window of the house in the hope no one would catch me.

So far, so good. I jammed the hat on Santa's head and had a feeling that it ought to be secured with a pin or something, but I hadn't come prepared. I hoped a strong wind wouldn't carry it away. Poor Mrs. Claus still wore exposed bloomers since her skirt had disappeared, and underneath her hat, her cloth face was bald as it could be. At least this time around, I didn't think Marnie had anything to do with the missing clothing.

I thought I heard footsteps inside the house. "Quick, Daisy!" We ran for the corner and turned right without looking back. Breathing hard, I paused and leaned against the brick wall of a building. Daisy wagged her tail, and when I bent to pet her, she licked the tip of my nose.

I slid down the wall a bit and hugged her. When I stood, she tugged me along the street, and stopped in front of the empty building where I'd seen Forrest the night of Bonnie's death.

The early dusk of winter had begun to descend on Old Town. I peered through the plate glass storefront but couldn't see much. Daisy's ears perked up, though, and I listened. Was that laughter?

Hurrying, Daisy and I jaywalked across the street. From our new vantage point, I had a better view of the second and third floors of the old building. In the semidarkness, white woodwork glowed against the redbrick walls. The glass panes shimmered, almost black, so the flash of a light inside was shockingly obvious. My breath caught in my throat, and I waited for another sign that someone was on the second floor. I was about to give up when I saw it. This time more than a flash — one window glowed with a warm light, steady and continuous, and then, the light clicked off.

I continued watching, thinking about Forrest — and Marnie. I pulled out my cell phone and called George's house. My mom answered the phone and launched into an excited discourse about Shawna.

"Mom," I interrupted. "Is Marnie there?"

A moment of silence followed on her end. "What do you want from Marnie?"

"Nothing. I just want to know if she's there."

More silence. "I don't understand you, Sophie, but I'm sure you have your reasons. Dad and Phil and I are here with Jen. We're playing Cat-opoly. Santa brought it to Jen for Christmas, well, late of course . . ."

"Mom!"

"George and Laci went to arrange for bail and pick up Shawna, but they told Marnie she couldn't go with them. I think Laci was afraid her mother might act up again — she's been so unpredictable. She's supposed to meet them in Old Town at your house. Isn't she there yet?"

"I'm out walking Daisy. Guess I'd better get home." I promised to call her later and hung up. With a last lingering look at the window, I hurried along the sidewalk with Daisy. Though if Marnie was where I thought she was — with Forrest — there really wasn't any need to rush home.

Nevertheless, Daisy and I kept up a good pace. Lights on our block twinkled in the cold air, but not a soul moved on the sleepy street.

Daisy entered the house first and broke away from me immediately, dragging her leash along the hardwood floors. In a sniffing frenzy, she pranced along the hallway, through the sunroom and the kitchen, and down the hallway again. I hung my coat in the bathroom to drip-dry, and when I came out, she pawed at the door to the study.

I opened it carefully, expecting the kittens to dash out. Instead, Mochie mewed mournfully from the top of the desk. "What are you doing in here?" Had I inadvertently locked him in? I shook my head at my own stupidity.

Daisy ran around the tiny room in frantic circles. It took me a moment longer to understand what was going on. Alice and Jasper were gone — basket and all.

TWENTY-SIX

From "Ask Natasha":

Dear Natasha,
With the kids home from college and four sets of grandparents (all remarried — sigh) dropping by for a few days, my beds will be like revolving doors. I don't have time to clean with hosting and cooking and entertaining. Help!
> — Drowning in Company in Sleepy Eye, Minnesota

Dear Drowning,
Cleaning is essential when you have a lot of guests. Take a cue from B&Bs. The minute your guests depart, strip the beds, and scrub the room and bathroom. Be sure to leave a basket of toiletries, reading material, a scented candle, and chocolates to make each guest feel special.
> — Natasha

I bent to see if Alice and Jasper were hiding under the desk, afraid of Mochie. That wouldn't explain the missing basket, of course. I straightened up when I didn't see them, wracking my brain to recall if Hannah could have been in the house.

By then, Daisy had moved on to the sunroom. She waited impatiently by the door that led outside. I opened it and she bounded out. I didn't bother with a coat, and followed her into the frozen lawn of the backyard. I shivered and rubbed my arms, but Daisy ignored the cold, intent on her mission. Her nose to the ground, she followed a straight line to the back gate. My heart sank. Unless I misunderstood her cues, someone had stolen Alice and Jasper. I looked more closely and made out what I thought might be new footprint tracks in the snow.

I called Daisy back into the house and mounted a room-by-room search anyway in the vain hope that the sweet kittens were hidden elsewhere — like in a laundry basket. Daisy and Mochie brought their expert noses along, but we didn't find the kittens. Scary as it was that someone had entered my house again, I was almost more afraid of Jen's reaction. Losing Alice and Jasper might upset her more than the prospect of her Aunt Shawna doing time.

Daisy's interest in the sunroom door led me to believe that the kitten giver and thief had entered through the sunroom. Were they the same person? Or had someone dropped off the kittens here, hoping they would be safe from someone else? It chilled me to imagine that anyone could mean harm to those darling, innocent kittens.

Making a mental note to buy a deadbolt for the door, I dragged a chair over, tipped it to rest on its back legs, and shoved it under the handle. At least it would stop anyone trying to come in that way.

I turned around and found Mochie and Daisy sitting in identical positions watching me. I had to admit that the house seemed empty and lonely without the kittens. "Don't bother looking at me like that. Mochie, you wanted them to go away, and Daisy, I'm sure you know who has the kittens from the person's scent." I was the only clueless one in the bunch. Purebred kittens were expensive. Could someone have stolen them to sell?

My heart heavy with fear for Jasper and Alice, I trudged upstairs to straighten up a room for Shawna and put clean sheets on the bed. Cleaning was not my forte, but stripping sheets and making beds weren't a big deal. I didn't know exactly what the plan was, but I thought it prudent to put Shawna in the tiny third-floor bedroom. If she decided to take off in the middle of the night, she would have two flights of stairs to contend with, and Hannah would be sleeping in the room next door.

I set fresh towels on Shawna's bed and traipsed down to the second floor. My mother had left the front guest room immaculate. I didn't have to do a thing except change the battery in the candle in the window. When I inserted a fresh battery, Daisy howled behind me. The howl quickly turned into a bark and she clomped down the stairs.

Alice? Jasper? Or had George and Laci arrived with Shawna? I rushed down to the foyer but didn't see anything. Daisy pawed at the front door.

I snapped on her leash and stepped outside. Daisy pulled with all her might, and I ran behind her in the direction of Natasha's house. Even though I held fast, I tripped on the uneven brick of the sidewalk, and Daisy broke away from me.

I stood and dusted off my hands. Something wasn't right in front of Natasha's house. The turquoise lights that had graced her front stairs appeared to be wrapped around a slender tree on the ground. I squinted into the dark as Daisy neared the odd spectacle, and I thought I saw Santa Claus. *What on earth?*

I stumbled along the sidewalk as fast as I could. The Santa figure became more clear, and I realized it was Mrs. Claus. Daisy reached her far ahead of me, and Mrs. Claus dashed around the corner, pursued by Daisy.

I arrived at the foot of Natasha's stairs only to discover that the teal lights didn't wrap a tree at all. Natasha lay on the sidewalk, coiled by the lights. The blinking pink and white lights above her cast a peculiar tinge on her complexion.

"Natasha?" I tapped her cheeks, but her eyes didn't open.

And then I saw it. Mrs. Claus had been strangling Natasha with her own Christmas lights. I rolled her over and unwound the cord from her neck as fast as I could. Why had I left my cell phone at home? Natasha needed an ambulance.

Placing my arm under her shoulders, I tried to lift her a bit and was rewarded with a sputtering cough.

"It's okay. You're going to be fine." I tried to sound reassuring.

I unwound the remaining lights and threw

them on the sidewalk. Natasha gripped her throat with both hands, choking and coughing. I considered slapping her on the back but thought that might make things worse.

"Should I call the rescue squad?" I asked.

She waved her hands and gripped her throat again.

I shivered uncontrollably. I had to get her inside, but she didn't seem fit enough to manage the steep curving stairs to her house.

Down the block a car slowed and parked in front of my house. I took a chance. "George?" I yelled.

My darling brother ran toward me at the same time that Daisy rounded the corner, proudly carrying something in her mouth.

"Do you think you can stand?" I held out my hand to help Natasha up.

George pounded toward us. "What happened?"

"Someone was trying to strangle Natasha with Christmas lights."

Natasha's dark eyes met mine. I'd never seen her so fearful.

George and I helped her stand up. With Natasha between us, we hobbled along the sidewalk. Laci opened the front door to my house and Shawna stood aside, her eyes huge.

We eased Natasha into a chair by the fireplace. Laci poured water in the kettle and set it on the stove to heat before she removed her coat, while George tossed kindling into the fireplace and started a fire. I rubbed Natasha's hands to warm them.

"Did you see her?" croaked Natasha.

"Her?" asked George.

"Definitely Mrs. Claus. I couldn't make out her face, though." Addressing Natasha, I asked, "Are you sure you don't want to go to the emergency room?"

She shook her head "no."

"Better call that jerk, Kenner," said George.

Shawna stopped collecting coats. "No! I've seen enough of him."

"Don't worry. You have an ironclad alibi this time," Laci assured her. "You were with us. There's no way you could have done it."

"I don't want to see him," she whined.

"You probably need a shower and a change of clothes," I said. "Why don't you do that, and when he leaves, you can come down and we'll make dinner."

"I don't have any clothes." Shawna glared at Laci.

"I told you I brought some of mine for you to wear tonight," her sister snapped back.

"Like they'll fit," Shawna muttered as she left the kitchen.

Ignoring the sisters, I dialed Kenner's number. As much as I didn't want to see him, he had to know about the attack on Natasha. His voice mail answered, and I left a message for him.

Natasha held out her hands as if asking for something.

"The tea isn't ready yet, sweetie," said Laci.

"Mirror," Natasha squawked before launching into a new fit of coughing.

At that moment, I knew she would be perfectly fine. I started for the bathroom to fetch a mirror, but Daisy lay in my path holding a piece of fabric between her paws. She didn't object when I picked it up. About four by five inches, three edges of the red material were frayed, as though it had been torn. The forth edge bore white faux fur. A smear of red marred it but looked more like red dirt than blood.

"Did you bite Mrs. Claus?" I whispered to Daisy.

She wagged her tail, and I finally noticed that her black whiskers wore a white frosting. Snow would have melted by now. I wiped it off with my finger and sniffed. Cream cheese?

I turned to Natasha with a big grin, hoping she might like Daisy more for saving her. "Looks like Daisy caught up to your Mrs. Claus."

I handed her the swatch of material. She fingered it and pronounced in a froggy voice, "Cheap fabric. Sleeve?"

That was my guess. Even though Mrs. Claus had tried to murder Natasha, I hoped Daisy hadn't bitten anyone. Kenner had already accused her of being vicious.

George grinned. "Daisy took a bite out of crime?"

We all moaned, and Natasha hacked again. I brought her the mirror and she examined her Audrey Hepburn–esque throat. George, Laci, and I clustered close for a better look.

"Gee, Natasha. The lights saved you," muttered George.

"I think he's right." The cord left an ugly red welt on her neck, but some of the tiny lights had left vertical impressions that suggested they'd prevented the cord from digging deeper.

The kettle screamed, and Laci hurried to make tea. I retrieved rubbing alcohol and cotton puffs and handed them to Natasha, not daring to apply the stinging solution myself.

Mochie looked on in the classic pose of an Egyptian cat. "No hissing at her today?" I asked. He must have realized something was amiss.

A rap at the door brought a growl from Daisy. I opened it to Kenner and launched into an explanation of what had happened.

Wordlessly, he bent to have a closer look at Natasha's throat. She handed him the cloth Daisy had ripped from Mrs. Claus's costume.

I'd never seen him so pensive. He turned to me. "Can you show me where this happened?"

Ugh. Alone with Kenner. I sucked in a deep breath and retrieved a warm down coat that made me look like the Pillsbury Doughboy. That ought to dispel any romantic thoughts on his part.

As we walked along the street, he said, "Certainly is curious that someone attacked Natasha right after Shawna was released from custody."

"You have to be kidding! My brother and his wife brought her straight to my house. However, I saw Ginger Chadwick cruising down the block late this afternoon." I felt a little bit guilty about diverting his attention to someone else, but it was the truth.

"That places her in the vicinity. Are you

sure you didn't get a good look at the assailant?"

That was the one thing I was sure about. "I never saw her face. Only the Mrs. Santa hat, jacket, and skirt."

"Hold it." He held a hand out in front of me like he was stopping traffic. "Someone is examining the crime scene."

Kenner was right. But I knew my ex-husband's shadowy shape from a distance. "It's just Mars."

He looked up at us as we approached. "What happened here?"

I started to explain but Kenner stopped me. "Exactly where were you for the last hour?"

Mars pulled back, his mouth twisting the way it did when he thought someone was being rude. "Vegas and I took her dad to the airport."

Great alibi. There were surely lots of cameras and time stamps to confirm his whereabouts. I launched into an explanation.

"Dear Lord!" Mars exclaimed. "All this time I've been teasing Natasha when she talks about Ginger wanting to kill her. I didn't believe it! Are you sure Natasha's okay?" He started for my house.

"What about Vegas?" I called after him.

He returned quickly. "Right! Gotta get used to that. I'll fetch her."

In the meantime, I showed Kenner exactly where Natasha had been attacked. "The lights hung on her railing, so her assailant must have taken them off and been waiting for her."

Kenner made a call for a forensic team. When Mars and Vegas emerged from the house, he shooed them away from the crime scene, but Vegas screamed and ran toward the gate that led to the backyard. In the eerie glow of Natasha's teal and pink lights, Vegas bent and picked up something over Kenner's protests. "It's the kitten basket!"

Twenty-Seven

From "Ask Natasha":

Dear Natasha,
I made a magnolia-leaf wreath this year but it didn't last. How do you get yours to stay nice?
— Turquoise Lover in Aliceville, Alabama

Dear Turquoise Lover,
Crush the stems of the magnolia branches and let them soak up a mixture of warm glycerine and water. Keep replenishing it as they absorb it. In a few weeks, the leaves will turn brownish and you can spray them with turquoise glitter. Try inserting some pink peacock feathers for an even more festive look!
— Natasha

Addressing Kenner, I said, "Would you shine your flashlight around a little bit? I hope the kittens aren't out here. They couldn't survive alone in this cold weather."

"What kittens?" asked Mars.

"It's the weirdest thing. Someone left gorgeous kittens in my house in this basket, but without a name on the gift tag. When I came home this afternoon, the kittens were gone."

Vegas disappeared through the gate. Unless Natasha had decorated the backyard with lights, I didn't think she'd see much there.

She returned in seconds. "It's too dark, but we have to look for Alice and Jasper! How did they get out here?"

Mars herded her down the street toward my house. "First we have to check on Natasha."

Vegas had said what I was thinking. I trailed after her and Mars, peering at houses in the darkness, hoping I would see those adorable kitten faces. Nothing about the kittens made any sense to me. Why had someone left them anonymously to begin with? And why had someone taken them? Had Natasha's assailant taken the kittens from my house? That would mean someone had stolen a key to my house — or it was someone I knew, someone who had a key.

I did know one thing for sure — Natasha

and Mars had a key.

Mars acted the duly concerned lover when he saw Natasha, kissing her forehead and checking out her neck, but I barged into the kitchen and folded my arms across my chest. When Mars had finished his soothing coos, I demanded, "What exactly might you happen to know about a couple of Ragdoll kittens?"

Natasha touched her throat and whispered, "Can't talk."

"Hogwash," said George. "She just told us how she had walked out of her house and down the front steps when someone bashed her over the head from behind."

Speaking in a very weak voice, Natasha said pathetically, "I passed out."

"When Mrs. Claus tried to strangle her," added George.

"The next thing I saw was Sophie." She lowered her head and sipped at a cup of hot tea.

Mixed emotions assaulted me. Natasha had been through a terrible attack, yet I couldn't shake the feeling that she knew something about the mysterious kittens. It seemed like more than a coincidence that the kittens' basket lay near her gate.

To my surprise, it was Laci who brought the subject back to the cats. "I thought it was quiet around here. Where *are* Alice and Jasper?"

"I don't know. When I came home, they were gone, and Vegas just found their basket where Natasha was attacked." I leaned menacingly close to Natasha. "Just tell me one thing. Are they outside in the freezing temperature?"

Natasha glanced around as if she was looking for a friendly face, someone to defend her. She must not have found one, because she whispered, "It wasn't my fault. I dropped the basket when I fell to the ground."

Dinner would have to wait. I bolted from the kitchen and collected flashlights. When I returned to the foyer, everyone was pulling on coats. I handed out the flashlights and remembered that Shawna was upstairs. "Someone needs to stay with Shawna and Natasha."

Laci winced. "Dad put up a lot of money for Shawna's bail. I promised to watch her."

George removed his jacket. "You go ahead and search. I'll stay here."

No one waited for further debate on the subject. Mars bemoaned the fact that he didn't have the special leash for Daisy that would give her more freedom to walk where she might smell a kitten.

I fetched the leash I'd given Mars for Christmas that Natasha had tried to regift to me. As we walked out of the house, I explained what had happened. Mars was appalled. "What was she thinking? Vegas, you stay close to me, okay?"

We spread out, walking up to neighbors' homes, peering behind bushes, calling "Jasper! Alice! Here, kitty, kitty."

I hoped their light fur would make them easier to spot in the dark, but the snow on the ground quickly extinguished that expectation. Deep in my heart, I knew they could be anywhere by now. In backyards, a block away — anywhere.

After an hour of searching, I heard Vegas shriek and ran in the direction of her cry. Under the Christmas lights of a house across the street from Natasha's, Daisy proudly carried a kitten by the nape of the neck, like Mochie had.

Mars let her carry the kitten back to our house, where the searchers gathered. Daisy deposited the kitten, its fur matted and wet, in front of the fireplace. Mochie zoomed in to sniff carefully, then took off at top speed running through the house.

Laci picked up the kitten. "It's Alice. Poor baby. She must be half frozen."

I brought her a soft towel, and she sat opposite Natasha, near the fireplace, gently drying the little cat.

"Soph, could you make some glühwein?" asked Mars. "I haven't had it in years, and it would warm us up."

The spiced wine drink had always been one of his favorites. I poured red wine into a pot, added sugar, heady cinnamon, cardamom, cloves, and slices of zesty lemon. While it warmed, I nuked some milk to make hot chocolate for Vegas and took coffee ice cream out of the freezer to make the next step of the bombe.

It didn't take long for us to focus on Natasha — and not in a nice way.

Mars eyed Natasha. "I think you'd better explain yourself. I'd like to hear this."

Natasha sat primly, her hands folded in her lap. "We were at a cocktail party, and a woman was going on and on about her ragdolls and how much she adores them. So I told her about the ragdoll I had as a child. I carried it everywhere — but I meant a doll. A *doll!* How was I supposed to know she was talking about cats?"

After a moment of shocked silence, everyone except Natasha broke into laughter.

"Tom Thorpe overheard the conversation and surprised me with the cats for Christmas. I didn't know *why* until Sophie's mother said they were called Ragdolls."

Mars clapped a hand to his head. "He must think I'm the most rude and ungrateful person in the world for not thanking him. That was a very thoughtful and generous gift."

I wiped my teary eyes and poured drinks for everyone. "Why did you bring them here?"

Natasha smiled her beauty-pageant smile. "They were a gift! You like cats."

Baloney! I wasn't buying it. "If they were a gift, why did you sneak them into my house? Why didn't you tell me they were from you?"

She chewed the corner of her lip like a kid who'd been caught lying. "All right! If they live here, they'll be close enough for me to pick them up and take them to my house when Tom comes over. He called this afternoon to say he would be dropping off some paperwork for Mars, so I came to get them."

I staggered backward. Natasha had had plenty of outrageous self-serving ideas in the past, but this was beyond anything I could have conceived. The worst part was that she didn't even seem ashamed.

"I can't have cats," she continued. "It's bad enough having to lock Daisy in a room every other week. There's still fur every-where."

My temper got the better of me. I could feel my face flushing hot. "That's it. Daisy is not going to your house anymore. Sorry, Mars. It's horrible to shut her in a room. We're ending this right now."

"We certainly are." Mars's tone dropped to his angry voice, very controlled but final. "You cannot continue to be the Queen Poobah of Old Town. I'm tired of living in a house where I have to hide all clues to my existence. The TVs are behind screens, my books may not venture out of my study, heaven forbid a magazine land on my night-stand. I'm not even allowed to use my mug that says DOG DAD. We don't reside in a museum, Natasha. We have Vegas staying with us and we're going to live like normal people. There will be no locking Daisy anywhere. If Vegas leaves her backpack in the foyer, you will not have a fit. If she doesn't hang up her clothes, you will not say a word."

I waited for Natasha's response. Mars and I had our share of arguments when we were married, but I couldn't remember him ever being this angry.

"Couldn't Daisy live here?" whined Na-tasha. "You could still run with her. I hate having a dog bed in the bedroom. I hate the fur she sheds all over. I have doggie place mats and she still manages to make a mess when she eats."

It wasn't easy for me to hear Natasha complain about my beloved Daisy. I didn't speak up, though, because I was more than willing to have Daisy live with me, instead of splitting custody with Mars. I busied myself slicing the coffee ice cream and pressing the slices on top of the chocolate ice cream already in the bowl.

Mars bent over and hugged Daisy to him. "You knew that Daisy came with me. I'm not giving up anything else, Natasha. Why is it that the things I want are always a nuisance, but you can bring all kinds of ridiculous projects into the house? Here's a bulletin, I love Daisy — your ever-present topiaries, fussy ribbons, and crafts — not so much. I wouldn't mind opening the windows and tossing them all."

It was Natasha's turn to be aghast. "You wouldn't!"

"Don't bet on it. You were willing to regift kittens."

Natasha fingered the welt on her neck. "I could have died tonight."

She had a point. I'd almost forgotten. Still she shouldn't have treated the kittens so shabbily.

A knock at the door rescued Natasha from further blame. Mars opened it, while I put the bombe back into the freezer. Marnie rushed in, pulling off gloves. "Where's Shawna? Isn't she here yet?"

"Is that Mom?" Footsteps pounded on the stairs and Shawna flew into the kitchen and her mother's arms.

"My poor darling." Marnie held her daughter at arm's length for a moment. "Let me look at you. Did they hurt you? Was it awful?"

"She's fine, Mom." Laci sounded weary, no small surprise given the events of the holiday. Laci gazed around. "Where did Vegas go?"

I peeked into the family room and found her sitting in the dark, except for the lighted Christmas village. "Why so glum?"

"I'm worried about what will happen to Alice and Jasper. They're just like me," said Vegas. "Nobody wants them."

Ouch! I sat next to her and put an arm around her thin shoulders. "You mean the world to your father."

"My mom ran off again."

"She's done that before?"

Vegas nodded. "They think I don't know, but I'm not a kid — her phone has been disconnected."

"Well, honey, we don't really know what happened. Maybe she couldn't pay the phone bill."

"She sent me to spend the holidays with my dad to get rid of me."

"I'm sure that's not true. Whatever is going on with her, I bet she loves you a lot."

"I'm in the way. That's what's going on with her. I'm like these kittens that no one wants. Jasper will probably die out in the cold tonight. That could be me."

"Did you know that Natasha's dad left her when she was younger than you?"

"Really?"

"Really. She had her mom, though, just like you have your dad. He'll come home to be with you as soon as he can. In the meantime, you'll like Mars. He's a lot of fun. And Daisy will stay with you every other week."

She leaned against me, and I gave her a reassuring hug. "There are so many people who care about you. Don't you ever think no one wants you!"

"What about Jasper?"

From the doorway, Laci said, "Instead of a big dinner, why don't we make sandwiches. That way, we can take turns going out to look for Jasper. C'mon." In the kitchen, she handed Alice to Vegas.

Alice already looked like a different cat. Her fur had dried and fluffed up, and she watched us with curious bright blue eyes. George, Mars, and Vegas took the first shift searching for Jasper, while Laci and I prepared our sandwich extravaganza.

When we set the potential sandwich ingredients on the island counter — turkey, ham, Brie, sharp white cheddar, mayonnaise, butter, mustard, horseradish, cranberries, lettuce, whole wheat bread, and kaiser rolls — I began to think a formal dinner might have been easier. As it turned out, though, everyone was psyched to make a sandwich with their favorites. The panini maker went into overtime business, but I had little to do other than set out trays of my homemade Christmas cookies. While Laci served the glühwein, I spent a few minutes making the raspberry center of the bombe. Golden egg yolks went into the bowl of my KitchenAid mixer and spun until they were thick and lemon in color. Meanwhile frozen raspberries thawed in a pot on the stove with sugar melting into them. They bubbled and I checked the temperature several times to be sure they were hot enough to cook any salmonella in the egg yolks. Moving fast, I added the raspberries to the spinning egg yolks. When they were fully mixed, I left them to cool and joined the sandwich crowd around the kitchen table. I felt a little bit guilty that Jasper and his whereabouts dominated the conversation when someone had made an attempt on Natasha's life. She seemed perplexed that she wasn't the center of attention.

Before I left to search for Jasper again, I stirred Chambord into the cool raspberry mixture, blended it with rich whipped cream, and poured it into the empty center of the bombe. When it was in the freezer, we donned our coats, leaving George to watch Shawna, Marnie, and Natasha, while we ventured outside in search of Jasper.

I planned to look in Natasha's backyard, but had a hunch Kenner wouldn't allow it. To bypass a confrontation, I intended to walk around to the back of the house and enter through the alley.

When I walked past the front of Natasha's house, I saw Kenner wielding a weapon that I recognized.

Twenty-Eight

From "Ask Natasha":

Dear Natasha,
Every year I think I'm organized because I toss wrapping paper, gift bags, and ribbons into big bags. Of course, I paw through them during the year to steal bows, tissue paper, and solid color gift bags, then when Christmas rolls around again, it's a mess. There has to be a better way.

— Fit to be Tied in Ribbon, Virginia

Dear Fit to be Tied,
Every home should have a wrapping center. Rolls stay put in long shallow drawers, and ribbons look adorable on mounted dowel rods. Scissors, tape, and craft items should all be stashed in readily accessible compartmented drawers. A long counter or table is a must. You'll enjoy wrapping

315

so much more when you organize!

— Natasha

I dashed toward Kenner to see the weapon up close.

He grinned at me, as though he thought I was eager to see him. Trying not to meet his gaze, I focused on the crutch he held. "Is this from the crime scene?"

"Do you recognize it?" he asked. "It's sort of peculiar."

It would seem that way out of context but I'd seen it in a Christmas display. "It's Tiny Tim's crutch. That's why there's a metal stake on the end — to secure it in the ground. I bet Mrs. Santa hit Natasha over the head with it."

Kenner stroked his mouth and chin. "Tiny Tim, huh?" He held it vertically. "Life-size and pretty realistic. The only place I've seen Tiny Tim this season is on Ginger Chadwick's lawn."

I was glad he figured it out, and that I wouldn't have to rat on her. "She must have dropped it when Daisy chased her."

"Better watch that dog. She has vicious tendencies."

"She does not! She's mostly hound, and she's as sweet a dog as you'll find anywhere. She loves everyone."

"Apparently not me or Ginger Chadwick."

So he thought Ginger had attacked Natasha! If they could tie her to the poison in the music box, she would be arrested and we would all breathe easier. Kenner turned to speak to another cop, and I took that opportunity to slip around the corner and down to the alley that ran behind Natasha's house.

I spent the next half hour creeping through the withered remnants of Natasha's garden. Bare rosebushes and twisting vines waited for spring, but no kitten hid among them. Cold air pierced my trousers, and my thighs felt leaden. Poor little Jasper. I left and walked slowly through the alley to the other end of the block, flashing my light in all possible crevices. I hoped Daisy would find him, because I was having no luck at all.

I rounded the corner and walked home. Orbs of flashlight beams skittered along my block like fireflies in the summer. I met up with Vegas, Daisy, and Mars.

"If you were Jasper, where would you go?" asked Vegas.

Good question. "I think I'd huddle under a porch, out of the wind."

"That's what Mars said."

"Daisy didn't smell him anywhere?" I asked.

Mars handed me the leash. "I hate to give up on the little fellow, but I think I'd better get Vegas and Natasha home. It's getting late."

Whoa! How paternal. I wasn't used to Mars thinking along those lines. He sounded like my dad.

"But you'll keep looking, won't you?" begged Vegas.

I promised I would. Daisy and I watched them walk to my front door to collect Natasha.

An hour later, my fingers grew stiff in spite of my gloves, and even Daisy had lost the spring in her step. I returned to my house and the warmth of my kitchen to thaw.

George, Marnie, and Shawna had very kindly cleaned up the kitchen. Laci stood in front of the fire, holding her hands out to warm them.

"Shawna has been telling us about her adventures in incarceration," said George, eliciting a dirty glare from Laci.

I dropped my jacket and gloves on a chair and joined Laci in front of the fire. There was something that had been bugging me. I turned my back to the fire and faced Shawna. "Didn't you tell the police that you regifted the music box?"

Shawna gulped. "I did, but not at first,

318

and by the time I did, they didn't believe me. See, when I first decided to give the box to Bonnie, I couldn't admit to Beau that I regifted it. What would he have thought? He loved his mother so much, and I wanted to give her something special." She lowered her gaze in shame. "I told him I found it at an antiques store just off of King Street."

Marnie rubbed her daughter's arm. "You know better than to regift, but under the circumstances, I think anyone would have done the same. Bonnie was hard to please, wasn't she?"

Shawna raised her voice in her own defense. "I'd bought her something else — fuzzy sock-like booties — and put them in a Christmas bag! But Natasha has divine taste, and the music box and wrapping were so beautiful. Bonnie loves . . . loved antiques, and I don't know a thing about them, but I know when something is pretty and special. So when the police asked me where I got it, I stuck with that story. I didn't want Beau to know the truth, and I thought it would be better to be consistent. Later, when I told the cops that Natasha had given me the box, Beau said I was lying. I guess it wasn't until my lawyer said other people were confirming Natasha's involvement that they checked it out."

I left the warmth of the fire to take the last container of ice cream from the freezer to thaw enough to slice it.

"Natasha is such a celebrity, too," said Marnie. "Saying she gave you an expensive gift was like saying a movie star gave it to you. No wonder they didn't believe you."

That figured, but if the gas was already present, why didn't it kill Shawna? "Didn't you play the music?"

"I turned the little handle, but it seemed sort of stuck, and I didn't want to mess it up since it looked like an antique. Besides, I didn't have it very long. I barely had time to rewrap it, though I thought I did a good job of using Natasha's fancy gift wrap."

It all sounded plausible to me. I sliced the ice cream and pressed it across the top of the bombe, which would actually be the bottom of the bombe when I turned it out onto a serving dish.

Shawna had been desperate for Bonnie's approval and a marriage proposal from Beau. Even if she had meant to kill Bonnie, which I doubted, she had been with George and Laci when Natasha was attacked, so it seemed more likely that Ginger might have been the clever person who installed the poison in the music box. I replaced the top of the bowl and slid it into the freezer to firm up for serving the next day.

Shawna and Marnie went up to bed, leaving Laci, George, and me to worry about little Jasper.

"I thought you were going home," I said to George.

He rinsed a glass at the sink. "Jen has three competent and doting grandparents keeping her busy. Laci is the one who needs me most right now. I'm sleeping with one ear open, just in case Marnie and Shawna try to pull a fast one and leave for Pennsylvania."

Laci held Alice on her lap and stroked the tiny kitten with a gentle hand. "Do you think Jasper can survive the cold?"

I opened my mouth to say "no way" but George spoke first. "Animals have instincts, honey. He'll curl up somewhere. For all we know, someone might have found him and right now he's fast asleep in a cozy bed."

Laci nodded and headed up to bed with Alice.

I wanted to think George was right. "Do you really think that?"

He looked out the window. "Don't you see the hollows under Laci's eyes? She has to get some sleep." He turned to face me, and patted Daisy. "The only thing we have going for us is that Marnie and Phil live in another state. I can't wait until they pack up their problems and take them home, and my family can get back to life without constant drama."

I checked the doors to be sure they were locked, and the two of us walked upstairs, followed by Daisy and Mochie. I changed into warm flannel pajamas that my mother insisted would keep me single for the rest of my life, and snuggled under the down comforter on my bed. Mochie walked over, settled on my chest, and purred. As I ran my hand over his silky fur, I wanted to cry about Jasper. I knew it wasn't Natasha's fault that someone bashed her over the head, causing her to drop the basket with the kittens, and I felt *sooooo* guilty for worrying more about Jasper than about Natasha, but she was probably in her bed, all toasty, and poor little Jasper might not survive the night. If she hadn't been so furphobic and hadn't carried the kittens back and forth, Jasper wouldn't be out in the freezing cold. Mochie had enough petting and stretched out near my feet. For one hour, I tossed and turned.

If there was anything I hated, it was being totally exhausted and unable to sleep. I finally gave up when I heard the front door shut. Hannah must have come home. Daisy bounded down the stairs ahead of Mochie and me, but when we reached the foyer, there was no sign of Hannah.

We walked through the dark kitchen and the sunroom, but I didn't see anyone. What if Marnie and Shawna had slipped past George?

I dashed up the stairs to the room I'd prepared for Shawna. Opening the door ever so quietly, I peered inside. A lump lay in the middle of the bed. That was an old trick. Every kid in the world knew to plump up pillows so it looked like someone was in the bed. I tiptoed in for a closer look. Shawna slept, emitting tiny little snores.

So why had I heard the front door shut? I returned to the foyer and opened the door to look outside. Laci scurried up to the door, holding her coat closed against the blustery weather. The wind blew wild snowflakes inside, prompting me to shut the door quickly behind her.

Smiling, she unfastened her coat and revealed Jasper. "I can't believe it. I went out to look for him again, and when I called his name, he came running up to me!" Tears rolled down her face. "You knew I would be looking for you, didn't you, Jasper?"

Daisy wagged her tail in approval, but

Mochie hissed and shot up the stairs.

I had a feeling Laci's tears were for more than the kittens, but I didn't mind one bit, especially since I had a feeling Jen would finally be getting the kittens she'd wanted so badly.

When Laci could bring herself to release him, Jasper chowed down on kitty tuna until I thought his little tummy couldn't hold any more.

"Everything is going to be okay now," murmured Laci. "This is a sign. My family will be fine."

I'd never heard Laci talk about signs. She always had her lists and seemed so no-nonsense. Maybe she had another side that she didn't show as often.

The kitchen door banged open and Hannah burst in, bringing a cold gust with her.

"It's horrible out there!" Laci shielded little Jasper with her hands.

"Is it?" said Hannah. "I hadn't noticed." She dropped her coat on a chair and floated to the fridge. "White wine, anyone?"

Laci's eyes met mine and we giggled. There was no denying the dreaminess of a new infatuation.

"Actually," said Laci, "I'd like more of the glühwein if there's any left."

"I missed that?" cried Hannah.

I poured the leftover wine into a pot to warm. "You missed more than wine." I placed gingerbread dogs and heart-shaped Linzer cookies on a platter and set it on the table. While Laci brought Hannah up-to-date about the kittens and Natasha, I revived the fire from the embers.

I divided the spiced red wine into three glass mugs, turned on the tiny Christmas lights, and doused the other lights. The fire crackled and cast shadows on the walls in my cozy kitchen.

"*Mmm,* I love the raspberry jam in these Linzer cookies." Hannah took another bite. "Well, I have to say that I never expected anyone to go after Natasha. This changes everything."

I gripped the mug in my hands to warm up. "Unless Natasha was attacked by someone who doesn't agree with her proclamation that pink and turquoise are the new red and green, I think the killer might have made a big mistake tonight. If we can find out who doesn't have an alibi, we've got him."

"Or her," added Hannah.

"Yes, please! Let's do that. If we could just nail the real killer, Shawna would be totally cleared." Laci sat back in her chair like she was tired. "And we know she didn't try to strangle Natasha because she was in the car with George and me at the time."

"Forrest and Ginger were in the area, because I saw both of them." I tried one of the gingerbread dogs, savoring the mild tang of the spices.

"And Tom was here to visit the kittens," mused Laci. "Who does that leave?"

I ate more of the cookie quickly so I wouldn't be tempted to mention her mother. Marnie had been mercurial at best, and I wasn't about to eliminate her from my private list.

"We can write off Emma and Dasher. They've been gone for days," offered Hannah.

"Tyler?" I said.

Laci frowned. "I have trouble imagining that Tyler or Edward could be involved." She raised her eyebrows and cocked her head. "But that's the point of all this. Maybe we can't cross them off as suspects. We can ask around, find out where they were when Natasha was attacked."

"Have we missed anyone?" I sipped the wine, thinking I should make some for Wolf when he came back.

"Uh, what about Phil?" Hannah leaned a bit like she thought she might have to duck.

Laci must have been more tired than I

thought. She barely fought back. "Dad? I don't think so. He's such a teddy bear."

"He was with Mom and Dad shortly before the attack on Natasha. He probably could have made it here, time-wise, but they would have noticed that he left. I suspect Mom will confirm he was with them the whole time." Now if only we knew where her mother had been.

Agreeing that we would ask some discreet questions in the morning, I tamped out the fire and Hannah cleared the table, while Laci looked for Jasper. She took him up to bed with her. Daisy and I walked upstairs, followed by Hannah, who whispered, "I thought Laci didn't want any pets."

"Sometimes they wriggle into your heart when you least expect it."

Hannah continued up the stairs and I peeled off to my bedroom, where I snuggled under my down comforter with Daisy and Mochie curled on top of it.

New Year's Eve morning, I slept late and was shocked to find I was the first one up. It had been a tough week for everyone — except Hannah, who'd been out late with Zack every night. She stumbled into the kitchen rubbing her eyes.

"Coffee?"

"No one else is up. I thought I'd walk Daisy down to the bakery to pick up some breakfast breads."

"Next year I'm staying at Natasha's house. I bet *her* guests wake up to bedside coffee and croissants."

"You can stay at her house anytime you like."

Hannah stretched. "Oh please. Even *I* make coffee for company."

"Come with me, and I'll buy you one." I didn't tell her that I'd set the coffee machine to start brewing in half an hour.

Inga Bauer would have been mortified to see her grown daughters schlepping along the street to the bakery wearing a colorful mismatched assortment of shapeless fleece pants and jackets, mufflers, gloves, and hats. The only thing that would have pleased her was that we were barely recognizable.

Daisy pranced ahead of us while Hannah and I discussed Natasha's close call.

"The more I think about it," said Hannah, "the more I think Ginger is trying to murder Natasha. She must believe that killing Natasha will magically open up a domestic diva slot in the cosmos that Ginger can step into."

"Don't you suppose there was more to it than that? You know Natasha can be imperious. Maybe she put down Dickensian decor. It's clearly Ginger's thing."

Hannah tugged at her muffler. "Do you think Natasha has some kind of dirt on her that Ginger doesn't want made public? If the cops thought I had tried to murder someone, I don't think I'd trot right back out and try again unless I needed to shut that person up."

Hannah had a valid point. Had Ginger been desperate enough to make another attempt on Natasha's life when the cops were already on to her?

We reached the bakery and I handed Daisy's leash to Hannah. "I won't be long."

A warm vent blew inside the door of the bakery, taking off the chill. I felt guilty about leaving Hannah and Daisy out in the cold, but gladly unwrapped my muffler and started to pull my hat off until a familiar voice caught my attention.

Not four feet away, standing with his back to me, Forrest Chadwick peered into the bakery case. It wasn't exactly the crack of dawn, but certainly early enough for me to wonder why he was in Old Town. Why wasn't he at work?

I pulled my hat down, whirled around, and wrapped the muffler up over my nose. I dashed outside and tugged Hannah and

Daisy across the street, where I hoped we could observe him without being noticed.

"Forrest is there!" The story of seeing him in Old Town in front of that empty building spilled out of me. "I bet he's buying breakfast for Marnie."

Hannah peered at me over the fuzzy edge of her muffler. "Being in a bakery doesn't mean anything, Sophie. Besides, Marnie is probably still at your house, fast asleep."

"There he is!" We watched as he passed us on the other side of the street. "He has three giant coffees and a huge box of baked goods."

Hannah crept forward. "What are you waiting for? Let's follow him."

TWENTY-NINE

From "Ask Natasha":

Dear Natasha,
Every day I waste time hunting for keys. We have three teenage drivers in the house, which mean keys can be in purses, pockets, and under the bed. How do I prevent key-mania?

— Dizzy in Dasher,
Georgia

Dear Dizzy,
Keys should be left close to the entry and exit point. Make your own key holder to match your decor. It's so simple! Paint a board that can be mounted on the wall. Stencil names on it, or a morning glory vine, or ivy! Screw cup hooks onto the board and you're done! The next one who does not return the keys to the assigned spot loses driving privileges for three days.

That should solve your problem!

— Natasha

Exactly as I'd expected, Forrest hurried back to the empty building. He extracted a key from his pocket, let himself in, and disappeared inside.

Hannah and I stared through the plate glass window, but the main floor remained dark and quiet.

"I know how to get to the bottom of this." Hannah squinted at the rental sign in the front window, pulled her cell phone out of her pocket, and pushed a few buttons. She exaggerated her Southern accent. "Mary Smith here, darlin'. I am standin' outside your adorable buildin' on St. Asaph Street . . ."

I cringed. Especially when she said, "What? Well, isn't that a cryin' shame? The whole buildin'? Upstairs, too?"

She hung up, clearly proud of herself.

"You know that Realtor must have caller ID."

"It's my cell. For some odd reason it always shows Virginia on caller ID. Besides, I got the scoop. The building has been rented by a Mr. Forrest Chadwick, who intends to open a bakery! What's more, he took the upper floors, too, because he plans to live upstairs with his son."

I sagged against the window. Did Ginger know? I couldn't imagine her being willing to live above a bakery. She'd mentioned wanting to move to Old Town, but she'd talked about a house near Natasha's. "I guess Forrest was checking out the competition at the other bakery. Why wouldn't he have told me when I saw him here the other day? Why act so secretive? And why three coffees?"

"Could we speculate about this back at the house by the fire?" Hannah handed me the leash. "This time *I'm* going into the bakery to warm up."

Once Hannah had purchased breakfast pastries, we hurried home. I confess I was relieved to know that Forrest wasn't involved in anything devious.

We walked into my kitchen to a chorus of complaints from George, Laci, and Shawna. I opened the boxes and arranged pastries on a large white serving platter before taking off my coat. George and Shawna dug in immediately, glad to have a morning nosh with their coffees.

Laci worked at the stove. "Just scrambling eggs. Nothing fancy."

I slid off my coat. "Where's Marnie?"

George did not sound happy when he

reported, "She left. Said she had an appointment."

Hannah sidled over to me and whispered, "Maybe you were right about Marnie and Forrest. But there were three cups of coffee. Who's the third person? Surely they wouldn't include Edward yet?"

George eyed us with the wariness born of being the only brother of two sisters. "What are you whispering about?"

I glanced at Laci, not sure how she might take my theory about her mother. "We saw Forrest buying three coffees and a host of pastries. Hannah made a call and discovered that he has rented a restaurant in Old Town to open a bakery, and he plans to live upstairs."

"Whoa!" George swallowed a piece of chocolate croissant. "They'll be selling their house then!"

I shot him a don't-be-dense look. "Can you really see Ginger living in a walk-up over a bakery?"

Laci spooned eggs onto a plate for George. "I can't say I'm surprised. Forrest has been miserable in his job for years. I guess he finally reached a point where he decided to make a change. Good for him!"

"Ugh, I hope Ginger doesn't keep the house. She's the scourge of the neighborhood. Having her next door without Forrest there to calm her would be a nightmare." George tasted his eggs.

"For his sake, I hope they're separating. Forrest has put up with Ginger far too long," said Laci.

George stopped eating and focused on Hannah. "Hold it, Lace. There's more to this. Hannah and Sophie wouldn't bother whispering if there weren't."

"We think he's having an affair with Marnie," Hannah blurted out.

The serving spoon in Laci's hand clattered to the floor. "You can't be serious!"

George laughed so hard he choked and had to drink juice to get his voice back. "Marnie is too old for Forrest. He's not *that* desperate! Who would trade a wicked witch like Ginger for a nut like Marnie?"

Laci glared at him until George muttered, "Oh, come on, Laci. Even you have to agree that Marnie is a little bit — unusual."

"My mother is still very attractive and a sweet and loving person."

Hannah frowned at me. "She is a little bit old for Forrest."

I guessed about ten years difference. It wasn't inconceivable. "Then where was she last night when you brought Shawna to my place?"

Laci plunked the egg pan on the stove. "What are you getting at?"

"I'm just wondering where she was all afternoon yesterday and where she is now?"

Shawna had been very quiet, but she finally murmured, "Yeah. Why wasn't Mom here waiting for me?"

Laci plopped into a chair and pulled her sweater tight as though she'd grown cold. "I hope you're not suggesting she had anything to do with strangling Natasha."

The thought *had* crossed my mind. "She did show a tendency to undress Santa Claus and wear his clothes, and I'm fairly certain the killer wore Mrs. Claus's skirt yesterday." Oops. I probably shouldn't have said "killer."

"You think Mom is the murderer?" Laci rose and paced the kitchen. "How dare you? She was never around that music box. No way."

"Except maybe when we left Bonnie's party, and Marnie went shopping on her own and then got drunk. She could have returned to the restaurant and tampered with the gift."

"I thought you liked me," whined Laci. "Why are you doing this?"

I stroked her shoulder, but she brushed my hand away. "Someone attacked Natasha, and it was most likely the same person who killed Bonnie. If we knew where Marnie was, we could eliminate her as a suspect."

Laci leaned against the counter, her hands on her hips.

George groaned. "Why don't you just ask her?"

Laci headed for the phone exactly as someone banged the knocker on the front door.

Daisy followed me to the foyer, and I opened the door to find Tyler on the stoop.

"Uh, hi. I heard Shawna might be here?"

I invited him in, and he followed me to the kitchen. When he saw Shawna, he said, "You look pretty good for a jailbird."

"Want some breakfast?" she asked.

"Just coffee. Forrest Chadwick brought us cupcakes yesterday, and I had a couple for breakfast. How do you feel?"

"Great!" Shawna poured him a mug of coffee, and I noticed that she didn't have to ask how he took it. "Is it okay if we drink these in your sunroom, Sophie?" she asked.

"Sure." I sat down next to Hannah and watched Tyler. From the adoring way he gazed at Shawna, I would have bet he didn't realize the rest of us were even present.

Laci hung up the phone. "Your mom says my mom picked up Dad. The bad news is that neither she nor your father know where they went."

I breathed easier. If Phil was with Marnie, she surely wasn't with Forrest. On the other hand, he had bought three coffees. Were they planning some sort of joint venture into baking?

"I didn't mean to accuse your mom of being a killer, Laci," I apologized. "I really thought she was having an affair."

"I hate this!" Laci poured more coffee for herself and joined us at the table. "No one trusts anyone else. Shawna can't leave town. We're suspicious of our own relatives and neighbors. It's just awful."

George yawned. "Ginger blew her top at Natasha. That's a fact. She probably tried to poison her. When that didn't work, she took the crutch from Tiny Tim in her front yard and drove here to bash Natasha over the head with it. Sophie saw her driving down the block, so we know she was in the neighborhood. Case closed."

Maybe George was right. Ginger's husband baked cupcakes yesterday. If they had cream cheese frosting . . . I rose and shouted into the sunroom, "Hey, Tyler! Did those cupcakes you ate for breakfast have cream cheese frosting?"

We all heard him yell, "Yes."

"That would account for the cream cheese on Daisy's whiskers when she tore away the Mrs. Claus sleeve during the attack on Natasha. Ginger must have gotten some on her sleeve," I speculated. "She just didn't anticipate Daisy ripping the fabric and bringing us a clue."

"It all fits together," said George. "Except for the cream cheese, Kenner knows all this, so they must be on the verge of arresting Ginger."

Shawna dashed into the kitchen, Tyler on her heels. "Someone broke into Bonnie's shop last night. The police just called Tyler!"

"Again?" I asked. What did Bonnie hide there that someone wanted so badly?

Tyler appeared dazed. He flicked a ring of keys in his hand. *Wait a minute.* Hadn't someone stolen his keys?

I smiled at him. "Car keys?"

"Yeah. Shawna, maybe we should walk over there."

"Office keys on there, too?" I asked.

He stopped flipping them. "Yeah. All my keys."

"Hold it!" said George. "Sorry, Shawna, you're not going anywhere without Laci or me."

"So come with." Shawna didn't seem

perturbed by George's requirement.

I, on the other hand, sat back and wracked my brain. Tyler had come to my house only once before. He picked up Shawna and took her to find Beau the day after Bonnie's murder. Yet hadn't he claimed his keys had been stolen the day *before* at Bonnie's party?

THIRTY

From "THE GOOD LIFE":

Dear Sophie,
My girlfriend just paid a small fortune to have a fancy closet system installed. I'm as green as my Christmas tree with envy. How can I improve my closets on a shoestring budget?
    — No Golden Rings in Golden Ring,
                                Maryland

Dear No Golden Rings,
There's one trick that will improve the appearance of any closet. Ditch the wire hangers and buy identical hangers for the whole closet. The uniform appearance makes all the difference. It won't cost a lot if you avoid designer hangers. Check box stores and discount chains for sturdy plastic hangers sold by the dozen.
                                     — Sophie

I jumped up. "I believe I could use a walk." Mostly I wanted to find out more since I suspected Tyler had lied about his keys.

We bundled up, shut the kittens safely in my den, left Mochie to snooze in the rays of sun beaming into the sunroom, and ventured out into the frigid weather. Tyler and Shawna led the way, with Hannah, George, Laci, and me trailing behind them. I brought Daisy along for the exercise.

George crammed his hands into his pockets and hissed, "No way am I letting him take Shawna anywhere. Did you see his SUV? It's loaded with stuff, like he's ready to take off."

Hannah giggled. "He's so smitten with her! I think it's adorable."

"How well do you know him?" I asked George.

"His dad, Tom, has lived in the house across the street from us for years. Tyler had an apartment somewhere, but when Tom sent Dasher away to military school, Tyler moved home. I think he lives in the basement or something."

"He's not as talkative as his brother." Laci zipped the jacket of her collar higher. "Or as rambunctious. You know how it is — older kids try to take care of the younger ones. Dasher was just a baby when their mom died. Tom says Dasher doesn't remember her. I think that's so sad."

"But Tom is a doting dad," George added. "He's tried hard to be Mom and Dad to those kids. Went to their games, was involved in the PTA. Always made a big deal out of Christmas. You saw their lawn with the ginormous Grinch and the train."

"He said Bonnie was a big help when his wife died," I offered.

George's mouth skewed to the side. "Tom was always very diplomatic. I got the impression he didn't like her, but he never said so."

Hannah nudged me. "Hey, your new boyfriend is here."

Perish the thought.

Kenner waited for us outside the front door to Bonnie's shop. While Tyler unlocked the door, Kenner nodded at us in a perfunctory greeting. "I'm sorry, I'll have to ask you to remain outside."

At least he was polite about it. We shivered and watched through the storefront window. When I saw Tyler shrug, I opened the door and stuck my head inside. "Tyler! Were you here after the auction?"

He thought for a moment. "No."

Addressing Kenner, I said, "We were probably the last ones in the shop, then. In fact, Hannah and Zack McGregor locked up."

The old Kenner would have snarled at me and ignored the facts. This time he shot an annoyed look at Tyler and motioned us inside. "Don't touch anything."

I should have waited by the door and allowed Hannah to check out the store, but restraint has never been my strong suit. Curious, I followed her to the rear of the shop. Shattered glass from the back window littered the floor. I pulled Daisy away so she wouldn't cut her paws.

Beside me, Hannah gasped. I swung around to face the storeroom where the auction items had been stored. Someone had ripped open the remaining boxes that contained closet and organizing materials. They'd been tossed aside in a haphazard mess.

"We left all this stuff boxed and neatly lined up against the back wall," said Hannah.

While Kenner conferred with her, I snuck over to glance inside Bonnie's office. The pile of papers on her desk didn't appear disturbed. If the intruder had gone through them, a few sheets of paper would surely have slid off onto the floor. Which clearly meant the person who broke in was looking for something sizable, something that would be in a box, not just a document.

I edged back toward Hannah, Tyler, and Kenner, and asked, "How did you find out about the break-in?"

"The guy in the next building reported it when he saw the broken window." Kenner eyed Tyler warily. "Got any idea who would want something from here?"

Tyler jammed his hands into his pants pockets and jingled his keys. "No."

I tried to suppress the grin that threatened to emerge on my face. Tyler had a tell. Just like gamblers who gave away the nature of the cards in their hands through subconscious habits, Tyler jingled something in his hand when he was lying. He knew who might have broken into the store, but he clearly didn't intend to spill the information to Kenner.

"There's not an alarm?" Kenner asked.

Tyler's hands remained still. "We didn't need one. Who's going to steal a closet rod? We're not like a regular store with a cash register or stuff thieves can pawn. Most of our clients don't even come here. We go to their homes because we have to see what kind of closet space they have to work with."

"So why the store?" asked Hannah. "Wouldn't it have been cheaper to rent a warehouse outside the Beltway?"

"Bonnie said the storefront gave us instant recognition and credibility," explained Tyler.

She'd been right about that. It seemed like everyone in Old Town knew her. Bonnie Scarborough's Clutter Busters was the first name that came to mind for organizing. I was itching to ask what would happen to the business now that Bonnie was dead, but it seemed unkind and a bit presumptuous. However, I knew someone who could get information out of Tyler, and she happened to be staying at my house. She might even be able to weasel out the truth about the keys. If I was right, and he was lying about losing his keys, that meant he might have been the person I saw removing items from Bonnie's shop.

On the walk home, I pondered the best way to convince Shawna to ask him questions. My ideas fizzled, though, when we walked into my kitchen.

Shawna removed her coat and folded it over her arm. "Do you think it's too soon for me to call Beau? I was hoping he'd make the first move once I was released from jail, you know, to apologize. Since I haven't heard from him, I thought . . ."

Laci shrieked. "No! Honey, it's over with

him. He accused you of murder and ditched you to rot in jail. He didn't make so much as a phone call to help you." She waggled her index finger at her sister. "That is not how someone acts when he loves you."

"I wasn't asking you." Shawna tossed her coat at Laci. "C'mon, Tyler."

He followed her to the sunroom. Laci dropped the coat on a chair, added her own, and disappeared in their direction. I caught up with her in my family room, where she'd slipped off her shoes. She hovered just inside the doorway and held a finger over her mouth when she saw me.

I should have been surprised that she would eavesdrop, but my entire family had already proven their inclination to spy — from my parents right down to Jen.

"Your sister is right, Shawna." Tyler's voice came through loud and clear. Laci flicked me on the arm, looking very satisfied.

"I wanted to spare you this," he went on. "You had every right to be angry with Bonnie. She stole your engagement ring from Beau's dresser drawer so he wouldn't propose to you over Christmas."

"How do you know that?"

"She told me. I know a lot about Bonnie. Maybe too much. Bonnie helped Dasher and me so much when our mom died. She was really good to us, especially to Dasher. She was the closest thing to a mom that he had. But she wasn't the wonderful person everyone thought. Dad used to say she had two faces. She was kind and caring to your face, but manipulative and wicked behind your back. Dad always warned us to tread with caution around Bonnie. In public, he pretended to like her, but he loathed her duplicitous ways." It sounded like Tyler uttered a bitter laugh. "She used to come to jobs where I was working and snoop through people's private things to get dirt on them."

"Why didn't you tell me this sooner?"

He mumbled something I didn't understand. I gathered Laci didn't, either, because she made a fist and frowned.

"What?!" Shawna sounded astonished.

He spoke louder, "Because I didn't want you to marry Beau."

Shawna drew a ragged breath. "You don't think I'm good enough for him, either? I thought we were friends."

"I think you're too good for him. When Bonnie stole the engagement ring, I didn't rat on her because I wanted you and Beau to break up. That makes me as terrible as Bonnie, doesn't it?"

Shawna's voice was barely audible when

she said, "Oh, Tyler!"

"Beau was a lot like his mom, and she wasn't always such a nice person. I was actually pretty relieved to find out that the killer was after Natasha. For a while there, I was afraid my dad might have killed Bonnie. The day of her party, she told him he would have to buy the business from her because she was going to get her own domestic diva business going with videos and books. I've never seen him so angry. He's the one who gave her the money to start Clutter Busters, and I did all the work."

"What's going to happen with it now?"

Good girl, Shawna! I didn't have to feed her my questions.

From the uncertain lilt in his voice, I could imagine him shrugging again. "It's what I do. I don't want to fight Beau for it. He's going to need a job, too, and he might just push me out."

"Why would Beau need a job? He works for that fancy law firm."

"Oh. We clutter-busted his boss's house. Beau only got that job because Bonnie found out his boss had a girlfriend on the side. Now that Bonnie's gone, I'd guess they'll dump him fast."

"But Beau must know the dirt on his boss. Won't that prevent them from firing him?"

"Beau never knew Bonnie did that. She swore me to secrecy because she wanted Beau to think he'd gotten the job on his own. It's not much of a confidence builder to know that your mom basically black-mailed someone into hiring you."

"I can't believe you never told me this stuff."

"You wouldn't have believed me. Bonnie fooled everyone. They thought she was so nice and sweet — you did, too. But all the while, she was calculating and tricky."

When we heard shuffling in the sunroom, Laci and I made a mad dash for the kitchen. Of course, she left her shoes behind. I pointed to her stockinged feet and chuckled.

By the time Shawna stomped into the kitchen, I'd grabbed the kettle to fill it with water, and Laci had picked up a section of newspaper. George and Hannah shook their heads at us like we were out of our minds.

"That was classy. Mom's going to hear about this," threatened Shawna.

Laci lowered the newspaper. "Oh, I'm so scared. If Mom had been here, she'd have listened, too." She jumped up, scampered over to Shawna, and threw her arms around her. "You and Dad had a very close call. Can you imagine what it would have been like being part of that family? The Bauers might eavesdrop and be generally nosy, and Inga might think she's Cupid's emissary, but Beau and Bonnie would have been a nightmare!"

"What?" cried Hannah. "What did we miss?"

I set the kettle on the stove. "Apparently Bonnie used people. Seems she was rather two-faced and very accomplished at it."

"Don't let Zack hear you say that!" Hannah threw her hands up. "Nothing makes him madder. We heard some people bad-mouthing Bonnie at the auction, and he told them off."

"I'm beginning to think it might be true." I searched a high cabinet for my fondue pots. "This isn't the first time I've heard she might have had an ugly side."

George snorted. "Rumors."

"Can you reach that?" I asked him. "If they're only rumors, how come I saw an engagement ring in her purse? I think Tyler's right. She stole it and was hiding it from Beau. And we did find Jen's Christmas present to Mom in her shop. Even Zack can't deny that."

Shawna sank into a fireside chair like she'd lost all the strength in her legs.

George handed me the fondue pots. "Where's Tyler?"

"He's in Sophie's den, calling his dad." Using both hands, Shawna shoved her hair out of her face, looking young and vulnerable. "If he had wanted to, Beau could have proposed without the ring. Or he could have used a substitute of some sort, couldn't he?"

It was the first realistic thing I'd heard from Shawna. I washed and dried the fondue pots and carried them into the dining room.

When I returned, Shawna was saying, "Someone who loves me would have come to visit me in jail. Would have tried to get me out. Would have believed me when I said I didn't kill Bonnie."

I looked at Laci. She knew where this was going, didn't she?

"Honey, a man who loves you wouldn't have let you go through that by yourself."

Apparently Laci didn't see what was happening. "George, could you give me a hand?" I asked.

He followed me into the foyer. "Why don't you store things where you can reach them?"

I opened the door and pushed him outside since I didn't know where Tyler was at the moment and I didn't want him to overhear me. "Shawna is in there convincing herself that Tyler loves her."

352

"You sound like Mom. Please don't start matchmaking."

"I'm not matchmaking! Didn't you say Tyler's SUV is loaded like he's planning to take off out of town? If Shawna thinks he's 'the one,' she'll be a lot more likely to go with him."

"Get your coat, Soph."

THIRTY-ONE

From "Ask Natasha":

Dear Natasha,
Our garage has become a catchall. It's so full that we can't even park in it anymore. My husband saves leftover parts from projects — plywood, old doors, extra tiles. On top of that, we have to stash our Christmas items there and, unfortunately, our washer and dryer are located in the garage. Help! I can't stand the mess.
— Living with Chaos in Candlestick, Georgia

Dear Living with Chaos,
Clean it immediately! You have a serious feng shui problem! A cluttered garage can block chi, bringing bad luck. Most people don't make enough use of the empty walls and ceilings of their garages. Have your handy husband use some of that plywood

to build storage boxes that slide into ceiling mounts. He can construct pulleys to raise and lower them. This is a wonderful method of getting bicycles out of the way, too!

— Natasha

Making an excuse about Daisy being restless, George and I grabbed our coats and hurried outside with her.

"Which one is Tyler's car?" We strode to the intersection.

"The dark blue SUV." George walked fast.

"You're sure it's his?"

"*Duh.* He parks it across from our house every night. Tom's garage is so packed with clutter that only one car will fit inside."

"But Tyler's in the organizing business. You'd think he would clean it up for his dad."

"Laci and I joke about it — it's like the reverse of the cobbler's son having no shoes."

Even though it had tinted windows, I could see boxes heaped in the back as we approached it. We peered inside. Tyler had thrown a blanket over some of the contents that filled the back two-thirds of his car, but it had slipped around the edges.

"He's definitely moving," said George. "I

see a microwave and a crock pot in boxes over here."

I looked through the windows on the other side. "I don't know. I see a bunch of candles in jars. They have Santas and silver bells on them, and red ribbons tied around the necks."

"What are you up to?" Hannah appeared out of nowhere and peeked over my shoulder. "Oh my gosh! These are the stolen Christmas gifts!"

"How can you tell?" George jogged around to our side of the car.

"Gee, that mug with Jen's picture on it is a good giveaway." Hannah poked a finger at the window.

My gaze drifted past the candles. Sure enough, a mug bearing a photo of Jen lay on its side.

"I have to call Zack!" Hannah said it with such fervor I wasn't sure if she was more excited about finding the gifts or seeing Zack.

"*Whoo-boy.* This is going to be another big blow for Shawna." George rested his gloved hand against the hood of the car. "I guess there's no way around it, though. If the creep stole the gifts . . ."

"He stole them from Bonnie . . . it doesn't make sense. We found Jen's gift to Mom at

Bonnie's shop." *Or maybe it did make sense. Sort of.* I waved my hands at them. "The person I saw loading boxes in back of Bonnie's place after she died was putting them into an SUV. I could make out the shape, but not the color. This dark blue would have been hard to see at night. Plus, I think Tyler was lying about his keys being stolen."

George frowned at me. "Why would Tyler unload the stolen stuff at Bonnie's, then load it up again and drive all over town with it in his car?"

Good question. "He didn't have anywhere else to hide it? He lives with his dad, so he probably couldn't take it home. Where would you stash stolen loot? Or maybe Bonnie arranged for the items to be stolen, and then when she died, he had to remove it all so it wouldn't look bad for the business?"

"I think I should call Zack. He'll get to the bottom of this." Hannah headed for the house.

George and I followed with Daisy.

"I can't wait until Laci's parents go home. I'd gladly skip the New Year's Eve celebration. The new year can't get here fast enough as far as I'm concerned. If only Shawna would move back to Pennsylvania with her parents. They make our family look sane," George grumbled.

We stepped inside the foyer, and as if to prove his point, Laci stood with her hands on her hips, her face flushed with anger. "Where's Shawna?"

"She's — with — you." George pronounced each word carefully.

"She must have escaped when I went to the bathroom." Laci buried her face in her hands. "I don't believe this."

"Where's Tyler?" I asked.

Laci's eyes widened. "I thought he went outside with you. Oh no! That silly lovesick fool would do anything for Shawna."

"They can't have gone far. We were just looking in his car." As soon as the words left my mouth, all four of us dashed outside and around the corner in time to see the brake lights flash as Tyler briefly stopped the SUV at the intersection.

"Oh, crud," muttered George. "Laci," he warned, "please don't cry."

She fought back tears. "Mom and Dad paid a lot of cash to bail her out of jail. They can't afford to lose it. Why would she do this to us?"

"Not to worry. I was just going to call Zack." Hannah started for the house.

"No!" Laci grabbed Hannah's sleeve. "You can't call the cops. They'll put Shawna in jail again. No, no, no."

George's head lolled to the side and his eyes left no doubt that, in his opinion, this was more of Laci's ongoing family drama. "We'll take our car and drive toward Shawna's apartment. Soph, you and Hannah check Bernie's restaurant and Bonnie's old office."

"Why would they go there?" Hannah asked.

Between gritted teeth he muttered, "Just do it. Maybe you'll get a lead."

Aha. It wasn't easy reading between the lines, but I guessed he was afraid they might be leaving the state — the gift thief and possible murderess — and there wasn't a darned thing he could do about it. It wasn't like he could cut them off at the pass. Tyler's work took him to all kinds of neighborhoods. He had to be very familiar with back roads.

Racing, we returned to the house. Laci grabbed her coat, I made sure the fire was extinguished and the stove was off, and we all headed out, promising to keep in touch by cell phone.

Hannah and I climbed into my car and turned in the direction Tyler had driven.

"This is ridiculous," said Hannah. "We're just doing this to placate Laci and George.

We'd have been equally efficient waiting at home."

I agreed. "There are some things we just do for each other. Surely you don't want to sit in the kitchen with a hysterical Laci and just hope Shawna returns?"

"What a nightmare. You know calling Zack is the right thing to do."

"What if they're just innocently getting lunch?" I pulled into the alley behind Bonnie's shop.

Hannah snorted. "You are so naive. *I* could use some lunch, though. That wasn't much of a breakfast. Is that Tom Thorpe?" asked Hannah. "For an older guy, he's really not too bad looking."

I parked the car and we stepped out. Tom paused to look at us, a hammer in his hand.

"Taking care of the broken window?" I asked, making conversation, since it was painfully obvious that he was doing exactly that.

"Tyler called me. He had to take Shawna somewhere. He's better at this sort of stuff than I am, but I guess the apple didn't fall too far from the tree — I'm pretty decent at building things, too." He hefted the hammer. "Too bad my younger son didn't get the handyman gene."

"Could I hold that for you?" I asked,

pointing to a piece of plywood.

"Thanks. That would make the job much easier." He hoisted the board, and I held it in place while he hammered.

"Did Tyler happen to mention where he was taking Shawna?" asked Hannah.

"Something about picking up clothes. I guess they're planning to celebrate New Year's Eve on the town tonight. Shawna has a lot to celebrate now that she's out of jail." Tom pounded nails, and from the corner of my eye, I could see Hannah making a phone call. To George and Laci, I hoped. Maybe it wasn't a crisis after all. Well, except for the fact that Tyler was in possession of the stolen gifts. *Uh-oh.* What if he'd talked Shawna into stashing the stolen items at her apartment?

"Thanks, Sophie. You're an excellent carpenter's helper. You have great timing, too. Mars told me about your rescue of Natasha. You know, I was there shortly before it happened. If only I'd stayed a little bit longer, I might have prevented Ginger from attacking her."

"Ginger?" Had I missed something? My family had a theory Ginger was involved but we didn't expect others to share it. "Do they know for sure it was Ginger?"

361

THIRTY-TWO

From "THE GOOD LIFE":

Dear Sophie,
I'm so impressed by all the gorgeous ideas people have for wrapping packages, but I'm no good at it. I don't have room for a wrapping station, either. Rolls of paper get crumpled in my closet, and I don't want to think about the tangled mess of ribbon under my bed. It's just hopeless!
— Klutzy in Jasper, Arizona

Dear Klutzy,
Develop a signature style that suits you. Pick a solid color wrapping paper or gift bag and always use the same ribbon with it — maybe a pink or red shot through with silver or gold for a little glitz. You won't have to store as much, people will always know the packages are from you,

and you won't have to worry about it anymore.

— Sophie

"The police found a Santa skirt in Ginger's trash today." Tom raised his eyebrows and nodded with satisfaction. "Looks like Ginger is the one who killed Bonnie and tried to murder Natasha."

My theories about Ginger fizzled. I'd been so inclined to believe that Ginger was guilty, but that one bit of news about the Santa skirt in her garbage changed everything.

Hannah's gaze met mine, and she blurted out what I was thinking. "It wasn't Ginger."

His brow furrowed. "How do you know that?"

"Elementary, my dear Watson," I quipped. "If you were the killer, would you leave such an obvious clue where it would be linked to you?"

Hannah pulled her long hair back. "Ginger could have grabbed the crutch off her lawn to use as a weapon and accidentally left it at the crime scene, but any idiot would know to ditch the Santa skirt."

"She's being framed," we said simultaneously.

Tom laughed. "You two should be detectives. What if Ginger left the skirt there on purpose, hoping to make people *think* she's being framed? She's not beneath that, you know. She's quite duplicitous in nature."

Like Bonnie. Ginger's overt hostility defined her. It hadn't occurred to me that she might be just as sneaky and deceptive as Bonnie, who cultivated an angelic image and hid her dark side. I'd thought Ginger wore her emotions and anger publicly.

"Who do you think tampered with the music box?" I asked.

"Aaagh." He rubbed his chin. "If I were a betting man, I'd have put money on Ginger. She's very unhappy with her life. People like that can be dangerous. They blame other people for their misery and have a need to strike out at someone."

"I hope that's not the case," I said. "Edward is such a great kid."

Tom clapped me on the back. "We can thank Forrest for that. He's a wonderful father. There isn't anything he wouldn't do for his children."

"Have you heard from your son and Emma?"

He regarded me oddly, as if he didn't like the fact that I'd brought them up. "No. I am sure they are already enjoying sunny beaches in Florida. Thanks for your help here, Sophie."

"Oh! I almost forgot. The gorgeous kittens you gave to Natasha and Mars for Christmas . . ." *How to say this in the best possible light?* "I'm afraid Natasha isn't a cat person."

Tom moaned. "Yes, Mars has informed me. I certainly made a big mistake with that gift. I was right there when she went on and on about the Ragdoll she loved so much as a child."

"It seems she was actually talking about a doll. She brought the kittens over to my place, and Jen is in love with them. I'm sure they cost a lot, though. Maybe we can pay you for them?"

"No, no. They'll have more fun living with little Jen, anyway. You know, I am not a young man. I have been around the block a few times, and yet, people continue to surprise me. If I had known Natasha wouldn't like them, I'd have given them to Emma."

I thanked him, we said good-bye and hopped into my hybrid SUV.

As I drove along the alley, Hannah said, "No wonder he's going into politics. Besides his good looks, there's something about him, an elegant way of presenting himself."

I sputtered at her words. "In the first place, you sound like Mom, and in the second place, he was lying through his teeth."

"You think you're so smart. Was his left eye twitching or something?"

"Who would give kittens to people living out of a van and traveling from flea market to flea market? He knows exactly where Emma and Dasher are. Edward said when Kenner arrived, Forrest went out the back door and ran over to Tom's house so the kids could get away. They didn't have time to load their van or pack. Then we saw Forrest picking up three coffees and taking them back to his new bakery-to-be. The two doting dads hid their kids right here in Old Town."

I cruised by the front of the building Forrest had rented. It looked the same. "What do you think?" I asked Hannah. "Third building from the corner?"

"Probably. What now?"

I stopped in front of a Chinese restaurant two blocks away, and handed Hannah my credit card. "Get take-out lunch for two, I'll try to find a spot to park."

"Let's eat in the restaurant."

"It's not for us, you dufus. It's for Emma and Dasher."

"I don't know what they like."

"Just get spring rolls, General Tso's

Chicken, and lo mein."

"Is that good for a pregnant woman?"

"Get anything you think she'll like. Go already!"

Hannah disappeared into the restaurant, and I drove around in search of a parking spot. It would have been faster to park at home and walk.

On my third trip by the restaurant, I found a slot and parked. My phone rang before I could step out of the car.

Mom's voice was as excited as if she'd won a lottery. "Sophie! You're missing all the fun. The cops are going through Ginger and Forrest's trash because they found a Mrs. Claus skirt in it. Jen thinks she's Nancy Drew and your father thinks he's Columbo."

"Did Marnie and Phil come back?"

"Thank goodness, no. Bonnie's death has been so stressful on them. I'm glad they're not here."

"How are Ginger and Forrest handling it?"

"Ginger infuriated your friend, Kenner. She hired some hotshot lawyer, and now neither Ginger nor Forrest will answer any questions! It's just like TV."

Even if Tom thought Ginger might try to make it look like she was framed, there was something peculiar about the skirt in her trash. "Mom, why would someone attack Natasha and then throw away the skirt but not the rest of the Mrs. Claus outfit?"

"Columbo thinks there must have been something incriminating on the other garments — like DNA. Nancy Drew says there's probably DNA on the skirt, too, but we won't know for weeks."

That didn't really answer my question, unless the killer didn't want anyone to see Red Velvet Cake on the jacket. I wouldn't know about it if Daisy hadn't torn off a piece.

"Oh, oh! I have to go. They're checking *our* trash now."

"Wait, Mom! Did you happen to see Tom Thorpe last night?"

She chuckled. "The whole neighborhood gathered on the street in front of the Chadwick house. I know for a fact that he was there. We all had a good laugh."

I felt like I was out of the loop. "What happened?"

"After dark, someone stole the pink and teal Christmas decorations from the community center, set them on Ginger's lawn, and plugged them in. It was absolutely hilarious!"

I bet Ginger didn't think so.

Mom hung up as Hannah opened the

back door of my car and shoved three bags of Chinese food inside. "How much do you think pregnant women eat?" I asked as she climbed into the front seat.

"The rest is for us. I'm starved! Thanks for buying."

Were all sisters like this? I put the car in gear and merged into traffic. A few turns and we rolled down the alley behind Forrest's bakery. "Which building do you think it is?"

"I'd bet it's the one with a sheet covering the window on the second floor."

I suspected she was right.

We clambered out of the car and Hannah grabbed one of the bags of Chinese food. "Now what?"

I looked for a bell. "There must be some way to announce deliveries to the back of the shop."

Hannah spotted it first and pressed the button. We heard a buzzer inside. On a hunch, I stepped back and looked up at the window with the sheet in it. Sure enough, a finger coaxed it aside. "Emma!" I hissed. "We brought food!"

For the longest time, nothing happened.

"We could buzz again," suggested Hannah.

At that moment, the door opened a crack.

Emma glanced around nervously. "Is anyone else with you?"

Hannah didn't waste time. She pushed the door open, saying, "I hope you like lo mein."

"Hurry!" Emma motioned me inside.

We found ourselves in a dated multipurpose area with pegboards and benches lining the walls, presumably for employee coats. A lonely white apron hung on a peg, carefully draped to display the name "Big Daddy's Bakery" and a Red Velvet Cupcake made of shiny bugle beads and sequins. Beneath it, not quite tucked away under the bench, stood a pair of men's boots. Rugged, they'd seen better days. As we walked past them, a tiny glimmer caught my eye. I didn't dare bend to examine them, but I gave them a little nudge with my foot to see better. A blotch of turquoise glitter gleamed on the toe.

The area opened onto a commercial restaurant kitchen. Stainless steel dominated the room, along with workhorse ovens and stoves.

"How did you know we were here?" asked Emma.

A male voice came from above somewhere. "They didn't know about me until now, you goose."

Emma peeked inside the bag of takeout. "We're getting a little crabby from being cooped up. Come on upstairs. This was so nice of you!"

We followed her up narrow stairs and could hear footsteps above us heading for the third floor. The second floor didn't offer much in the way of creature comforts. A bean bag and a couple of wicker chairs provided the only seating. A television rested on a box.

"So, how *did* you know we're here?" repeated Emma. "Do the cops know?"

"We saw your dad picking up coffee." I wandered toward the front window. The hardwood floors gleamed. It would be a nice room once it was furnished.

"Stay away from the windows, please!" The panic in Emma's voice ripped through me. I hadn't realized how taxing it must be for them to hide out in plain sight.

"Where's the van?" I asked.

Whispering, Emma said, "In the alley. Dasher went out last night and switched license plates."

"You're an idiot, Emma!" The angry voice came from above. "Why not tell them everything?"

I bit my lip to keep from reacting. Did he think if we didn't see him, we couldn't report his presence to the police?

She forced a smile. "Could I offer you something?" She looked around. "Dad made these Red Velvet Cupcakes. They're my favorite, and from the way I've been craving them, I think they're the baby's favorites, too. He made a small batch in a hurry while Mom was out. She doesn't like him using the kitchen."

We looked at the three cupcakes sitting on a paper plate, and I hated to eat them when she obviously loved them so much.

As though she read our minds, Emma said, "Oh, but you have to try one! He made them with organic ingredients and no red dyes, because of the pregnancy and all."

"I'd love to have a husband who baked." Hannah took one and split it with me.

"Me, too," whispered Emma. "I think it makes Mom feel inferior because he's so good at baking. They came out great, don't you think?"

"Delicious," I assured her. "Will he offer these in the bakery?"

Her face fell. "How could you know about that? My mom and Edward don't even know. Mom thinks he's still going to work every day. Please don't tell her. She'd turn in Dasher in a heartbeat. And me, too, probably."

I smiled reassuringly, but I had a bad feeling her mom wasn't her only problem anymore. Dasher hadn't said one nice thing to her since our arrival. Had she subconsciously selected a mate who treated her as poorly as her mother did? "Who'd have thought the music box you gave your mom would cause so much trouble?"

"She never should have bought it. We could have lived a week on what she paid for that thing." Dasher's voice came from the stairwell loud and clear.

Emma dropped into a wicker chair, her expression weary. "He doesn't know what it's like to have a mother. All he had was Bonnie. I thought Mom would cherish the music box, and love me for it. Dad told me her colors this year were red and gold, and I wrapped it so beautifully."

Emma knew her mother's color scheme? I tried not to show a reaction to her statement, even though it troubled me. If Emma had wrapped the gift correctly in red and gold, but it was wrapped in red and green when Ginger received it, then she had almost certainly been the intended victim. The murderer must have unwrapped it, installed the gas, and then wrapped it back up again. What other reason could there be to rewrap it?

She glanced at the stairs before whispering, "The truly awful thing is that I know I should feel terrible about Bonnie's death, but the thing that hurts the most is that Mom regifted the music box. It was like she was getting rid of me by giving it to someone else."

Tears came to my eyes and I was furious with Ginger for being so heartless. No wonder someone wanted to do away with her.

Striving to sound casual so she wouldn't know I was trying to reconstruct what happened, I said, "Edward told me you sent your gifts ahead of time?"

Emma spoke in a soft voice. "We didn't think we'd have the money to come for Christmas . . ."

"We would have if you hadn't spent so much on your mother!" No matter how softly Emma spoke, Dasher didn't miss a word.

". . . so we wrapped everything up and Dasher took it all to the post office to pack in one of those flat-rate boxes. A good thing since the music box weighed so much. I was afraid Mom might intercept the box and throw everything out if we sent it to my parents, so we shipped it to Tom and put in a note asking him to give my family's gifts to my dad."

Interesting. Dasher, Tyler, Tom, Edward, and Forrest all had access to the gifts and could have tampered with the music box intended for Ginger. But whoever did it had made a huge error that narrowed the field of contenders.

I listened to Hannah chat with Emma for a few minutes so it wouldn't be too obvious that I was itching to leave, then suggested we'd better get going before someone recognized my car and wondered what I was doing there.

When we were safely in the hybrid and headed home, I spilled my theories to Hannah. "The killer didn't know about Ginger's Christmas package color scheme. That eliminates Forrest and Edward. They would have known for sure."

"Are you going to call Kenner?"

I guessed I would have to. Why wasn't Wolf home yet? Kenner would think I wanted a date for New Year's Eve tonight. I hated to reveal Emma's whereabouts, but I couldn't see any way around that — unless we managed to give Emma a heads-up and get her out of there. Of course, once they had the killer, the police wouldn't care about Emma.

"It could still be Ginger, you know."

"I don't think so. If I can believe Edward, and Ginger came home to rewrap the music box and give it to Natasha that night, then she didn't really have much time to set up the poison inside. Plus Ginger would have been smart enough to ditch the Mrs. Claus outfit in its entirety in the river. No, Hannah, I think the killer tripped himself up by using the wrong wrapping paper."

"The music box!" cried Hannah. "Tom said Dasher isn't adept with his hands. Whoever installed the poison in the music box had to be clever and very good at tinkering with things."

"I wonder if it's true that Dasher isn't good with his hands. He and Emma make a living selling their artwork."

"There are all kinds of art. He might be a great photographer, for instance, and completely inept at sculpting wood or making poison music boxes."

I stopped for a light and looked over at my sister. "Or Tom could have said that about his youngest son to throw us off his trail."

THIRTY-THREE

From "Ask Natasha":

Dear Natasha,
My husband is on the verge of leaving me because of my shoes! I adore shoes, but they're all over the floor of our walk-in closet. I can't get rid of them. Help!
— Aching in Tar Heel, North Carolina

Dear Aching,
Buy an old dresser with deep drawers. Paint or stencil it to match your decor. Divide the drawers into shoe-size sections with narrow planks of cedar. Your shoes will have a lovely dust-free home and they won't be underfoot anymore.
— Natasha

"Dasher tampered with the music box figuring he had an alibi because they were out of town!" exclaimed Hannah. "Sounds like something a worm like him would do."

"Seems like Emma would have told him about her mother's gift wrap rules, though. I think we've narrowed it to Tom and Tyler." I pulled into a parking space near my house.

"Tyler!" exclaimed Hannah. "Sophie, we're supposed to be looking for Tyler and Shawna."

I rubbed my eyes. In my excitement at narrowing the suspects, I'd completely forgotten about Shawna. "We're already home. Maybe we should make sure they didn't come back?"

We plodded along the sidewalk and were almost at my house when we heard doors slam and angry shouts.

It wasn't hard to find Laci and Shawna screaming at each other on the sidewalk.

"Mom and Dad paid a lot of cash to get you out of jail. I'm not letting them lose it!"

Shawna spat back, "Oh, right. Did it ever occur to you that I might need a few things from the drugstore — like makeup and a toothbrush? It's not as though Tyler drove me out of state. You had no business dragging me out of the store. Like it wasn't humiliating enough to go to jail? My own sister has to hunt me down and embarrass me in public, too? And then to make me ride back with you and George like a child!"

"You couldn't have told me where you were going? Would that really have been too much to expect of you?"

George slid a hand over his face, dragging his features down like a Dali painting. "Could we at least take this inside?"

George tried to steer Laci along the sidewalk. Hannah and I brought up the rear, walking behind Tyler and Shawna. They all came to an abrupt and silent halt at my front door. I unlocked it and watched as they filed inside, thinking about how I could get Tyler to confess.

Daisy greeted everyone with doggy glee, wagging her tail so hard it went in a circle. *How could Natasha not adore her?*

I opened the door to the den and the kittens scampered through the foyer, but Mochie bore down on them at rocket speed and all three cats scrambled toward the kitchen.

I snagged George's sleeve. "I talked to Tom about the kittens, and he was okay with giving them to Jen. We might buy him a nice gift since they cost so much and he's not charging us."

George leaned to the side — I presumed to be sure Laci was in the kitchen and wouldn't hear him. "This has been such a wonky holiday. Jen will be overjoyed. She deserves something special. I still can't believe that Laci changed her mind about the kittens."

"You can thank Jasper for getting lost and running to her in the dark of night."

George peered into the kitchen again. "It's going to be miserable hanging around here watching Shawna. So here's my plan. I'm taking Laci, Shawna, and Tyler to the six o'clock movie. At least they won't yell at each other in the movie theater. We should be back around eight thirty for your fondue dinner. Luckily Mom and Dad will be here tonight for dinner and the New Year's Eve fireworks. More people will make it easier to keep track of Shawna so she can't pull any more stunts. Want to come to the movie with us?"

George knew I had to fix everything for our New Year's Eve dinner. Still, it was nice of him to ask. "I'll hold down the fort. What are you going to do with Shawna the day after tomorrow, when we all have to go back to work?"

I saw terror in his eyes. "Mom and Dad will have to help out, I guess. I don't think we can trust Marnie and Phil to keep Shawna in check."

We ventured into the kitchen, where Laci

and Shawna glared at each other, and Hannah unpacked Chinese food. She'd bought enough to feed an army.

I was handing out white plates with ornate yellow and red borders, which Mars's Aunt Faye had brought back from Hong Kong, when Hannah brushed by me and whispered, "I'm calling Zack about the stolen gifts in Tyler's car."

The time had come, I supposed. She scuttled off to make her call, and I tried hard not to stare at Tyler lest I alert him. Poor Shawna. Dumped by Beau, thrown in jail, and now her new crush, Tyler, would be arrested for stealing the gifts and, worse, maybe for murder.

Shawna shed her shoes. "I am half frozen." She peeled wet socks off her feet. "Did you bring me socks and shoes?"

Laci winced. "Your feet are two sizes larger than mine, and you know it."

"How did you get so wet?" asked George.

"Not all the sidewalks are clean. I guess I stepped in snow," muttered Shawna.

Guilt saddled me. I hadn't cleaned my sidewalks the way I should have.

"Man, this floor is cold. I want to go home and get clothes! Socks and shoes and my fuzzy slippers!" Shawna groaned.

Tyler stood. "I'll take you. We can go right

381

now. You'll feel much better once you have your own stuff."

George moaned. "Let's not start that again."

We had to keep him and his SUV here until Zack arrived.

Laci jumped up and barred the door. A futile move, really, but quite dramatic. "You're not going anywhere. We just engaged in a wild-goose chase. How can you be so immature? Don't you understand what's at stake here?"

"Like you would wear the same outfit for days on end, Miss Clothes Horse?" Shawna mimicked Laci's voice and mannerisms perfectly, as though she'd been doing it for years. "Oh! I must go to the mall and buy new clothes." Then Shawna reverted to yelling. "I was in jail! All I want is go to my apartment and get a few things."

"In the first place, I have never been a clothes horse." Laci had regained her composure and spoke with the calm sensibility that she used when reasoning with Jen. "You're talking about things I did when I was a teenager. However, you appear to be overlooking the fact that I hadn't been arrested for murder, I wasn't out on bail, and neither the cops nor a bail bondsman cared what I did or where I went." She returned to her seat at the table. "Make a list. I'll drive over to your place and pick up what you need."

It seemed reasonable to me, but Shawna screamed, "So you can snoop in my apartment? I think not."

"Would you rather George went?"

Shawna didn't respond. It seemed to me that she didn't have a lot of choices.

Hannah returned to the table and appeared comfortable with her deception about calling Zack. She smiled and joked about sisters who fight.

To drag out lunch and keep Tyler around, instead of offering Christmas cookies for dessert, I promised my company warm chocolate chip cookies from my stash in the freezer.

I heated the oven and cut the frozen dough into slices, which I quartered and placed on a baking tray. Once they'd been eaten, I would have to rely on Shawna's allure to keep Tyler around until Zack arrived.

I needn't have worried. About the time Tyler bit into his second cookie, he and Shawna had started grinning at each other, and from the little chuckles they tried to hide, I had a feeling a game of footsie had commenced under the table.

To keep myself from pacing, I washed

dishes, spending most of the time looking out the window toward the street. When Hannah jumped up and ran to the front door, I breathed easier. She intercepted Zack before he knocked, and after a mushy kiss that made me miss Wolf, she escorted him in the direction of Tyler's SUV.

George dried dishes beside me, but he didn't miss Zack and Hannah strolling arm in arm away from my house. He nudged me with his elbow at the same time that Laci said, "Is that Zack?"

What seemed like an eternity of horrified silence followed until I blurted out, "He's Hannah's date for New Year's Eve." Never mind that he was hours early. To distract everyone from Zack's presence, I asked, "Tyler, did your dad find a date for tonight?"

Tyler turned his head toward me and blinked. "Dad? He doesn't date."

"My mom has been trying to match him up with someone," I explained.

"She won't have much luck. Women have chased him since Mom died but he likes being the single guy without any 'entanglements,' as he calls them."

I didn't think I should be the one to break the news that his father had a change of heart. Plus, Hannah and Zack hurried toward my house wearing grim expressions. I braced myself for the confrontation between Zack and Tyler.

Zack opened the door to the kitchen and held it for Hannah, who entered saying, "It's cold out there. How about some hot lattes, Soph?"

Okay, so they were going to take the casual approach. Did Zack intend to play the good guy and weasel the truth out of Tyler? I put rich Dallmayr House Blend coffee on to brew, fumbling a bit because I was antsy about Tyler's imminent arrest.

Hannah brushed by me. "You won't believe this."

I followed her into the foyer, where she hung coats in the closet.

"Everything is gone. The back of Tyler's car is completely empty."

THIRTY-FOUR

From "THE GOOD LIFE":

Dear Sophie,
I thought our storage problems were over when we built a shed in the backyard. Now I'm afraid to go in there because of the mice and squirrels. How do we keep them out of the birdseed?
— Musaphobic on Snake River

Dear Musaphobic,
Eliminate anything mice like to eat. Try not to store garden seeds, birdseed, dog food, or anything edible in the shed. If you must store those items, put them inside old-fashioned metal trash cans and weigh down the lids. Mice will eat through plastic. Most importantly, seal all holes, no matter how small, and make sure the doors shut tightly.

— Sophie

"Tyler must have been on to us." I closed the closet door and leaned against it.

Hannah grimaced. "Zack wants to play it cool and see what he can find out."

"Find out?" I hissed in a whisper. "They obviously pulled that stunt to get away from us and unload the stolen goods. Think they took everything to Shawna's place?"

"Or back to Bonnie's."

"That can't be. *We* were there."

"They might have waited for us to leave. Remember, we picked up Chinese and paid a visit to Emma."

"Did you tell Zack about Emma?"

The corners of Hannah's mouth twitched down. "Technically Bonnie's murder isn't Zack's case. It's your boyfriend who is looking for them."

"Would you stop calling him that? Someone is likely to believe you." I could understand why she wanted to justify not turning in Emma and Dasher. Of course, we didn't know if Kenner had put out a warrant for them. Maybe they weren't wanted at all. On the other hand, what if there was another murder and I was wrong about the suspects? If Emma and Dasher were the killers, it would be our fault for not revealing their whereabouts. "What if we're dead wrong and they kill someone else?"

"What are you whispering about?" George emerged from the kitchen and Hannah caught him up to speed. "I wish Wolf were back. He's always so sensible about these things."

"Look," said Hannah, "the killer was after Ginger. All we have to do is let her know that the killer might still be around. That way she can watch out."

George's eyes turned up to the ceiling when he growled, "I think she knows *that!*"

Laci bustled out of the kitchen. "Well! This is about the rudest thing I've seen in a long time." She made no effort to whisper. "We have company, you know. George, I think we'll have to put off going to the movies."

We traipsed into the kitchen like scolded children. I poured milk into a pot to warm it, but my mind was on Emma. It wasn't fair of me to exclude her from our list of suspects just because I felt sorry for her. Then again, someone had changed the wrapping paper. Didn't that clear Emma?

I whipped cream, then mixed heady vanilla and a generous amount of decadent Bailey's Irish Cream into the milk, and poured it into the coffee Laci had already poured into mugs. A dollop of rich whipped cream topped each latte, and Laci followed behind me tapping a sprinkle of nutmeg on the billowing white cream.

We carried the mugs to the table and handed them out. I nestled in the window seat, cupping a mug of latte in my hands. How could I draw Tyler into giving us information? As casually as I could, I said, "Tyler, it must have been great seeing your brother again."

"Yeah, it was."

Argh. He wasn't the talkative type — at least not to me. I tried again. "Did you have a chance to spend time with Dasher while he was here?" That might have been too much. He flicked an annoyed glance my way.

Shawna preened. "He was too worried about me. Tyler called me in jail every night except last night. He went to a rock concert with Emma and Dasher. That's why he didn't know I'd been released."

The change in Zack's expression was barely noticeable. His eyes gave him away, though, when he studied Tyler. Zack must have known that Forrest claimed Dasher and Emma had left the area the day before.

I heaved a huge breath of relief. A cop now knew that they were still around. Hannah and I didn't have to turn them in after all. Giddiness overcame me and I joined in the silly banter around the table.

Snow began to fall again, heavily this time. Laci reached a hand toward her sister. "If you want me to pick up clothes at your apartment, I'd better go now. It's coming down hard."

Grudgingly, Shawna wrote out a list of items for Laci. If they found the stolen Christmas Eve gifts in Shawna's apartment, would George be able to convince Laci to rat on her sister? I doubted it.

George and Laci bundled up and headed out in the mini-blizzard. Although I didn't want to shovel anything, Mom and Dad would be arriving in a hour or two, and I knew I had to clear the walk. I delayed as long as I could before pulling on a coat and boots. I let Daisy out to play in my fenced backyard while I retrieved the snow shovel. She romped through the snow with genuine joy. Thick snowflakes stuck to her black fur like a winter coat, but she didn't mind, racing around the yard and burying her nose in the white powder. She accompanied me to the potting shed in the very rear of my property.

I stopped cold. I should have had to clear snow away to open the doors but it had been trampled under the new fluff. I pulled the left half of the double doors open, expecting to find my snow shovel just inside, leaning against the wall. Instead, I nearly fell over a pile of neatly stacked boxes, mostly covered by a blanket.

I whisked the blanket off them. A microwave and a crock pot sat in unopened boxes on top of the pile. Wincing, I used the tip of my forefinger to flip the lid on an open box. Christmas candles in jars. There was no doubt about it — Tyler had moved the contents of his SUV to my potting shed. My blood pressure soared. Shawna must have helped him. They staged that little escape so he could unload the ill-gotten goods.

Furious, I stomped back to my house. How dare they pawn those things off on me? What if Shawna and Tyler denied any knowledge of the stolen items in my potting shed? Would Zack believe me? Surely he would believe Hannah. Or would he be doubtful like that grim Kenner, who thought I made up stories just to see him? The trek across the snow did little to help me cool off.

Daisy looked up at me, wagging her tail. A white strip of snow bridged her nose. "You're right. I've had enough of this pussyfooting around."

Daisy and I entered through the kitchen

door. The lovebird couples had eyes only for each other. This time, I didn't mince words. I stared straight at Shawna. "I have taken you into my home and this is how you repay me?"

Shawna shrank back in her chair. "I . . . I don't know what you're talking about."

"Oh, I think you do. You and Tyler took us on a wild-goose chase. You ran away so we would follow you. Then you doubled back and unloaded the stolen Christmas gifts into my potting shed!"

Tyler's eyes roamed the room like he sought a hidden exit. "You must be mistaken."

"I have witnesses that those items were in your car."

Hannah cocked her head. "I saw them."

Fixing his gaze on Shawna, Tyler waved his hands in denial. "I didn't steal anything."

I went for the jugular. "Then why do you have a mug with Jen's picture on it?"

Shawna appeared to be on the verge of tears. "You have to tell them. Tell them the truth, just like you told me."

Tyler grabbed his head with cramped fingers. "All I'm trying to do is save the people I love!"

Save the people he loves?

I jabbed a finger in the air at Shawna.

"Did you have anything to do with the missing gifts?"

A slow smile crept over Shawna's lips. "You love me?"

Oh, brother. I glanced at Zack. He was the cop — why didn't he say anything? But he was grinning at them.

"Tyler had to remove the stuff to save Bonnie's reputation," said Shawna.

Something in Tyler's pocket jingled, and I knew that wasn't quite the truth.

"It was me you saw that night, Sophie." The jingling stopped, and he scratched Daisy under her chin. "Everything was in such chaos when Bonnie died. I forgot all about the stolen stuff in the shop. She was planning to sell it to some guy. Then when you needed access to the office for the auction, I panicked and loaded it all into my car. I heard Daisy howl and took off, but I didn't know where to hide it." He leaned toward Zack. "Shawna had nothing to do with any of this, I swear. She didn't know about it until she saw my car today."

"Your keys were never stolen?" I asked.

"No."

Zack's forehead creased. "You expect me to believe that Bonnie stole the Christmas presents?"

Tyler hesitated. "I don't know the extent

393

of her involvement. All I know is that they showed up in the shop and she planned to unload them."

"It was my idea to put everything in your potting shed, Sophie," explained Shawna, beaming like she'd aced a test. "That way, the items would be discovered and returned."

At least she meant well, even if she could have landed me in a heap of trouble. I was still angry with her, but I guessed if someone had announced that he loved me, I might want to believe him, too. Who else did Tyler love and want to protect? His dad? Somehow I couldn't imagine Tom stealing anything. Besides, he was front and center at the Christmas pageant in his role as Santa Claus. Dasher? Emma? Jen liked Emma and implied she was well liked by the neighborhood kids. Had Tyler nursed a secret crush on Emma like he had on Shawna?

"But that's not everything. Where are the rest of the presents?" Hannah asked.

Tyler's hand remained on the table, clenched in a fist. "They were sold. I guess some stuff doesn't sell very well. I never saw any electronics or the computer Ginger made such a fuss about, but there are tons of candles."

Zack sighed. His demeanor reminded me

of Wolf. He took it all in and processed it without the drama that Kenner usually brought to a situation.

"Let's have a look, then." Zack stood up.

I didn't wait for them to pull on their coats. I headed out front to shovel the walk. The snow had stopped, and Old Town lay under a clean, fresh blanket of white. As twilight fell, candles glowed in windows and cozy lights flicked on. The cold air nipped my face, which was still hotter than normal.

Ordinarily, I'd have been enchanted, but Shawna's little stunt, and the fact that the killer hadn't been apprehended, left me feeling anxious. I returned to the kitchen, where Hannah and Shawna both looked glum.

"What happened?" I asked.

"Zack and Tyler are transporting the presents to the police station. Now neither of us has a date for New Year's," whined Shawna. "Couldn't you have waited one day to discover the boxes in your shed?"

Well, if that wasn't the height of audacity! "You'd better be glad I wasn't arrested for possession of stolen property."

"Could that really happen?" she asked.

Hannah snorted latte. No wonder no one who knew Shawna thought she could have rigged the music box with poison gas.

"Can you babysit for a while?" asked Hannah. "I'd like to shower and change, just in case Zack makes it back."

"Sure."

"I have some phone calls to make. I'll be in my cell upstairs," announced Shawna. I listened to the sound of her footsteps going up the two flights. At least I could set the table and putter around the kitchen. My old stairs would creak if she tried to get away.

I stood in the archway leading to my dining room and tried to switch gears from murder to dinner. I considered using a black tablecloth, but had done too many events with a black theme, and it seemed too deathly for the fresh start I hoped the new year would bring. I decided on a white tablecloth shot through with silver threads and flicked it out onto the table.

The knocker on my front door sounded. Thank goodness. It would be easier to keep an eye on Shawna once everyone arrived.

Daisy accompanied me to the door. When I opened it, instead of my family piling in, Ginger Chadwick marched into my foyer, unbidden.

THIRTY-FIVE

From "Ask Natasha":

Dear Natasha,
I live in an older home and the only storage in the bathroom is an ugly medicine cabinet. My husband would like to replace it with a modern mirror, but it's the only storage we have and it's overflowing! I'd love to rip out the whole bathroom and start over, but our daughter's college tuition comes first. Any suggestions?
— Vexed in Vixen,
Louisiana

Dear Vexed,
The standard distance between wall studs is eighteen inches. If you remove the Sheetrock between two studs, you will find a floor-to-ceiling space about three inches deep. Add shelves and a door and you've got perfect storage for all those little

bathroom items.

— Natasha

"Where is she?" demanded Ginger.

"Shawna?" What would Ginger want with Shawna?

"Are you always so dense? I don't care about Shawna. Where is my daughter?"

Alice and Jasper zoomed down the hallway toward the open door with Mochie after them. I closed it in a hurry.

Ginger glanced at the cats, and her nose flared as though she thought they stank.

"Emma!" she shouted. "Emma, where are you?"

Without so much as a "please," Ginger stomped up my stairs toward the second floor.

"Excuse me. Excuse me!" Where did she get off inspecting my house? *What nerve!* "Mrs. Chadwick! I have to ask you to leave."

Nothing stopped her from her quest. I toyed with the idea of racing ahead of her and pushing her down the stairs, but prudence and propriety stopped me from following through.

They didn't stop *her,* though, and the next thing I heard was a shocked scream from Hannah.

The door shut with a bang, and I heard

Ginger's footsteps continue as she probed my bedrooms. She wouldn't find Emma, or anything else of interest for that matter, so I returned to the dining room and continued with my silver and white table decor, but I was seething inside. In the middle of the table, I clustered silver candlesticks with white candles. Shorter white pillar candles studded with silver stars led away on either side. A coil of silver stars on a wire stretched nicely through the length of the centerpiece, adding the illusion of movement. On top of that I draped a long garland of mirrors and glass beads that would reflect the candle-light.

An angry voice accompanied clomping down the stairs. Hannah, dressed in a sexy black sweater with touches of gleaming silver and a pair of black trousers, reamed Ginger out for bursting in on her bath.

My hands on my hips, I spoke harshly. "How would you like it if I barged into your house and poked my nose around?"

Ginger stopped at the foot of the stairs. Her mouth pulled into a bitter slash. "The domestic diva business must pay exception-ally well if you can afford a historic house like this."

The woman simply couldn't say anything nice. What an offensive person! I ignored her thinly disguised slight. Since she'd been so rude, nothing would coax me to explain that Mars and I had inherited the house from his aunt.

"I am not in the habit of searching houses. Just so you know." Ginger started for the door.

"Hold it there, honey." Hannah nabbed Ginger's elbow. "I think we deserve an explanation."

Ginger sucked in air so hard her chest shuddered. "I have followed my husband to Old Town on several occasions, but he always loses me. I can't imagine that he's having an affair. Who would want a fat, unhappy man with a boring job whose only joy is baking? While I was out recently, he baked Red Velvet Cupcakes, which are Emma's favorites. He's here, somewhere in Old Town tonight, and I suspect he's sheltering the daughter who tried to kill me. Surely you understand that I cannot sleep, or do anything else for that matter, until she's safely behind bars."

"Why would you think she was here?" I asked.

"Your father was helping Forrest in our garage, and I overheard your mother say something about you babysitting a trouble-maker. Besides, there has to be a reason

Detective Kenner is sitting in a car outside, watching your house."

Hannah and I rushed to the dining room window.

"Where?" I asked.

Ginger hadn't budged from the foyer. "Second car from the corner directly across the street."

A twinge of guilt nagged me. She might be rude and insulting, but she was obviously afraid and taking in every detail.

We couldn't see much in the dark, but the streetlights offered sufficient glow to make out the shape of a head in the front seat of that car.

I returned to Ginger in the foyer. "Look, you may not care for me or my family, but I think you should know that Hannah and I suspect you were the intended victim of the poison fumes in the music box — and we don't think Emma is the culprit. You ought to be very careful."

She focused enraged eyes on me, and I braced for a tongue-lashing. "I'm not stupid. The facts are undeniable. My daughter thought she could murder me from afar, thus providing herself with an alibi. When I didn't die, she tried to frame me by sending that ridiculous Dasher to impersonate me and attack Natasha, in the hope I would be arrested. Clearly, that hasn't happened, either. Emma and Dasher lurk in this town somewhere, plotting their next strike against me — but I shall find them first. Those two will rue the day they ever hatched a plot to kill me."

"Mrs. Chadwick," I said, "I don't think Emma —"

She interrupted me. "You think I don't know my own daughter? Emma was groomed to go to Cambridge. She has a higher IQ than most of the people you will meet in your lifetime. She's pregnant with the devil's spawn just to spite me. I know what she's capable of, and mark my word — I will find her before she knows I'm looking for her." She opened the front door and paused. "Besides, everyone else loves and admires me."

I closed the door behind her, and though we shouldn't have, Hannah and I burst into shocked laughter. "She's delusional," I gasped. "The devil's spawn? What an awful thing to call her own grandchild."

"Should we warn Emma?" I asked.

Hannah's mouth twisted. "I don't see why. Ginger obviously doesn't know where Emma is holed up or she wouldn't have come here."

Hannah retreated up the stairs to do her

hair and makeup. Still shaking my head over Ginger, I hustled to the kitchen to cut hard, nutty Gruyère and slightly fruity Emmental cheese into small chunks so they would melt easily for the cheese fondue later on. I poured canola oil into a pot and set it aside, ready to be heated for the meat fondue. Next I cut lovely lean steaks into inch-size cubes and stashed them in the fridge.

While I worked, I couldn't help thinking of Ginger. Surely she wouldn't harm her own daughter — would she? I didn't have Emma's phone number so I couldn't call to warn her.

I washed and dried mushrooms, sliced crunchy red peppers, and broke cauliflower and broccoli into small florets that would be fabulous dipped in the cheese fondue.

Maybe I could call Forrest or Tom, and one of them would warn Emma. But what if I was wrong? What if Emma did try to kill her own mother? Or more likely, what if Dasher was the murderer? No, that couldn't be. At least not if the wrapping paper was relevant. Though it was possible that Dasher hadn't known about it, but I thought that unlikely. Emma was pretty chatty and would have mentioned it to him. That still left Tyler and Tom as possible culprits.

I debated my options as I washed and tore

curly red leaf lettuce for a salad, sliced red onions and black olives, and separated sections of clementines. I mixed them all in a bowl and put it in the fridge until later. I was on the verge of making a vinaigrette when I heard a commotion upstairs.

"Jen alert!" shouted Hannah as she raced down the stairs.

I scooted to the family room. Where were Jasper and Alice? What a time for them to hide.

I dashed through the sunroom, Mochie and Daisy at my heels, delighted about the excitement. No kittens. I passed Hannah in the foyer.

She held the kittens' empty basket. "You can't find them?"

I shot up the stairs and looked in my closet. Once again, the little furballs had gone for my laundry basket. I scooped them up, hurried down to the foyer, deposited them in the cute basket, and paused to catch my breath before I opened the door for my parents and Jen.

I have to admit that I love the feeling of friends and family arriving. Magically, all the competing voices aren't noise, and all the people aren't in the way. It's a warm, happy moment every time.

Hannah held the kitten basket out to Jen.

"I think these are for you."

Jen's squeal made the moment even better. "Are you serious? Mom and Dad are letting me keep Alice and Jasper? I can't believe it!" She pulled the kittens from their basket and clutched them to her.

As Mom, Hannah, and Jen moved toward the kitchen, I hung up their coats.

"Need some help taking down Christmas tomorrow?" asked Dad.

"That would be great!" The dreaded chore would go much faster with his help.

He handed me his coat. "After the cops left, I gave Forrest a hand storing their Dickens carolers. Those things are heavy!"

"Did he mention anything about a divorce?"

Dad's expression of shock lasted only a second. "Oh. Now I understand. He didn't mention a divorce, but he said something odd that makes more sense now. I can't say I'm surprised. His wife is rather caustic. Did you see Natasha's column this morning?"

I rarely paid her column much attention. "About feng shui?"

"Half the people on George's block cleaned out their garages today! When I was helping Forrest, Ginger charged into their garage, waving the column and insisting Forrest build a wall of cabinets in their garage for storage. She had a fit that we covered the carolers with plastic bags and stashed them in the corner."

"*Eww.* Didn't that look a little bit creepy? Like people in cocoons?"

"That's what Forrest said. 'Like pod people waiting to emerge and finally live their lives.' But he didn't do what she wanted. When Ginger left the garage, he chuckled and said, 'It doesn't matter anymore.' Maybe that's what he meant — that they're divorcing."

Maybe. Then why were the little hairs on my neck prickling and why did a shiver run through me? "Did he say anything else of interest?"

Dad raised his eyebrows. "Wait until you hear this! The strangest thing happened when we left George's house tonight."

Mom appeared in the doorway. "Are you telling Sophie? Come in the kitchen so Hannah can hear, too."

We shuffled into the kitchen, where Mochie looked on like a sourpuss as Jen cuddled her new babies.

I scooped him up and whispered, "They're going home with her tomorrow." He rubbed his head against my chin, and I hoped he understood he was still the top cat in my life.

Dad scratched Daisy behind the ears and sat next to the fireplace. "We drove out of the subdivision behind Forrest. I wasn't paying particular attention to him, and we were separated in traffic. Your mother wanted to stop for some champagne, so I waited in the car while she and Jen went into the store. Forrest had parked his car in a remote corner of the parking lot and — right in front of my eyes — he got into a white van and pulled out."

"A white van?" said Hannah.

"To evade Ginger?" I set Mochie on the floor. "He must know she's been following him."

"Unless" — Hannah's eyes met mine — "he's looking for Ginger to finish her off."

Mom gasped. "Forrest? He's far too nice!"

"But Ginger is just odious. The most perfect person in the world couldn't stand the way she treats her own children. Who could blame Forrest for wanting to get rid of Ginger? I barely know her, and today *I* wanted to wring her neck. How can she be so awful to Emma? We should have realized it all along," I said. "He was in an ideal position to plant the poison in the music box. When she was dead, he would be able to pursue his dream of opening a bakery. It seems so obvious now."

"What about the wrapping paper?" said Hannah.

I shrugged. "I guess I was wrong about that. Or maybe he used the wrong stuff on purpose, so she would open it sooner. Then, when that didn't kill her, he attacked Natasha and planted the Mrs. Santa skirt in their trash to throw suspicion on Ginger. If she was in jail for Bonnie's murder, Forrest could do whatever he wanted."

Hannah's eyes grew wide. "We have to warn her."

"Did she say where she was going?"

Dad scowled at us. "Shouldn't you report this to the police and let them take care of it?"

He was right. "Of course. Kenner's parked outside." I walked to the foyer and pulled on my coat and boots.

Hannah reached for her coat. "I'm coming, too. In case he doesn't believe you."

We ventured into the cold night and jaywalked across the street. I stopped in the middle of the road. Why did Kenner's car look so familiar? A plain dark-colored sedan, there was nothing striking about it. Until I remembered where I had seen it before — on George's street on Christmas Eve, slowly following me.

Kenner saw us coming, but I rapped on

his car window anyway. When he rolled it down, I couldn't help challenging him. "That was you on Christmas Eve!"

"What?" Kenner looked straight ahead and avoided my eyes. "I don't know what you're talking about."

"You followed us. You've been tailing me. That's why you pulled me over on Christmas Day." I leaned toward him. "That's how you managed to get to the crime scene so fast. You knew exactly where I went. Were you sitting outside in your car waiting for me to leave Bonnie's house?"

"No. Once I knew where you were going, I drove to the police station."

"So you admit it! That's stalking!"

Kenner finally met my gaze. It was the first time I had seen a softness to his face. He seemed almost wistful. "It's not stalking to watch out for someone."

That shut me up. I stared at him in shock. "It's Christmas, what did you think was going to happen?" But as soon as the words left my mouth, the truth dawned on me. "You didn't have anywhere to go for the holidays. You didn't have anyone to share them with, so you were watching my family?"

His jaw tightened, and I knew I'd hit a nerve. "I'm sorry, Kenner." For a split second I considered inviting him to our fondue dinner, but Hannah nudged me and hissed, "Ginger!"

I spilled everything we knew about the Chadwicks. "We don't know where Ginger went, but she's planning to do harm to Emma, and Forrest is after Ginger. There's going to be a massacre in that family tonight." I gave him the approximate location of Forrest's bakery, and he pulled out into the street behind a line of slow-moving cars whose drivers were probably in search of parking spots.

"It will take him forever to get there."

Hannah groaned. "He has a siren, for pity's sake. Why doesn't he use it?"

Without another word, we rushed toward the bakery on foot, pounding the freshly fallen snow and trying to avoid icy patches. Traffic grew heavier as we neared the center of Old Town. The sidewalks remained surprisingly clear of pedestrians, though. I guessed the cold weather prevented idle strolling through the scenic town.

We cut through the alley behind the bakery. Lights glowed near the back doors of most of the buildings. I hit the buzzer and bent double to catch my breath.

Hannah braced herself by placing a hand against the brick building and gasped, "I have got to get into better shape."

I turned my head toward the door. "They don't know how important this is." I rang the buzzer five times in a row to convey urgency.

"What if Ginger is already here?" asked Hannah. "What will we do then?"

I had no idea. I just hoped Kenner would arrive soon if that was the case.

The door creaked open. My breath coming hard, I stood up straight to face Emma. She grasped the edge of the door with both hands, and two of her bangle bracelets, adorned with scattered diamonds, caught the light.

"What's wrong? Is Dad okay?"

The words stuck in my mouth. How do you tell someone her mother might harm her, and her father is after her mother? Even worse, her bracelets mesmerized me. The way the stones glinted, they looked like real diamonds.

"Your mom's looking for you," Hannah blurted out.

As she did so, I grabbed Emma's arm and pulled her outside. "She's not in there, hiding behind the door, is she?"

Emma blinked at me. "No. We're fine. It's just Dasher and me. What's going on?"

"Where did you get the bracelets?" I demanded.

"Sophie!" Hannah's tone scolded me.

Emma didn't seem to mind my abrupt question. "Dasher gave them to me for Christmas."

Dasher. The worm who complained bitterly about how much Emma spent on the music box. The same worm who'd barely had enough money to come home for the holidays.

Hannah nudged me. "Tell her about her mom!"

I felt fairly foolish as I explained what had happened. There was no emergency, no imminent attack. Her mother was looking for her, but since her father was driving a different car, the likelihood that Ginger would locate Emma by following him was almost nil. Ginger was the one we needed to warn. If Forrest found her first, he might finish the job he'd started. "Just be careful, okay? If your mom should come knocking on the door, don't let her in."

She burst into tears. "Nothing I do will ever please her. I try so hard. She wouldn't have had a turkey to eat for Christmas if we hadn't had extras. I snuck it over to my parents' house in the middle of the night and stashed it in the fridge. I bet she even complained about that."

That cinched it. No one else on the block had a turkey after the food was stolen. Yet they had extras? "Dasher raided the houses and stole the Christmas gifts, didn't he? That's why he could afford the bracelets. That's why you had extra turkeys."

Emma shuddered. "No. He wouldn't have." But her voice faltered. "He . . . he sold some things, some art to a friend of his."

"I don't think so, Emma." I wanted to be kind, but saying the father of her child was a thief wasn't easy. "He went out last night. He decorated your mom's house with the turquoise and pink things she despised, and then he broke into Bonnie's office to retrieve the stolen gifts he stashed there with her." Why didn't I see it sooner? Bonnie had an ugly side, and she helped raise Dasher after his mother died. They were in cahoots.

"See?" Emma said hopefully. "That's just not true because he didn't bring anything back."

"Because Tyler had moved it all out," said Hannah.

The slow crackle of tires on snow alarmed all of us.

"It's not a van," said Hannah. "Is it Ginger?"

I shielded my eyes against the bright lights

413

of the car.

"It's Kenner."

Emma covered her mouth but it didn't stifle her shriek. "You ratted him out!" She barreled inside and slammed the door. We could hear her yelling, "It's the cops! Quick, bring my coat. We can go out the front!"

I leaned against the door. How could we have muddled everything so badly? Would Kenner take Emma off to jail for evading the police? Or for aiding and abetting Dasher? I sighed. At least she would be safe from her mother there.

Emma still screamed inside. "*Please* tell me you're not the Christmas-gift thief."

Silence followed. I guessed Dasher was trying to explain. Then Hannah and I heard Emma yell, "You moron!"

"We needed money, Emma. Did you think your mother was ever going to give you one thing for our baby? We were entitled to their stuff. Your brother's brand-new computer brought in a nice chunk of change."

"Why would you spoil Christmas for the whole neighborhood?"

"For somebody with a high IQ, you can be really stupid. If I only hit your parents' house, the cops would have guessed it was me. Besides, we needed the money. All those people can replace what we took."

414

Hannah and I didn't wait for Kenner to park. I ran over and rapped on his window. "Dasher is the Christmas-gift thief. He's heading out the front way."

We ran around to the front of the building just in time to see Emma and Dasher escape through the front door. They dodged traffic to cross the street, passed us on the other side, and disappeared into the night. In a matter of minutes, they would be among the throngs of revelers on King Street. Kenner wouldn't find them, but Ginger might.

We had turned to walk home when we heard a scream.

THIRTY-SIX

From "THE GOOD LIFE":

Dear Sophie,
I'm itching to buy one of those gadgets that holds sports balls so they don't roll around everywhere, but my husband thinks they're too expensive and take up too much space. How do I store balls so they're not in the way all the time?
— Tripping Over Balls in Candlestick, Georgia

Dear Tripping Over Balls,
Buy an inexpensive hammock and hang it in your basement or garage. Toss the balls inside and you're done.
— Sophie

Hannah and I stopped. "Did you hear that?" I asked.

"It didn't sound like a Happy New Year

scream. Which direction?"

I pointed toward the corner where I had run into Forrest. We jogged along the sidewalk to the intersection.

"There!" Hannah pointed toward the Santa and Mrs. Claus whose clothes had been taken.

Under the shield of darkness from the curving stairs, it appeared that two people struggled. We sprinted toward them like crazy women. As we neared, one of the shadowy figures raced away, running like he meant to save his life. Tall and heavyset, there was no question that it was Santa Claus.

We found the other person sprawled on the sidewalk. It was Ginger Chadwick. Forrest had found her before we did.

At that moment, the front door of the house opened and light spilled out. "Hah! I've caught you now, you hooligans!" Another light shone down on us. "I told my wife if we left Santa out here, you would be back." He sounded elderly, and against the light escaping from his house, it appeared he brandished a large candlestick over his head.

My focus moved downward. Ginger's body lay crooked, her head bent at an unnatural angle.

"Should we do mouth-to-mouth?" asked Hannah.

Mustering every ounce of strength not to sound hysterical, I looked up at the man above us. "Would you please call an ambulance?" It came out as little more than a whisper.

Still, the old man heard it. He shouted into his house for his wife to call for help. "Who is that down there?"

"We should do something," Hannah knelt next to Ginger.

"I don't think we should touch her. Her neck might be broken." I joined Hannah on the ground. "Is she breathing? Can you tell?"

The light vanished as quickly as it had arrived. Seconds later, the old man joined us and flashed his light directly on Ginger. "Good Lord in heaven. I knew I heard something out here. Is she alive?"

Ginger's eyes blinked but she didn't move a muscle.

A hand gripped my shoulder, and I looked up to see Kenner leaning over us. "An ambulance is on the way."

The words were hardly out of his mouth when we heard the sirens.

In moments, Hannah and I had backed up to make room for the rescue squad. Kenner pulled us aside to learn what we'd seen. Not much, unfortunately.

They put a brace around Ginger's neck and immobilized her on a gurney. In spite of her condition, as they rolled her toward the ambulance, she said, clear as a bell, "It was Dasher."

"She's just pure evil," exclaimed Hannah.

Kenner asked, "You're absolutely certain you saw Dasher leave with Emma?"

"They took off in the other direction. There's no way it could have been him. Plus, the guy who did this to Ginger was tall and heavy," I added.

"Forrest." Hannah and I said his name together.

Kenner nodded. "Love is a very strange thing. It's not the first time I've seen a woman protect the husband who just tried to kill her."

The grinding sound of a car that wouldn't start resounded farther up the block.

Kenner's mouth twitched. "It's going to be a long night. Happy New Year to both of you."

At least he knew who to look for now. Old Town wasn't very big. If he put out an all points bulletin, the cops would nab Forrest quickly. We wished him a Happy New Year and walked toward the sound of the stalled car. I wondered what time it was and whether my mother had served the fondue to everyone else.

"He's not as bad as I thought," whispered Hannah.

"Who?"

"Kenner. I mean, he's kind of gaunt, with those sunken cheeks, and he looks like he couldn't smile for anything, but he's okay."

"You're turning into a police groupie."

"Oh, gosh! I wonder if Zack is at your house."

We passed a little alley where someone still tried desperately to start a car. Kenner pulled his car up behind it, and the driver of the stalled car got out.

Hannah elbowed me. "It's Tom. Oh my gosh, he looks great!"

He did. We joined Kenner and Tom at the open hood of his car.

"Beautiful sweater!" gushed Hannah.

"Thank you. Emma made it." Tom's chest puffed out a little bit as he showed off the white sweater with slate cables knitted into it. "I'm late to pick up my date and now my car won't start."

Kenner leaned forward under the hood. "What is this? Did you put it in here on purpose?" He withdrew a mass of blue fluff and shone his flashlight on it. "*Eww.* Mouse poop. Mice moved into your engine. Looks like they shredded a blanket and made a nest." He bent closer with his light. "Nuts? They've done a number here. They've carried almonds into your engine. Didn't you have trouble driving here?"

"Maybe you should have kept those kittens, Tom!" Hannah giggled.

Tom looked like he'd bitten into a lemon. He held up his hands as if he wanted nothing to do with it. "The engine sounded like it was grinding but everything else was okay. Thanks for your help. I'll take a cab and call my auto club to come out here and take care of this tomorrow."

"No, no," insisted Kenner. "Give me a minute here. Sophie, would you mind turning the key to see if the car will start now that I've removed these blanket bits?"

"Sure." I opened the door, slid into the driver's seat, and twisted the key to the right. For a second, I thought it might start, but then it made the sick grating noise.

"Wait a second, Sophie," called Kenner.

I looked around — Tom was a car pig. He couldn't pick up a date in this car. Two soccer balls rolled on the floor of the passenger side. The seat contained fast-food containers, mail, the hammer he'd used earlier, an open bag of almonds, and three cupcake wrappers, just like the ones Forrest used on his Red Velvet Cupcakes.

I studied them. Tyler told us Forrest gave them cupcakes. There was nothing sinister about that. But their presence explained how someone might have gotten cream cheese on the sleeve of a Santa Claus jacket. Tom ate them in his car. He hadn't known about Ginger's matching gift wrap rules, and after installing the poison in the music box, he'd rewrapped Emma's gift in the wrong colors.

When I looked up, Tom stared in at me. His friendly smile had disappeared. I had a very bad feeling that an entire Santa Claus suit might be found in his trunk, and that the sleeve would have a piece torn out of it. "Kenner!"

In a split second, Tom bashed the hood of the car on Kenner's head — so hard that I cringed for him.

"Hannah, watch out!" I screamed.

It was too late. Tom wrapped his arm around her neck, much as I imagined he had done to Ginger. Had I been alone, I might have locked myself in the car, but I couldn't let him choke Hannah or, heaven forbid, break her neck.

Moving slowly in the hope he wouldn't notice, I slid the hammer up the sleeve of my bulky winter jacket, gripping the heavy head in my hand so he wouldn't see it.

I stepped out of the car. "Let her go, Tom. She's not Ginger." What did he expect to do? Kill all three of us right here in the alley? He couldn't drive away.

He forced Hannah to walk toward the trunk with him. Suddenly, I knew what he meant to do. If he could wedge all three of us in the trunk, he could get away. I couldn't think straight. Would he stop if I reasoned with him? If I sympathized? If I gave him a way out?

"You know Forrest wants to kill Ginger," I said.

He stopped propelling Hannah forward, and I thought I might have thrown him off guard.

"Forrest doesn't have the guts. He should have eliminated her years ago to save our children from her wrath. She is the reason our children can't come home! She is the reason my son had to be shipped away to a military school. They weren't planning to come for the holidays this year because of Ginger. They sent a box of gifts, including the music box for Ginger, and that was the last straw for me. That sweet girl bought her mother such a lovely gift, even though my son told me that it blew their budget and they had to eat beans and rice for a month. But Ginger was full of venom. She had to be killed, like the poisonous snake that will bite you if you let him live."

I tried to buy time. "What about Emma? Weren't you afraid she would be arrested for the posionous gift?"

"That was the beauty of it. Once the seal broke and the chemicals mixed, they would dissipate in the air, and no one would be the wiser about the cause of her death."

Would he leave us alone if he thought he accomplished his goal? "She's dead now. Your son and Emma and your grandchild can live in peace."

"Don't think you can fool me. I saw the ambulance."

"They always send an ambulance. What — you think they send a hearse when someone dies?"

"Open the trunk!" It was a command.

What if I didn't? Where was everyone? Didn't anyone ever come down this way?

Like he could read my mind, Tom said, "If you scream, I will tighten my arm just a hair, and your sister's pretty little neck will break."

Hannah's eyes caught mine. She was terrified.

I needed him to bend over so I could

smack him in the head with his hammer. I wasn't tall enough to give him a good blow otherwise. Reluctantly, I opened the trunk.

It looked worse than the front seat of his car. He wouldn't be able to fit us in there unless he emptied it. How old was this car, I wondered. Maybe the trunk had an interior latch to open it. Or maybe not. I couldn't take a chance.

"Get in."

"Me?"

"Get in!"

I stepped on the bumper and pulled myself up. Crouching, I placed one foot in the trunk. I wasn't sure what I hit with my boot, but I had to take a chance. It was now or never. Watching him from the corner of my eye, and praying that I wouldn't hit Hannah, I stood up as straight as I could and swung at his head.

The hammer connected with the back of his head, stunning him enough for him to loosen his grip on Hannah. She tore away from him, coughing. I hauled my hand back and swung at him again, just as he turned to face me. His nose crunched when the hammer hit him. I winced at the sound and he went down.

Somehow, I didn't think he would be so good-looking anymore.

I sat on him, ready to use the hammer again if necessary. "Hannah, check on Kenner and see if he's got a phone or a radio on him."

"He's out cold," she yelled.

She returned to the rear of the car and flashed me a nervous smile. She couldn't fool me, though — while she gave information to 911, the phone in her hand shook like a leaf in the wind.

THIRTY-SEVEN

From "THE GOOD LIFE":

Dear Sophie,
My sister-in-law regifts everything. Our family is tired of receiving junk that she doesn't want. She just sent me a music box, which is very beautiful, but has her name engraved on it! How do we tell her to quit regifting?
— Unappreciative in Jolly, Kentucky

Dear Unappreciative,
Do not turn the handle to play the music! Send the music box back with a note saying you're sure she must have sent it inadvertently since it bears her name.
— Sophie

The police finished with us at eleven thirty. Tom had clammed up, but everyone thought he had attacked Natasha to throw suspicion on Ginger. When he hadn't been able to kill Ginger, he'd tried to get rid of her by putting her in jail. He'd planted the crutch and the Santa clothes to implicate her.

We'd called my house to assure everyone that we were fine. While Hannah and I explained our story to the police, the rest of our family and Laci's family had enjoyed the fondue. They generously decided to wait until after the fireworks to cut the New Year's Bombe so that we could join them.

With less than half an hour to go to the new year, Hannah and I walked toward the Torpedo Factory, an actual torpedo factory that had been converted to an art center. Running was simply out of the question.

Kenner had been taken to the hospital with a nasty concussion, but both he and Ginger survived. The doctors didn't think she would be paralyzed from the injury. Ginger's broken neck would take a while to heal, but Emma's broken heart would take much longer.

The year hadn't ended on a happy note for her. Dasher had been arrested and hauled off to the Fairfax County Police Department. Police were on the hunt for some of his old hoodlum contacts, since it was unlikely he'd pulled off the Christmas-gift heist all by himself.

No one could believe that Bonnie had been a fence. However, after Hannah and I told our story, I overheard one of the police officers mutter to another one, "Bonnie Scarborough fencing stolen goods — hard to imagine, but it does explain some things. You watch, it will turn out she's been doing it for years."

We wound our way through the crowds to the waterfront, where our family gathered. After hugs and assurances, Hannah and I told them the whole story.

"Can you imagine," said Laci to her mother. "They thought you were having an affair with Forrest!"

"He *is* a handsome man, but I think I'll stick with your father."

Phil wrapped a proprietary arm around Marnie, and they looked every bit the adoring couple, like my parents.

Laci avoided my eyes when she asked her mother, "So where have you been going? You keep taking off, and no one knows where you are."

Marnie shifted her shoulders like she was doing a little dance. "Surprise! Daddy and I are moving here! We've been looking at houses."

"Here?" choked George. "Here as in Old Town?"

"No, silly. We want to be near you and our only grandchild. We found an adorable town house, but now that Tom's house might be coming on the market . . ."

George's eyes literally rolled back into his head. Laci and I steadied him. He came around in seconds, but a glazed look remained in his eyes as though he couldn't believe what he'd heard.

Jen and Vegas hung on the railing overlooking boats that still glittered with Christmas lights. George and Laci watched the girls, and Shawna clung to Tyler as though he was the one she'd wanted all along. He had some legal issues to clear up, but apparently Dasher had been decent enough to clarify that Tyler hadn't been involved in the theft of the gifts. Hannah found Zack looking for her in the crowd. They held hands and had eyes only for one another.

A bit farther away, I spied Forrest with Emma and Edward. Rude and unfriendly as she was, I was still glad Ginger had survived. I didn't think her marriage had, though. With the baby on the way and Dasher in jail, I guessed Emma and Edward would move in over the bakery, and help Forrest realize his dream.

As the one-minute countdown to the new year started, an arm slid around my waist. After the night I'd had, I reacted strongly, whipping around with my fingers tightly wrapped into a fist. My hand stopped inches from Wolf's face.

He grinned at me and tilted his head toward mine for a kiss.

Fireworks exploded over the river. "You're just in time," I said.

He stood behind me and wrapped his arms around my waist. His chin nuzzled my hair, and I relaxed in his embrace. "I see Shawna's out of jail. How was your Christmas?"

"I'm glad it's over."

RECIPES & COOKING TIPS

Bread Machine Cinnamon Buns

12 tablespoons butter (cold and cut into
  tablespoon-size pieces)
4 1/2 cups flour
2 large eggs
1/2 cup sugar
1 teaspoon vanilla
dash salt
1 package yeast
1 cup warm milk

For the Cinnamon Sugar Inside the Buns
1 cup sugar
2 tablespoons cinnamon

Topping
1/2 bar (4 ounces) cream cheese (softened
  to room temperature)
1/4 cup powdered sugar
splash of milk or cream

Place the butter, flour, eggs, sugar, vanilla, and salt in the bread machine. Sprinkle the yeast over the top and add the warm milk. Set the machine on manual so that it will go through the first rising but won't bake the dough. If it looks too sticky, add a little bit of flour.

After it has risen, punch down the dough, remove from the bread machine, and divide into equal portions. Roll one half of the dough into a large rectangle, dusting with additional flour as needed. Mix 1/2 cup sugar with 1 tablespoon cinnamon and spread over the dough. Roll the longest side inward until you have a long log. Cut into roughly 1-inch slices. Grease an 8-inch cake pan and fit the rolls in, but not too close to each other. (Disposable cake pans work very well for this and can be easily transported.) Allow to rise a second time until the rolls have completely filled the pan and doubled in height.

At this point, you can slide the pan into a gallon-size freezer bag and freeze up to a week. Repeat with the remaining half of the dough.

To bake, preheat the oven to 350 degrees. Bake 25–30 minutes, until the tops are done and a tester comes out clean.

Beat the cream cheese with the powdered

sugar, adding milk or cream as necessary to achieve a spreading consistency. Spread over the cinnamon buns and serve.

NEW YEAR'S EVE RASPBERRY BOMBE

3 pints premium-brand chocolate ice cream
2 pints premium-brand coffee (or vanilla) ice cream
1 cup whipping cream
1 1/2 cups frozen raspberries
2/3 cup sugar
6 egg yolks
1/3 cup raspberry liquor Chambord (or one airline-size bottle)
1 large mold or aluminum (freezable) bowl

Slightly thaw 2 pints of the chocolate ice cream and slice into 1/2-inch rounds. Using your fingers, press the ice cream into the bowl or mold until the bottom and sides are covered, filling in little crevices as needed. Cover and freeze until firm.

Slightly thaw the 2 pints of coffee ice cream, slice into 1/2-inch rounds, and press on top of the chocolate ice cream until covered. Cover and freeze until firm.

Beat the egg yolks until thick and lemon-colored. Leave in the mixer. Meanwhile, stirring and taking care not to burn, cook the frozen raspberries with the sugar until the mixture registers 236 degrees (or makes a soft ball when dropped into water) on a candy thermometer or thermapen. Immediately beat the egg yolks and slowly pour the raspberry mixture into them as they are beating. Continue to beat about 5 minutes, then allow to cool. When cool, add the Chambord. Pour the cool raspberry mixture into the mold. Cover and freeze until firm.

Slightly thaw the remaining chocolate ice cream and slice into 1/2-inch rounds. Cover the bottom of the bombe with the ice cream. Cover and freeze until firm, at least 6 hours. Overnight usually works well.

To serve, dip very briefly in warm water and turn the mold onto a serving platter (save yourself a lot of trouble and use one that you can put into the freezer), loosen the edges, and the mold should slide off. Serve and enjoy!

BAKED EGGS ON SALMON

1/4 cup heavy cream
2 tablespoons butter
8 large eggs
1 teaspoon chopped rosemary
1/4 teaspoon thyme
pinch of sage
salt

kaiser rolls, halved, or a sliced baguette
1 package smoked salmon

Preheat the oven to 400 degrees. Crack the eggs into four teacups or small dishes. Pour the cream into an 8-by-8-inch baking pan (glass works well), and add the butter and the herbs. Bake in the oven for a couple of minutes, until the butter has melted and the cream is a little bit bubbly. Slide the eggs into the pan so they're spread out and salt as desired. Bake 5 minutes or until the whites are set and the yolks are to your liking.

Meanwhile, lightly toast the bread. Top each half roll or slice of bread with a portion of salmon. When baked, scoop one egg and a portion of the egg white out of the pan and ladle onto the salmon. Serve.

RED VELVET CUPCAKES
6 large eggs, separated
1 cup sugar
1 teaspoon vanilla
3/4 cup flour
1/2 cup milk
2 tablespoons apple cider vinegar
1/3 cup beet powder (available at health food stores)
1 tablespoon Hershey's cocoa powder

4 tablespoons butter, melted
1/2 teaspoon cream of tartar

Preheat oven to 350. Add the vinegar to the milk. In a small bowl, mix the cocoa powder and the beet powder. Beat the egg yolks with 3/4 cup sugar until thick and light colored (about five minutes). Add the vanilla and the flour and mix well. Add the beet powder mixture and beat. Add the milk mixture and beat. Slowly add the melted butter and beat thoroughly. Set aside. Beat the egg whites with the cream of tartar. When they begin to take shape, add the remaining 1/4 cup of sugar. Beat until stiff but not dry. Fold a dollop of the egg whites into the red batter to lighten it. Fold a dollop of the red batter into the egg whites. Merge the two and fold gently but thoroughly. Spoon into cupcake liners. Bake 18 minutes.

OLD-FASHIONED RED VELVET ICING
1 cup milk
5 tablespoons flour
1 cup butter
1 cup sugar
1 tablespoon vanilla

Combine the milk and flour and cook until thick, stirring constantly. Cover with plastic wrap and store in refrigerator until cool.

Cream butter with sugar. Add cooled milk mixture and vanilla and beat until fluffy.

GLÜHWEIN

1 bottle inexpensive red wine (750 ml)

2 cups orange juice

3 cinnamon sticks (or 2 teaspoons cinnamon)

1/2 teaspoon cardamom

4 whole cloves (or 1 teaspoon cloves)

3 tablespoons sugar (add more to taste, if necessary)

The key to glühwein is to let it steep so the flavors mingle. Put everything into a pot and heat, but do not bring to a boil. Stir occasionally. Let steep at least 30 minutes or up to 1 hour. Feel free to add what you like and have on hand. It's an evolving recipe that changes!

ABOUT THE AUTHOR

Krista Davis is the national bestselling author of the Domestic Diva Mysteries. Her first book, *The Diva Runs Out of Thyme,* was nominated for an Agatha Award. Krista lives in the Blue Ridge Mountains of Virginia with an Ocicat named Mochie and a brood of dogs. Her friends and family complain about being guinea pigs for her recipes, but she notices that they keep coming back for more. Visit Krista at her website, www.krista davis.com, and the blog www.mysterylovers kitchen.com.

We hope you have enjoyed this Large Print book. Other Thorndike, Wheeler, Kennebec, and Chivers Press Large Print books are available at your library or directly from the publishers.

For information about current and upcoming titles, please call or write, without obligation, to:

Publisher
Thorndike Press
10 Water St., Suite 310
Waterville, ME 04901
Tel. (800) 223-1244

or visit our Web site at:

http://gale.cengage.com/thorndike

OR

Chivers Large Print
published by AudioGO Ltd
St James House, The Square
Lower Bristol Road
Bath BA2 3SB
England
Tel. +44(0) 800 136919
email: info@audiogo.co.uk
www.audiogo.co.uk

All our Large Print titles are designed for easy reading, and all our books are made to last.